MAX ABADDON

And The Path Of Blood

Justin S. Leslie

J.S.L

Paperback ISBN: 979-8-9918422-2-8
E-book ISBN: 979-8-9918422-1-1

Contact Information
Email: Abaddonbooks@hotmail.com
Facebook: @Maxabaddonbooks
Website: www.JustinLeslie.com

Copyediting by Happily Ever Proofreading LLC

"Tempus edax rerum."

Time, the devourer of all things....

OVID METAMORPHOSES

PROLOGUE

Neon lights reflected on the dark, pooled water of the Seven-Eleven's parking lot in Soho. The sounds and bustle of downtown London at night echoed as the familiar slurp of the one and only Hermes draining the last of his slushy joined the ruckus.

"Kids," Hermes huffed from the bushes, which were leaking smoke and creating a light layer of fog in front of the glowing convenience store. Truth be told, he was intrigued by the fact that the UK now had 7-Elevens. A new treat for the island of kings and queens.

"Yo!" one of the taller young men barked, part of a group of college kids who were in the area for a night on the town. "Halloween ain't for another two months, bruv." He turned to his group and added in a lower tone, "Look at these clowns," while pointing at Hermes, who was dressed like a lounge singer in the 1970s as he feverishly skimmed the bottom of his slushy.

Al, the shifter alligator, was in human form and was wearing a sparkling green suit from head to toe, slurping his own cup and holding a tin of biscuits. The two were often found traveling together to Seven-Elevens around the world, taking on new slushy flavors.

"I don't see any clowns," Hermes replied in his off-putting voice.

"Oy, look at that one. He looks like a shiny bugger," another of the college kids shouted. The group of drunken twenty-somethings were getting each other wound up.

This was the point at which Al took offense, after the slight to his favorite suit. "Hermster," Al mumbled under his breath. "Think I should ruin their night?"

"Oy, look at the other one. He looks like a disco queen's butler."

Hermes sneered, side-eyeing Al with a slight grin. Knowing what this meant, Al stepped out of the shadows of the foggy hedges. One thing Al could do was make an entrance.

Standing to his full height, Al pulled his suit coat tight, strutting into the light as he morphed his teeth to that of an alligator's but in a human mouth, followed by him slitting his now green eyes.

"Um . . . uh," the previously fearless leader of the group stammered.

"What's wrong, boys? Don't like my suit?" Al smiled, showing every pointy tooth in his mouth.

"You magic types?" A boy from the back of the group spoke up, garnering an odd look from the rest of the young men. Within seconds, it was clear he wasn't part of the drunken crew and had just exited the convenience store.

"I see we have one smart one in the group," Al huffed as Hermes continued to slurp on his empty drink. It wasn't lost on the Greek deity that the young men making fun of his clothes had no clue who they were in the presence of.

"Uh, he ain't with us," another of the young men spoke up. "Matter of fact, you need to mind your own business, bruv."

Just as Al was about to put the icing on the cake, three loud bangs boomed throughout the night, forcing even Hermes to stop his slurping.

Al froze, sniffing the air and quickly turning to Hermes. "Trouble, and not these rats." Just as the words passed his green lips, two massive, clawed hands reached through the shrubs, grabbing Hermes—a mistake that immediately cost the creature one of its arms.

Having the ability to move faster than any other god known to man or the gods themselves, Hermes was lethal in a fight. At least a fight with a normal monster. Turning, Hermes squared up with what he could only describe to himself as a miniature version of an ugly Titan. Massive arms and legs were offset by giant tentacles wrapping around its shoulders, protruding from its back. He had seen this type of creature before but couldn't place it.

Hermes, seeing he had taken too much time, shifted to strike the beast in front of him as a field of energy burst from a short staff in its hands, sending the Greek god flying into a tailspin.

"Not my friend!" Al erupted through the hedges, not allowing the creature to turn as he morphed into his version of an alligator nightmare buzz saw. His now elongated snout snapped on the fat head of the one-eyed monster while its tentacles wrapped around Al. It was a war of attrition to see which of them could squeeze the hardest before the other popped.

While Al and Hermes were preoccupied, another creature rolled into the group of drunk kids, tearing through the ringleader in a blender of misting gore and clothes. After letting out an earsplitting shriek, two more of the young men went flying through the night, landing in bizarre positions from the majority of their bones being liquefied.

Now standing in front of the young man who had guessed that Al and Hermes were, in fact, not regulars, the creature let out another roar as silver erupted from the kid's hands and eyes. The two remaining drunk college students took the distraction the young man named Tristen had given them, allowing them time to flee the area, saving their lives.

"No more," Tristen said through gritted teeth. "Leave them alone. It's me you want."

This time, the creature didn't hesitate. Tristen unleashed a flow of silver flashes directly at its chest, pushing it back several feet, but it once again started to charge after the brief encounter.

Just then, eerie music started flowing through the night, and the beast slowly stopped its charge, coming to a complete halt. Out of the hedges, Hermes walked out holding a shepherd's flute to his lips. One of the Greek god's powers was the ability to charm monsters using a flute given to him by the shepherd of the first flock of sheep he ever saved.

Tristen froze in place, seeing Hermes in all his glory. Blond hair flowed over gold-and-white armor like water. While everyone who had met Hermes always saw him as a cranky old man, in reality, he was a Greek god. He just preferred wearing the face of an old man to keep people from asking him for autographs—something he was convinced would happen even though no one knew what he truly looked like.

Hermes was on an epic quest that could not be disturbed. One that was self-imposed. A journey so important that even the gods themselves were not involved. That quest was to sample every flavor of slushy the Seven-Eleven had to offer. Being that different countries had different flavors, he was more than halfway done.

Al walked out of the hedges holding the head of the other creature, seeing his partner in crime no longer in disguise. Hermes turned, holding up his hand as Al handed him the head.

"Where's the rest of it?" Hermes asked, but Al shook his head.

"Gone. It evaporated. I got its head before it also dissolved into the ether," Al replied before both men turned back to Tristen.

"You . . . You are an Ethereal?" Tristen stammered as the sounds of sirens blared in the distance.

Hermes nodded. "I am Hermes. The regular authorities are coming, and they will see the bodies."

Tristen scanned the scene. Pieces of the young men lay strewn across the parking lot. Glancing up at the CCTV camera, it sparked as Al snapped his fingers, frying the device.

Al turned to Hermes. "He was trying to help the others. We must take him with us."

"True," Hermes said thoughtfully, morphing back into the old leisure-suit-wearing man.

Tristen, seeing this, took a step back. "I didn't do anything."

"I'm not so sure about that," Hermes replied as flashing blue lights speckled the night sky. The police were getting closer. "You said these things"—Hermes looked down at the head —"were here for you. Why?"

Tristen shuffled. "It's just . . . It's complicated. Look, can you get me out of here?"

Hermes nodded. "Al. Call that Dick Holder guy."

"You mean Inspector Richard Holder? He retired from the Dunn," Al replied as the sound of tires screeched a block over.

"He can still help," Hermes declared as Al pulled out his phone, holding it up. Satisfied, he turned toward the young man. "Tristen, I need you to come with us."

He held out his hand as Tristen hesitated, looking at the severed head in his other hand before reaching out to the Greek god and winking out of existence. All that remained was a puff of smoke.

CHAPTER 1

Home Again, Home Again

The familiar aroma of books offset by the smell of fresh paint flowed through the stacks as I walked toward the freshly renovated offices of the Atheneum. Since returning to the real world, things had been relatively calm, much to my enjoyment.

After days of Petro telling his family and the other Pixies of his bravery while once again saving the world and the Under, he had decided to put a care package together for Dit—Bo's hairless demon raccoon who, once upon a time, had tried to eat him.

Yawning, I scratched the back of my head, closing the notes I had finally completed on the Timegate. While still recovering, I had taken the time to get things in order for what I supposed was an adventure for another time.

"Bruther," Phil's voice echoed through the stacks before he finally spotted me in the small alcove beside the Postern. Since returning, things had calmed down enough to have everyone come back from Devin's keep. With the ability to go there through the Everwhere, the trip was still just a few short gates away.

"Sup," I replied, leaning back.

"Trish called. She's reopening the apartment and wants us to stop by later for a libation."

Smiling, I glanced down at the folder, seeing Phil shake his head from the corner of my eye. "Sounds good. Trish said she was doing some work on the place to avoid any further issues," I said, wondering where Petro was.

"Bruther, that time gobbledygook can wait. You just got back six months ago. Anywho, Ed also called. Said something about that Dick Holder fella wanting to talk to us."

"That's a name I haven't heard in a while. Wonder what's up. Oh, and before I forget, Leshya stopped by earlier. She wants you to go to the Everwhere and talk with Sheyla. She said she's ready."

Since finding Phil's long-lost wife's soul, it had taken a while for Ed and the others to work out a way for her to be in the Everwhere. All this time, Leshya had been a craft built from pieces of her soul. Gramps had done this to one day reunite the two; something that wouldn't happen now that Leshya had grown into her own being and he was gone.

"Yes, I heard we should be good to go starting tomorrow."

"You're not going to run off and leave us, are you?" I asked, raising an eyebrow. This was a very real possibility.

Phil looked at his worn combat boots. "Ah. I know she'll always be there waiting for me. We will have more than enough time. With everything getting back to tops and bottoms, I'll make time."

Satisfied, I stood, handing Phil the folder. "I want you to go through this. I think I have it figured out."

"I owe you, bruther, and you know that. I might not like it, but I'll do what I can. Not sure what help I'm going to be."

I smiled. "Just make sure I'm not doing something crazy. You know . . . something that will cause more problems."

"Ha," Phil blew out. "You mustn't have been paying too much attention to the past couple of years. I'll look it over; I think we already know you're taking that trip—Goolsby's letter and all proving that."

Nodding, we walked into the main hallway, turning into the newly refurbished crucible room. A new version of the box sat on a desk in front of new monitors and the familiar layout of desks and offices. A good bit of death had occurred in this room, not to mention my run-in with Darkwater's daughter, who had ended up as an octopus-like creature. This had been the very room where we had taken our last stand when fighting off the Soul Dealers.

"Right!" Ed's voice boomed from the break room, the location where I'd first met Petro and where I'd saved him from the freezer. "Check the place out. They finally opened up the old offices and brought the crucible room back online."

Ed turned the corner, holding a cup of steaming coffee.

"Ed," I grinned. "I heard you would be back today. How's the Council?"

"Better. Ana Vlad says hello. Aslynn was also there, asking about you. I told her you now have a girlfriend; she just snickered."

Shaking my head, I did indeed agree that I was now in some sort of relationship with Gabby, a Vampire once living in Salt City. "That reminds me," I started, "we're heading to FA's; you want to join us?"

"Sure," Ed replied, punching several buttons on the box as it fired up. "Inspector Holder will be in town tonight, as I am sure you have heard already. Not sure what's going on, but he was insistent."

Jenny walked in next, coming from the entrance to the underground labs and heading toward Ed, placing a light kiss on his cheek. "There you are. I was looking for you."

"I know," Ed replied as only he could. While he was a powerful Mind Mage, he clearly could no longer read mine. "We're just talking about heading to FA's."

Jenny clapped her hands. "Perfect! I've been wanting to stop by after Trish's reopening. The girls will love it." She was referring to Lacey and Macey, her two Pixie partners in crime.

"I'm sure they will. That reminds me, have you seen Petro?" I asked, seeing Ed bring up the marshal's OTN map of Jacksonville, Florida.

"I heard he was filming videos for his newest social media profile. Something about tales from the freeze. The girls were helping him. Neil is in the dining room with Casey, working on a few potions," Jenny relayed.

"Let's round the crew up and head that way," I said as several dings flashed on the OTN map of Jacksonville. The nostalgia filled me with a relaxing calm I hadn't experienced in a long time.

"What's all that, then?" Phil asked, screwing up his face.

"OTN reports. Crazy how we haven't been paying attention to this stuff," Ed breathed out. After a few quick keystrokes, James's name flashed on the screen. "Looks like James is on the job. We need to have him over for old times' sake," Ed followed.

"What's that one next to Riverplace Tower?" I asked, crossing my arms over my chest.

"Right." Ed punched more buttons. "Looks like an unregistered gate. And the other, while we're at it . . ." He continued pressing buttons, being out of practice. "Oh, a murder."

"Murder?" Jenny asked, pressing for more information. Someone was typing in the system at the same time, words filling the screen. "Oh shit."

The screen flashed. *"Reported murder of other."* This was a term for magical types. *"Possible regular involvement."*

Just as the words stopped, Petro zipped into the room. "Sup, yo!" Reading the room, he dropped to the table. "Why the long faces?"

I pointed at the screen. Petro read it out loud before shaking his head. "What does all that mean? Does that mean they were involved on the regular?" Petro followed this with his patented hip gyration.

"No," I breathed out, realizing it wasn't our issue to handle. "It means a regular killed a magic type. Ethereal, V . . . who knows."

"Oh shit, boss. Are we on the case?" Petro asked.

Since being preoccupied with other issues, the CSA and marshals had put together a robust team capable of handling localized issues such as these.

"No. James is entering the information; the locals have it covered," I said, shifting back to the evening's plans. "Hey, we're going to FA's; you joining us?"

"You bet your nuggets. I heard she has a new cook and everything." Petro took off, lightly dusting the table.

Ed turned off the monitor. "Right. I think I'll call Frank and see if he wants to join us. I believe he's with Angel. Are we gating there?"

"Yeah." I clapped my hands. "I got everything back to normal with the Postern; might as well start using it again. I even got all the gate stones for the Evergate, minus the one for Petro's brothers."

Jenny patted me on the back. "How's everything with the Timegate?" A few glances were exchanged. "Don't be so coy, everyone. We know Max is going to use it at some point."

"It's going. I believe I figured it out; it's just not the time to get into it yet. One adventure a year is enough."

Jenny smiled. "Well, you'll know when the time is right. On a separate note, I went through the evidence room and labs. Everything is in order. A little mess in the evidence room, but it might give Max and Phil something to do."

"Hey, what about me?" Petro asked while she nodded.

"*And* Petro," Jenny added.

"Enough of this lollygagging. Let's get this party started!" Phil boomed, singing a soccer fighting song while walking out of the crucible, leading the charge to FA's.

CHAPTER 2

The Fallen Angel Rides Again

T he familiar scent of buttery steaks and tangy copper from the ceiling tiles filled my senses as we made our way to the bar. Familiar faces and some new ones shuffled around the room as Sarah beamed a smile, pointing at Frank and Angel already sitting at the bar. Next to a high-top table with a reserved sign on it, several seats leaned forward, making a small section for the crew.

Petro zoomed past with the rest of the Pixies, landing next to the serving station. Trish was ready, quickly pulling several small caps from under the bar. She beamed as we all made our way through the crowd.

Hands were shaken and backs slapped as everyone set into a cadence of general conversations. While I had seen everyone since returning, we hadn't all truly been together in a social setting.

"Max," Frank greeted as Angel smiled through her ruby-red lipstick.

"Hey, lover boy," she said, fang slipping.

Ever since connecting with Gabby and our subsequent relationship, the rest of the Vs had treated me as if I was part of some special club. Even the usually bland Frank was more inviting, regardless of the fact we were already friends.

"Frank, Angel, it's been a while. How's the CSA and the Night Stalkers?"

The two rolled their eyes at the same time. Angel spoke first, taking a sip from a martini glass. "Same as always. There is too much to do and not enough time to do it. Things have calmed down some over the past couple of weeks, so we have both been catching up on paperwork."

"Sounds exciting," I said, grabbing the Vamp Amber Trish slid in front of me. "Looks like FA's is back up and running. Any word on who the new chef is? I heard she fired Paul or whatever his name was."

The two shrugged before Frank leaned forward. "Rumor is it's a historical figure and his Pixie. I think they said his name is Ben."

The gears started cranking in my head as I cocked my head. "The stair master? Benjamin Franklin?"

Angel chuckled as only she could. "The one and only. I guess he and his Pixie are somewhat notorious cooks. It sounds like he is filling in until a longer-term solution is found. Truth be told, I think she isn't going to be happy with anyone other than Amon . . ." She trailed off as the door swung open.

The entire bar turned at the authority with which the door opened to find Ana Vlad, followed by her brother, the one and only Dracula, Vlad himself.

"No shit," Frank huffed, standing up. The rest of the Vs in the bar followed suit, showing reverence. As I was already standing, I obviously fit in. Gabby would be proud; I would have to get a selfie.

"Right, Ana!" Ed bellowed, and more smiles were exchanged. This was, of course, followed by the crushing presence of Vlad.

He looked the same as the last time we'd met, wearing a flowing cotton shirt buttoned just enough to show the top of his chiseled abs. Flowing hair and pants completed his look as every woman's eyes in the bar, including Jenny's, locked onto the man. Or V, for that matter.

"Hello, everyone," Vlad spoke as Ana walked to Jenny and Ed, exchanging pleasantries. "I'm not here on official business, and it is my honor to be in your company."

With those words, the rest of the Vs and other patrons relaxed. Vlad was not only respected but also feared in a way that was hard to articulate. Before I could react, Vlad walked up to Frank, Angel, and me.

"Vlad." I smiled while he also let out a toothy grin.

"Max, I see you don't disappoint. How's Gabby?" he asked, motioning for a drink that appeared before he could pull his hand back.

"She's good. I talked to her earlier, and she's coming into town tomorrow."

Nodding, Vlad grinned at Angel. The two obviously knew each other. Frank shifted, showing their moderately hidden relationship.

"Ha, ha," Vlad chuckled. "So glad to see you two together. Not like it was going to stay a secret for long." Vlad paused, letting out a long breath. "I know I said this was a simple visit, but we are here on business. Ana has something to talk to all of you about later, and I thought I would tag along."

"Business?" I asked, finally sitting down.

"Yes, they want to take you to the Council holding chambers and show you the round table and all that King Arthur stuff. They have it mostly completed, and I believe they are looking for your team to find the last piece."

While I knew this was coming, I also knew there was no real lead on the last piece. It was a push to get us involved. I glanced at Ed, seeing his face. Ana had already dropped the news.

"Vlad, the thing is, I'm not sure what is going to happen," I said, taking another light sip of my Vamp Amber.

Again, Vlad let out a light chuckle. "You are always thinking you're the one who's going to save the world." Vlad stopped as Frank and Angel smiled, knowing I had. "Anyway, this is more about refocusing the Council's efforts. Truth be told, they are at a loss for the location of the last piece, and they know it will soon be needed."

"We all know that," I pointed out as Phil walked over.

"What's this all about? Do you mind buttoning your shirt, bruther? Some of us have to keep the hope up."

"Phil." Vlad grinned, turning. "I'll never keep up with you. I heard the news." He was referring to Sheyla. "If there is anything we can do, let me know."

"Ah, bruther, we have that all sorted. Just odd to see you out and about."

Vlad nodded, showing mutual respect. "With recent events, I need to make my presence known. Ana insisted. There needs to be some sort of order to things."

Angel and Frank both nodded in understanding. I needed to talk with Gabby; she would know what this meant. I stood tall with all my newly found stature. "Vlad, this is a celebration for Trish. Let's not detract from that. I promise when we have time, we'll help."

"I know," Vlad finished, turning to greet a group of Vs at the far end of FA's dining room.

"What was that all about?" Frank asked first. I shrugged.

"Things have changed. We all knew things were going to change. All I know," I said, holding up my glass for a toast, speaking up so the rest of the bar could hear, "is that FA's is back open for business!"

Hearing this, the rest of the group also joined the cheer, holding up their glasses. The Pixie crew did so as well, buzzing around the bar.

"Max," Vlad said under his breath, coming closer once again and leaning over. "Do you know what you are?"

This question took me off guard. I shrugged. "A little."

"You know what demons are?"

I took in the comment while working through his statement. "Yeah. I suppose."

Vlad let out a full-on belly laugh, drowned out by the rest of the bar's usual cadence of noise. Frank, Angel, and Phil were the only ones listening.

"They are the Fallen. You know there is not much of a difference between you and others like Gabriel. Just remember that." Vlad smiled, turning to the rest of the bar and lifting his glass.

With my cheer over, the rest of the bar started to get back into the flow of having a good time. Ed eventually made his way to me, motioning me over.

Vlad, seeing a group of Vs by the fireplace awkwardly burning in Florida, smiled before walking to the group. Frank and Angel both lightly bowed their heads, giving Ed and me some room to talk.

"What's up?" I asked, seeing his face morph. I decided to pack Vlad's comment away for later.

"I just received a message from the marshals. You know that alert we saw earlier? It appears there is another event with regulars and a lone sensitive. Something's going on in town. I put a call in to Goolsby; he'll know." Ed shuffled. "I'm not trying to kill the mood, but it may be something to keep an eye on."

"Event?" I asked as Ed breathed out.

"Right, there's been two deaths of magical types at the hands of regulars. Not earth-shattering stuff, but something we may need to check out."

"Sure," I said before pointing at the kitchen, wanting to change the topic. "You know Ben's back there cooking?"

"Really?" Ed replied, taken off guard by the comment. "I wondered what the old bugger was up to since his fitness channel was shut down."

Smiling, I grabbed another Vamp Amber, which Sarah

dropped off. I needed to talk with her. "We can talk about it later. We still have Dick coming into town."

Ed saluted before walking off as I turned to Sarah. "How are things going? I haven't talked with James recently. He good?" I hadn't talked to either of them in some time.

"Good. I'm sure Vlad told you the news. It sounds like things are starting back up soon, and we will be expected to help. As for James . . ." Sarah trailed off, not wanting to talk about it.

Smiling, I took my drink and downed it in one gulp. "Fair enough. He's busy as always, I take it. Listen, I want to set aside some time to catch up. I'm not sure when that will be, but I wanted to let you know if there's anything you need, don't hesitate to ask. If time permits, I want to go to the Everwhere and take you with me."

Sarah nodded. "Of course, I'd love that. Max . . ." She hesitated. "We need to talk about other things. You know, I get the Everwhere, but let's be real. My sister, while important to me, is not my priority. Keeping things going here is."

"You always have things figured out. I think it's time to get a few more of these Vamp Ambers in me," I insisted. Without hesitation, she set two more down in front of me, placing her hand on mine.

"I'm glad you're back, and I'm glad this place is back open. We can take that trip when time permits. No rush."

I placed my other hand on top of hers, patting it. I cared for Sarah as if she were my own sister. While she had mostly kept out of the fighting, she had carried a heavy burden.

CHAPTER 3

Dick Holder

Dick grinned as he saw us walking into the Atheneum's dining room. A plate of what the Brits called biscuits and a pot of tea sat in the middle of the table. Ed, Phil, Petro, and I all entered the de facto meeting space while Jenny and the Pixies headed to the stacks to look for an old potion book.

"Oy! Look at this lot," Inspector Holder bellowed.

"Dick," I replied; I couldn't help but to smile at the man. We had been through a good bit together, including my first real experience as a magical type. Chloe had also happened to be working for him when we first met. "You look great. The missus taking care of you?"

In reality, he used to hate the magical community and often ignored it, but once the shoe dropped with the Balance and he realized his wife was a witch who focused on cooking, things changed.

"The missus is on point as always with the meat and potatoes. She has me on this special tea. Let me tell you, blokes, it's *highly* invigorating. Either way, thank Leshya for the tea. It's been a while since I've been here. It feels like old times," Dick replied. Truth be told, his wife had been giving him a rejuvenation potion.

"Right," Ed started. "We just got back from FA's; it looks like the Vs are getting everything situated. I take it you don't mind us talking about it?"

Ed was testing the waters, but Inspector Holder just let out a chuckle. "Listen here, lads. I got over that years ago. I'm more than aware of the situation with those Scarlet Court blokes."

"Right, Ana Vlad and her brother made a public appearance. It sounds like things are moving in the right direction." At the mention of Ana's brother, Dick scowled. Even though he was more accepting of the magical community, mentioning Dracula was less than appealing.

"Hmph," Dick grumped. "Listen, I think we need to chat it up a little. I didn't come here alone; Tristen is in the crucible room playing TV games."

"You mean video games?" Petro interjected.

"Yeah, right. Listen, he's special—and I mean special. Like the young ones," Dick stated, letting his overly long eyebrow hairs reach his forehead.

I sat leaning back at the table, letting the statement sink in. Phil smacked his lips. "Like the young ones Lilith and the Thule Society did all that nonsense with?"

Dick nodded. "Long story, but it checks out."

"Petro, go get our guest," I requested as Petro saluted, zipping out of the room.

"Right. Why are you bringing him here? And why is he with you?" Ed asked, breathing out heavily.

"Well, that Hermes bloke and Al, that greenish thing or whatever, brought him to the Dunn. I got the call, and here we are." Dick slurped the rest of his tea, wiping crumbs off his shirt.

A light knock interrupted the conversation as Petro flew in. "Come in," I said, looking at the young man who stepped through the door.

Glowing blue eyes and youth not a day over twenty looked at us with a focused gaze as his chiseled jaw flexed. With cleanly cut blond hair, the young man absolutely fit the general type for the older kids Lilith and the Thule Society had experimented with. I didn't like calling them what they truly were; they were in many ways like me—I had just been created from the correct recipe.

"What's your name, young man?" Ed started as Tristen walked farther into the room.

"Tristen. My name is Tristen. Hey . . . I know who you are," he said, pointing at me. "That means the Pixie is Petro."

"And I'm Phil," Phil added not to be left out.

"You guys are famous. I mean. I've seen you guys on TV, and well, I heard that you saved some of my brothers and sisters."

While he was nervous, he wasn't scared of the group in front of him. If anything, his voice held relief at the fact that he was somewhere he wanted to truly be.

I stood up. "If you mean the ones Lilith and the Thule Society had, then yes. We were not able to get the older kids, but as for the younger ones, they are safe. Close by, actually."

This perked up the young man. "Really? Who? Can I see them?"

I glanced at Ed, letting go of the hold protecting my thoughts so his voice flowed through my mind. "*Not yet.*"

He was right. This could be many things. He could even be here to take the other children.

Lilith wouldn't do this, I thought.

"Maybe after we figure out a few things. You're safe now. Why don't you tell us how you got here?" I asked, seeing Tristen relax in his seat.

Petro dusted lightly, flying out of the room to tell the others what was going on. We had worked together so much that it was almost second nature to understand each other's actions.

Phil walked toward the kitchen. "I'll get you a soda pop, bruther."

Tristen let a grin slip. "That would be great. I don't know where to start."

I cleared my throat, sitting back down. "How about you no longer being with Lilith? We know most of what happened there."

Tristen's smile drooped slightly as Phil set a drink in front of him. Within seconds, the young man slurped down the entire can. "Thanks."

Phil shook his head. "I'll grab a couple more for you."

"Thanks. It's something about the sugar; it sort of fuels me," Tristen noted. I would let Jenny know this when she started inevitably poking and prodding the young man.

"Right. Proceed," Ed urged.

"Well, I have to say that I left before you guys saved the younger children."

"Before?" I asked as he nodded his head.

"Yeah, a few of us decided to get away. There were three of us."

I leaned forward. "Were?"

Tristen's eyes lowered to the table. No more words were needed. Something had happened. "Lilith was not as strict with us older kids; it wasn't that hard. Rachell was a strong Gate and Chaos Mage all bundled into one. She came and got Billy and me one night, and we left. I would rather not get into the details, but they didn't make it."

"Listen, Tristen, we aren't trying to bring up bad memories, but it may be important," I said, giving a gentle smile. Petro landed in front of him, lightly dusting.

"You got this, bro!" the Warrior of the Freeze added.

"A group of Mages or whatever came after us." Tristen paused. "Lilith didn't send them." He seemed to show some respect for Lilith. Truth be told, it was mostly the rest of the Thule Society goons who were into the really gnarly stuff. Lilith was just looking for a means to an end, building an army strong enough to take up the inevitable fight against the Old Gods.

"I see. You made it, and the others didn't," Ed interjected.

Tristen nodded.

"Ever since then, I've been on the run, and every once in a while, they find me."

"Who finds you? You sure it's who you think it is?" I asked as he shrugged, popping open another of the sodas Phil had brought him.

"I don't really know. All I do know is that they are looking for others as well. At least, I think so."

"Okay," I stated, having more questions than I would likely get answered in one sitting. "So, what are your plans now, and how did you meet up with Hermes and Al?"

"One of those creatures they sent caught up with me while I was out one night. They killed several local regulars before I could stop them."

Ed leaned forward this time. "How did you stop them?"

"I used my powers. I'm not that smart on how to use them, but I'm strong and can do a good bit."

"Right, we will set some time for you to talk with Jenny. How did these creatures find you?"

Tristen shrugged again before scrunching his face. "I think it has something to do with the magic I use. I know I'm different."

Petro snickered. "You'll fit in just fine here, then. That big lug over there"—Petro pointed at me—"he's so different he can barely keep a girlfriend."

"Okay, enough of that," I refocused the conversation. "Dick, you were right to bring him here. Are you good if we take care of him for a while till we get this figured out?"

Inspector Holder noshed on another biscuit while talking. "That was the plan. I have to go back and get things settled with that little altercation he just mentioned."

I nodded as Tristen sucked down his second soda. "What else can you tell us?"

"Usually, when I travel, it takes a few weeks for whatever is following me to catch up. If I stay here, can you help me?"

"*If*, bruther?" Phil bellowed. "I'd like to see them try anything here. It's been a little slow around here lately, minus all the saving the world muck."

"He's right," I added, focusing on the young man. "You can leave, but I think you would have already done that if you weren't concerned."

Tristen again nodded. "Yeah, I'd like to stay here."

I leaned back in my seat. "Honesty is something we will need here, so I'm going to be honest with you: I'm going to have a little chat with Lilith about all this."

Memories of my conversation with Lilith while dealing with the Dark Carnival flashed through my mind. *There is one child you may be particularly interested in.*

Tristen shuffled nervously in his seat. "You can do that?"

"Considering we're family, yes," I replied. "She's been rather cooperative lately, and sort of owes us a favor."

"Family?" Tristen asked, not fully knowing everything.

Petro spoke up. "Oh yeah. His gramps and Lilith bumped uglies. You know. The old in and—"

"Petro," I huffed. "She is my grandmother."

Tristen's face screwed up, only to settle on understanding before he spoke again. "I mean, she was never truly bad to us. It was the others."

Phil kicked his boots onto the table. "Well, last I saw one of those nobbers, they were hanging on Hades's wall."

Tristen again looked confused, so I spoke up. "You're safe here, Tristen. We have very powerful allies. At least, I like to think we do. We are the ones who took Mengele and most of the Thule leadership out."

"I see," Tristen said as Dick stood up, letting out a belch.

"It's been roses to see you all again," Dick bellowed. "Keep in touch. And Max," Dick shifted to a serious, caring tone, "I'm glad things worked out. I was all pins and needles when I heard you got hurt."

"Missed you too, sunshine," I replied as the round man's chuckle shook his belly.

"Ed." He tipped his hat before walking out of the room.

I turned to Petro. "Can you set him up in one of the rooms and give Tristen the grand tour?" Shifting my focus, I stood, walking to Tristen. "I need you to hang about. Don't get into any trouble, and I'll be back later tonight."

"No worries, boss. I'll have Neil hang out with him. Say . . . you don't mind Pixies, do you?"

Tristen beamed a smile. "I've heard all about you and your friends. I can't wait."

I paused, realizing I hadn't set ground rules for Petro. "Petro. No nudy magazines. No booze. No sneaking peeks into anyone's room." I paused, thinking through what other things Petro and the other Pixies were liable to do. "And no pranks."

Petro screwed his face up. "Me? I never . . ." He winked as he took flight. "Boss, would I ever do anything like that?" He again paused. "No nudy magazines?"

"None," I confirmed.

"Alright, kid," Petro started. "Let's show you around. Boss here just sucked all the fun out of the room. That's okay, though. He's usually right."

Tristen looked perplexed. "Okay . . ."

"Right. Let's plan on meeting in the crucible room in the morning. I have a few errands to run," Ed said, standing up and joining everyone else in leaving the room.

CHAPTER 4

The Long Dark Hamburger
of the Souls

I sighed, gazing at the beachfront restaurant with its outdoor bar and several tables, both inside and outside the building, situated. After being torn down, it had been mysteriously rebuilt in the exact image of its predecessor, though I had a feeling there had been a permanent change of ownership.

Lilith made an appearance every time I walked into this establishment. It was like going to a McDonalds: you always knew what you were going to get.

The tightly dressed, familiar hostess smiled as I walked in.

"The usual?" she asked, her fake smile shifting as she guided me to my table.

"Yeah, minus whatever the chef puts in the food this time," I replied as she just nodded. "No." I stopped, knowing the rules much better these days. "Promise me."

She rolled her eyes as a young man leaving looked her up and down, taking in all her exposed skin. "You have my word."

Smiling, I followed her to the same table I had been sat at during my previous visits.

"I would like a bur—" I started to order but she walked off. "Okay."

I smelled her before I saw her, the odor of the dark, leathery Onyx cigarette wafting in front of me. The click of her boots ticked as she came up behind me before sitting down.

"Hello, Max," she drawled out. The last time I was with her, she and Goolsby were snapping back and forth. Petro said it was "pent-up frustration," but I think they were flirting in some sick way.

"Grandma!" I exclaimed, letting a smile rip as she stayed stoic before finally letting a little fake grin slip.

"Yes, it's nice to see you in one piece." She took a drag of her cigarette.

"Well, I'm feeling much better. Ah," I said as a waitress dropped off a hamburger and fries on a nearby table. It smelled amazing.

"You eat enough of those, and you might just go back there." She pointed to the ground. "So, to what do I owe this pleasure?"

"Straight and to the point; they say I got that from you. Fair enough. Does the name Tristen mean anything to you?"

Lilith became animated, leaning into the conversation. "Perhaps. Who do you think that is?"

She was trying to seem aloof, but it was too late. The name had grabbed her attention. I leaned forward, joining her, and decided to get to the point. The initial meeting to see if we were going to kill each other was over.

"One of yours. Ran away some years ago. I talked with him today; he's safe."

"Safe? Are you sure?" She motioned for a drink. "Where is Tristen?"

"First, some answers."

A drink appeared within seconds, and she sipped on a tall glass of wine before leaning back. "Okay. No strings attached."

"There are always strings attached. Who are his parents? Or was he one of those test-tube babies?"

She sighed. "Remember when you were dealing with all that

Dark Carnival nonsense? Well, remember when I told you there was one child you would be particularly interested in, and you never mentioned it again?"

"That was Tristen," I concluded. "You didn't answer the question or mention it again either."

"Yes, his parents. He is special, you know. Very special . . ." she drawled. I was starting to wonder where this was going.

"If you tell me he's somehow my son, I've already gone through that rodeo."

Lilith smiled. "Oh no. You see, Tristen is, as I said, special. He's not like the others. Not at all."

"Okay, enough of dragging this shit out, Grandma. Oh . . ." I drawled out as a supremely delicious-looking hamburger was dropped off at the table.

Lilith reached over, putting her cigarette out in my fries.

"What the hell?"

"I don't like the fries. Just eat the burger."

"Let me guess: they are enchanted, or if I eat them, I'll wake up in a tub full of ice with no kidneys."

"New management, what can I say? No, it's not what you think. You see, Tristen is very, very old; he was just asleep for a very long time. He is the offspring of Hades and Titania." Lilith leaned back, letting the information fry my brain.

"So, that means . . ." I drawled out again.

"He is a true god. I once heard an amazing story about an amazing child told to me by Tom. Let's just say it was not a simple task to obtain Tristen and wake him up in time to make it seem natural, like he was part of the team."

Lilith cocked her head as I took a massive bite of the burger. Grease ran down my hand in a way that only happened with the greatest of burgers.

"I eat when I'm anxious," I said with a full mouth. Her face screwed up at my almost Phil-level display of sloppy eating. "Continue."

"Tom and I worked together to get him out of his prison. The Crystal King was keeping him; I'm sure you know what happened to him. Tom and I became close during this time. And..." Lilith pointed at me.

I wiped my face off. "So you went and got Tristen, then took your time waking him up. Something doesn't add up. Why?"

"Why not? But before you ask, your mother was part of the deal. He wanted to be part of what I was doing, but you already knew that. With a daughter, it was clear that a grandson would need to be born to complete the chain. Your mother is a very powerful witch, stronger than even she knows, but it had to be a boy."

I finished cleaning myself up before responding. "You're saying Tristen is similar in that way. He was part of a chain. A perfect child."

"One capable of great things, or..."

"Or great destruction. Yeah, I get it. People say the same thing about me. So, he doesn't know. How about Hades?"

"That bumbling cow. Who knows? He has made his rounds, but Titania—now, that is special. Tristen is her only offspring. Maybe you should ask him his full name sometime."

"So, is she looking for him? Is that what he was talking about?" I asked, getting genuinely interested.

"She's the one who locked him away. He was, well, a threat to her. But no, she would not go after her own." Lilith bit her bottom lip, looking up as if grasping for a thought. "Shit."

"Shit? That isn't good. If you don't know something, it can't be good. Or it could be." I shrugged.

"The Crystal King was holding him. The knights of the Old Gods came to his keep and to him. I get the Pillars situation, but perhaps, just perhaps, they were looking for something else."

"Or someone," I followed.

Lilith leaned forward. "Take care of the child. I have done all I can for the ones still with me. If someone knows he's here, then who knows? Maybe you didn't get all of the knights."

"This is bad. What do we do?"

"We? I'm not sure. You? Find the last piece of the round table. War is coming."

"Everyone keeps saying that. Maybe you're right. But I don't know where the last piece of the table is," I said as true concern swept over her face.

"It's not *where* but *when*. You know, the children with me are no longer kids. Before you judge me, they are allowed to come and go as they please. They have chosen to stay. They understand how important they are."

"Like the Avengers or something," I lightly joked. It landed flat. "*When*. Are you saying it's in another time?

"You have a Timegate, don't you? Maybe it's set to go to a specific time for a specific reason. Have you ever thought about that?"

"Yeah, I figured that much out; I was planning on using it soon. What does it do? Go to another time on another plane?"

"The Planes are like pages of a book—all part of the same story but on another page, with the Everwhere holding it all together like the spine."

"Jenny said something like that. She said they are like pages wrapped around Earth. You know more than you're telling me."

Lilith snapped her fingers, and the waitress walked over. Seeing the mess on my plate, she picked it up after handing Lilith a purse. After a brief pause—in which she worked some magic on the bag—she pulled out a book. "Here."

The book was covered in green leather with gold-encrusted flourishes and etchings. It felt like holding a brick as I took it.

"I'm afraid to ask, but what's this?" I asked.

"The story of King Arthur. The real story."

"The real story? I think I already know that one."

She chuckled. "Yes, just like the Bible is the same as it was originally written before the church and Gabriel got their hands on it."

Lilith mentioned Gabriel in a manner that showed respect for his name.

"There's more to the story."

"Oh yes. Much, much more. Just ignore the bits about the female daughter of the Lord of the Underworld."

"You've always known where it was? The last piece of the table?"

"Yes," was all she said, standing up. The conversation was over.

"You know, when you're helping, you're not that big of an ass."

"Hmph. Tom would disagree." She chuckled, fading into dust.

Was she making a joke about her ass? I shook my head, also standing up as the waitress walked over, slamming the check on the table.

"I thought it was on the house?" I asked as she frowned.

"Before you ruined the fries. And for the record, they were just fine."

CHAPTER 5

It's Regular Day

"Grab your shoes, we're going out," I said as Tristen looked at the book Lilith had given me sitting on the table.

After leaving that day, Tristen had spent most of his time in the stacks. I had spent most of the next day explaining the conversation I had had with the others. Phil was less than amused about having to deal with another world-affecting situation after reconnecting with Sheyla, and apparently, Petro and Tristen had found the adult section in the stacks.

Ed, Jenny, and the rest of the crew had left for the Council halls to meet with Ana Vlad about some recently acquired artifacts, plus fill them in on current events, including the arrival of Tristen. While it was nothing serious, it was still their job as part of the Artifact Retrieval Team.

"Where are we going?" Tristen asked as Phil walked into the small alcove next to the Postern with Petro on his shoulder.

"It's regular day. We go out and do normal things," I replied as Phil dropped into a chair, slinging his boots on the table.

"It's a real gas. We go out and act all normal, then someone sees Petro and, well, the evening's over," Phil added.

"Yeah," Petro jumped in. "We get slushies and maybe watch a movie. Maybe we can go to the strip—"

"Nope," I barked, knowing what he was going to say. Truth be told, we had never gone to an adult establishment, but it was on Petro's wish list.

Tristen cleared his throat. "You know you guys look like something out of a movie, right?"

"Perhaps," I replied, leaning back. "With all that being said, we also have plans to make."

"Aye, we know, bruther."

"Another quest!" Petro belted out as Phil and I moaned.

"A quest?" Tristen asked.

I leaned forward. "You heard some of it. We have two things to get our hands wrapped around. First, the final piece of the round table. Second, keeping you out of trouble."

"You think it's safe for me to go out?" Tristen asked as Petro and Phil all shrugged.

"About that," I huffed, standing up. "It just so happens that Angel and Frank are going to be in the area, as well as several marshals and a few others."

Phil scrunched up his face. "What's all this nonsense? I thought it was regular day?"

"It is. We just might not be doing anything too regular. I mean, we are for sure getting some slushies. Maybe a few cheap tacos." I grinned, focusing on Tristen. "There's nothing to worry about." Petro and Phil both groaned this time as I continued, never liking when I made that statement. "While you're in the Atheneum, you are shielded from whatever has been following you around. They doubled the wards in the building."

"Aye, he's right. This place is tighter than a toad's tooter now. All new and updated."

Petro snickered. "Do toads have butts?"

"Shit. Do they?" I asked as Phil shrugged. Tristen just stared at us like we were crazy.

"I'll ask Gagle," Phil said.

"Google. You mean Google?" Tristen asked.

"Aye, bruther. Gagle."

Petro and I snickered. "Alright, the point is to see if we can get a better understanding of what's going on, Tristen. If something has been chasing you, we will likely be able to tell and maybe figure out how to stop it. Hell, we might just get a nice evening out with plenty of folks in the area just in case Phil gets some whiskey in him."

Phil grinned. "Hogwash. It's a regular night. That means I do regular things."

"You drink every night there, chief," Petro added as Phil smiled.

"You know," Tristen spoke up, maturity cutting through his youthful face. "I heard stories about you guys. I doubted them at first, but you guys use humor to detract from the fact that you've seen so much, done so much to help others."

I flattened my lips. The kid was thoughtful, and every word he'd just said was true. But in all fairness, I had once watched Phil fight a ghoul in his underwear, only to have them end up singing old Irish drinking songs after Phil had won.

The ghoul had been terrifying a group of farmers for years, but after making a deal, it was now gainfully employed watching over several of the farms' herds. It had sent Christmas cards, even if they only had smudged stick figures.

"I wouldn't say all that," Petro spoke up. "I mean, I may have saved the world a few times, but who's counting."

"You're counting, bruther." This time, even Tristen joined in with a chuckle.

After a few seconds, Tristen spoke back up. "What I'm saying is I was skeptical at first. But I trust you. I trust all of you. It's all true—the demons, the angels, the Old Gods, everything. But I have to ask: Why am I here?"

I licked my lips, knowing he was being serious. "When a Greek god brings you to Inspector Holder"—I was using official titles to prove my point—"then he, after talking with the

Council, brings you to us, it means something. Hermes and Al knew something was up. I still need to talk with them. The fact that you are tied to Lilith means something, and you mean something." What I was failing to tell anyone, including Ed and the others, was just who his parents were.

"That reminds me. Phil, Petro, can I have a word in private?" I motioned to the door to the Postern.

"Uh, sure, bruther," Phil replied, turning to Tristen. "Be ready to go once we get back."

Tristen nodded as we walked through the door, closing it with a resounding thump. Walking to the center table, I picked up the small eye for the dragon inlay in the door. This would cut off all communication into and out of the Postern.

Petro landed on the table as Phil scratched his beard.

"Spill the beans, boss," Petro urged, sounding like he also wanted to go out.

"Yeah, so Tristen's parents—"

Phil cut me off. "He's one of those test tube babies?"

"No, he—"

Petro cut me off this time. "You're related?"

"No." I paused to see if they had any more guesses to interrupt me with. "He's old, and I mean *very* old. Well, sort of. He was just woken up, so to speak, not too long ago. His parents are Hades and Titania."

Both Phil and Petro's mouths puckered into a shit-festering, "Oh . . ." in unison.

"Yeah, that. The thing is, according to Lilith, Titania gave him to the Crystal King to watch over. Not sure about that one."

Petro raised his hand as if asking for permission to go to the bathroom.

"Go ahead," I said.

"The Fae queen ain't all tulips."

"Roses, bruther. Roses."

Petro waved off the correction. "Yeah, those. What I'm saying is she has been and can be incredibly cruel. She fought in the wars, and if memory serves, when her brother went to claim the throne, she ensured he wasn't able to."

"Able to?" I asked. Petro nodded.

"Well, the story goes that the Council, once upon a time, when they first figured out how to go to the Plane, sent an emissary. It is said that it was the same emissary that she fed to an ogre."

"Aye," Phil cut in. "They talked about this at the Guild. She also fed her bruther to the same ogre, then sent the smelly back of bones back to the Council with a little message."

I furrowed my brow, not liking the direction this was going.

Petro finished the story, which I probably needed to read. "Then the ogre did the darndest thing: He got in front of the Council, then puked them both back up in front of them like Phil on a Friday after happy hour. All that was left was bones and their clothes."

"Damn," I huffed. "Yeah, I know she's not as nice as she seemed, but to have your own child imprisoned?"

"Well, at least the lass didn't feed him to an ogre. No, she sent him there to be safe. While she might be immortal, a blade is a hell of a way to change that," Phil added.

"Keep it in the family when it's convenient for you. I get it. You guys know we will have to talk with Hades at the very least. I feel more comfortable starting there," I suggested as the others nodded. Petro buzzed to the door, pulling out the stone.

"I'm hungry, boss." Phil nodded, agreeing with Petro.

CHAPTER 6

The Cost of Conformity

The Black Beast's engine roared as we pulled up to the unassuming beachfront tiki bar. On many occasions, I had come here for the peace and quiet. It was set in a relatively calm section of the beach, and since it was fall, all the snowbirds had yet to return to their condos for the winter season.

"I don't understand why we didn't just gate here?" Tristen spoke up as I pulled into the parking lot. Most of the time driving had been spent listening to Planes Drifter's greatest hits.

"Regular day," I replied, patting the dashboard. "Plus, I need to get her out and drive every now and then."

"This place looks dead, boss," Petro said, pointing at the nearly empty parking lot tucked between two condos.

"Yeah, I thought it would best to stay out of the city for our first run out," I replied, finally cutting the engine off.

Bill smiled as we walked in. An old man sat in his usual seat, a regular at the restaurant. The man tipped his hat before losing interest in us and focusing on his beer.

"Been a while." Bill nodded as we took a seat at the bar.

"Yeah. Good to be here. Got a little busy for a while," I joked as Petro landed on the bar.

"Hey, man. Max told us about this place. He said you guys make great tacos?"

"Prince Petro, what an honor. And Phil." Bill again smiled. Phil had come with me on one occasion, only to run into the ocean to go swimming after one too many cocktails. "Need me to get a batch whipped up for you guys?"

"Yeah, sure thing. And a round of Miller Lites if you have them." I glanced at Tristen. "And . . ."

"I'll take a sweet tea, thank you." Tristen replied, being too young to drink, taking in the view of the ocean. Happiness crept into the edges of his eyes as we all collectively let out a sigh. In reality, he was likely millennia, if not centuries, older than we were.

Bill turned to a young man behind the bar working in the small kitchen. "Three and a half gold coast plates." He was choosing the tacos for us. I loved this place, and Bill was always right.

"So," Bill turned. "What's been going on?"

Before I could open my mouth, Petro started up like a spinning top.

"Max was in the Under—you know, Hell—for a while and saved the Devil, who is his great-great-grandad. Then, his girlfriend—Oh, she's a super-hot Vampire lady—" I cut him off.

"All right, enough of that."

Bill shook his head. I couldn't tell if he believed all that or just thought it was another crazy story being told at a bar, and the fish was really only five inches long. "We've been busy. How about things around here?"

Bill shrugged. "Well, Mrs. Tillman, who owns the condo next door, lost her dog about three months ago. It was a huge scandal. Everyone thought it got out and went in the water and got eaten by a shark."

This was the entire point of regular night. We all leaned in, already drawn into the story.

"Then," he continued. "Her ex-boyfriend, who comes here every so often, shows up for a drink, and she sees the dog barking in his car. Next thing you know, the seventy-year-old Mrs. Tillman comes over with a .357 Magnum and starts shooting at him. Craziest thing I ever saw here."

The old man at the end of the bar chuckled, adding, "She almost blew his foot clean off. When the cops got here and realized what was going on, her son showed up. He's the local sheriff." Bill let the old man continue telling the story. "The only person who got in trouble was her ex for pet endangerment and theft. No one seemed to care his foot looked like a meatloaf."

We all let out snickers. While it was a simple story, this was the whole point of regular day. No Vampire assassins, no angels, and no world-ending problems.

"What was the brave dog's name?" Petro asked.

"Yoyo the Shih Tzu," Bill replied.

"Here's to Yoyo!" Petro raised his cap of beer.

"To Yoyo!" we all joined as Bill filled up the old man's glass. I was fairly certain the old man, much like me at FA's, had never once paid for a drink in his favorite haunt.

"This is nice," Tristen said after we scarfed down our first round of tacos in utter silence. While not up to Amon's standards, they were as good as shrimp tacos not made by a hellion general turned chef could be.

"Yeah, boss. I see why you like it here," Petro piled on, patting his belly after eating an entire shrimp.

"Do you think we can go out like this more often?" Tristen asked, to which I nodded, licking the sauce off my fingers.

"As long as things stay calm, yes," I replied as Phil and Petro both shook their heads.

"What?" I huffed.

"You had to go ahead and say it. Phil, my man, how long do you give it?" Petro asked while Phil bobbled his head, looking at his castor.

"Probably be best if we head home, bruthers . . ."

As was the norm, as soon as the words left his mouth, the old man at the end of the bar pointed toward the ocean. "What's that?" He squinted his drunken eyes.

I rubbed the gate stone in my pocket, quickly pulling out my phone and making a call. "Angel, you seeing this?" I asked, knowing they were close by.

"Where?" her silky voice replied as Frank said something in the background.

"Something's coming on the water." Petro, of course, snickered at the phrasing. "That doesn't look normal," I added.

"No, it doesn't. Head toward the beach," Angel instructed.

While I wasn't sure what she was getting at, when Angel or Frank asked you to do something, you did it. The trust had been earned.

"Bill, we have to go. I might leave my truck."

Bill nodded. "Sure thing. Is everything okay?"

"Maybe, maybe not. Are there a lot of people around?" I asked, confirming my reason for coming here in the first place, which hadn't included having this place wrecked by coming face-to-face with whatever had been chasing Tristen.

"Most everyone's gone," Bill replied.

We started heading toward the exit to the beach as Phil dropped a hundred-dollar bill on the table. "Does this cover the goods?" Phil asked as Bill slid the money back, pointing at the picture of Max and him from his first visit to the bar.

"On the house. That picture gets me all kinds of folks in here."

Phil grinned at the man, leaving the money on the bar and pointing at the old man. "Maybe this will cover some of his drinks."

"It's going to take a lot more of that," Bill joked before seeing the seriousness on our faces.

Tristen spoke up after making it several condos down from

the bar. "What's going on?"

I stopped just as Angel and Frank walked out several feet in front of us. "Something's coming. I know it looks far away, but if I'm right, something just gated in."

Petro started sniffing the air. "Too much salt in the air for me to tell."

"Are we safe?" Tristen asked, staring at the growing light dots on the water.

I pulled out an Evergate stone. "Yeah, we'll be fine.

"The marshals are coming. You should go and let us see what this is," Frank said, checking the action on his pistol.

Angel, on the other hand, pulled out a katana. It was one of Two's—her Night Stalker persona—favorite weapons. "Agreed," she said, punching something into her phone.

Agreeing but also not wanting to leave, I activated the Evergate stone, only to have nothing happen.

"Hey, guys, the gate stone's not working," I barked just as the two spheres arched into the air, heading directly toward us. Turning, I grabbed Tristen by the arm. "Can you handle yourself?"

"If you mean fight, then yes," he replied, nodding.

"They're coming right at us," Phil barked as the two blue spheres thumped into the shallow water. "So be it." Phil grinned as a sheen of gray haze covered his body.

The water glowed as if aliens had decided to announce their existence to humankind. Two hulking figures emerged, water flowing off their figures. Flat, wide torsos with large, elongated arms lurched forward, running at full speed toward us.

"Those aren't like the last one," Tristen warned as Frank and Angel jumped in front of us with no hesitation. They collided with the creature to our left, leaving us its companion.

I quickly pushed Tristen back while Petro took flight several feet overhead. No words could describe what was standing in front of us. The hulking monster had the body of a wide crab with the arms and legs of a massive land-walking beast.

I yelled, "*Ignis!*" as my hellfire whip slapped onto the sand. At the same time, I pulled a ball of hellfire into my hand, launching it. The sand hissed at the heat, creating a ball of smoke.

The creature, not liking this, shot several light blue darts of energy toward us. Before I could move, Phil ran forward at full speed while Petro darted toward the creature with his sword drawn. I needed to figure out how he had stashed it away.

I stood with my hellfire whip sizzling in the sand as Petro jabbed into one of the creature's four eyes, taking flight after hitting his target. Phil, reaching the beast, sounded like a bell being rung as he launched it several feet into the water, finally turning to me.

"We got this, bruther!" trailed into the night.

To my left, Angel and Frank had effectively cut off all of the other creature's arms and legs, and Frank was now lighting a smoke. For her part, Angel stood over its body, silvery blood dripping from her blade.

Petro came to hover next to my shoulder. "Get ready," I advised.

Directly in front of us, the silvery glow of the last of the angry crustations rippled through the water like an enraged shark about to beach itself.

With all our focus on the last of our problems, a cracking howl erupted from its armless and legless counterpart. Pulsing like a transformer winding up to blow, Tristen screamed, releasing a massive silver pillar of energy from a spell, slamming it into the creature, which rocketed hundreds of feet into the ocean.

Before it could land, a massive explosion rocked the night sky. Tristen ran forward. "Don't let it get out of the water!"

Shifting my approach, I pulled in my hellfire whip and launched several balls of hellfire into the water, bringing it to a hissing boil. It was evident the creature couldn't launch out of the water and was pushing its way through the loose sand.

The silvery glow faltered as I pulled back my will. "Can you do that again?" I asked Tristen, who nodded.

Spreading my hands, the water started shifting, creating a path. Flopping fish glistened under the bright moonlight just as the glowing monster came into clear view.

"Now!" I shouted at Tristen, who again launched another pillar of whatever magic he was using directly into its chest. This time, a large chunk of its head evaporated, the clear signs of boiling water on its glowing skin showing.

The fight was over as its body went limp.

"Phil, grab that thing," I huffed, the strain of keeping the water back creeping through my essence.

"Ah, bollocks," he huffed, running into the sand.

Angel and Frank stood beside each other, watching as Phil chucked the remnants of the body on the beach. As always, I knew just what Phil needed.

A bath.

He looked me in the eyes. "No, bruther!"

I let the wall of water around him crash down on his sides as he flailed for several seconds before finally standing up and realizing his head was above water.

"Kenny Loggins looking, but muncher!" Phil exclaimed as I almost toppled over laughing at the creative insult.

"First of all, I don't look anything like Kenny Loggins," I started as Frank chucked Phil a pack of dry cigarettes. While he had slowed down, he still carried a pack for times like these. In reality, his violent assault on nicotine gum had been just as offensive as him lighting up a smoke in places such as the grocery store or in the middle of a public library, as he once had.

"Ah, bruther, this will do. I'll remember that. Yes, one shenanigan owed." Phil grinned, knowing it was funny. Petro was snapping pictures with his small smartphone while snorting, proving the point.

"Tristen, what the hell was that?" I asked as Angel and Frank walked up to the now dull body.

"I don't know. It just happens," he replied, looking sheepish.

Knowing his lineage and having been around other angelic types, I had a feeling I knew precisely what he had done. This would need to be discussed with Devin, or even Trish.

"Yeah, that was some cool voodoo," Petro said, finally landing on my shoulder.

"Just take it easy. It's safe," I reassured him. He nodded.

"No more regular night? Or was that supposed to happen?"

"Both," I said as Phil started blowing smoke rings into the night.

"You're going to want to see this," Frank called as we made our way over to the body. He reached down, pulling out a large object from its back before quickly dropping it on the ground. The sounds of sirens started echoing behind us, meaning it was also time to go.

"Petro, that look familiar?" I asked as he took a sniff, wrinkling his nose.

"Oh yeah, boss. It's from the Crystal King's place."

Nodding, I took a clearing breath. "Yeah, that's what I was thinking. I saw a ton of those fall out of the rock gorilla things."

"What does that mean?' Angel asked.

"The knights of the Old Gods were using them to control Ordius's guards, or whatever they were."

Seeing my flat expression, she slipped on a glove and picked it up. "So this isn't good. Or by chance . . . ?"

"No." I glanced at Tristen, activating the gate stone. "This might be moving things up a little."

"What things?" Phil asked, finally walking over.

"The round table. We have to get the last piece of it," I replied, walking through the gate.

CHAPTER 7

Special Operations Unit
Alpha. So It's a Thing

Under the Council halls, in an area I didn't know existed, sat the special operations unit headquarters, also known as the home of the Night Stalkers. Sleek lines and exhaustive organization made the space look like something out of a movie.

Tech I hadn't seen previously and randomly sealed rooms all culminated on a massive room with all the currently owned pieces of King Arthur's round table put in order, the one remaining gap in the circular device making it resemble a smiling hockey player.

The entire crew, including Goolsby and several members of the Supreme Council, were present. Ana, Davros, Mouth, Carvel, and Jamison were flanked by the one and only Aslynn.

"Right," Ed cleared his throat. Tristen was in another room talking with a group of Night Stalkers about his prior run-ins with the creatures. They were already dissecting the one we had captured, working on how to stop them effectively. "It appears we have a situation that will need to be resolved sooner rather than later."

Davros cut him off, flailing his hand around the room. "Yes, yes," he growled. "This is the first real report of one of the Old

Gods' scouts being on Earth."

"Correction." I raised my hand.

"Yes?" Davros let me continue.

"I believe Tristen. This isn't the first time. Think about it." I looked around the group as Mouth rolled his eyes. "We figured the knights of the Old Gods had gone rogue after centuries of being on their own. With that control crystal, as Dr. Simmons called it," I said, using Jenny's official title, "they had been working to take over the Plane on their own. I believe these are somehow the leftovers."

"Perhaps," Davros drawled out. "Perhaps not. Either way, as Ed stated, we can no longer wait to obtain the final piece of the table. It is my understanding you know where that is."

"When," I corrected. "It's a long story, but Lilith said it was in the past. Though I don't know what all that means."

Jamison stepped forward. "That means the table is in the past until you get it."

"He's right," Aslynn added. It had been several years since I had seen the two together. "We've dealt with time before. It was sloppy, but as we learned, meant to happen."

Goolsby, in an odd show of interest, spoke up, holding out his hand. "This letter was given to my distant family by Max here. It's the only reason he . . . well, why I'm here. That can't be changed."

I had also given Devin a letter which had helped me find Chloe, a letter he said he couldn't share the last part of. At some point, I would do this. Maybe during my attempt to find the last piece of the table. As Goolsby said, that couldn't be changed.

Yeah . . . I had watched *Back to the Future*—all of them.

"This isn't a quest to find your daughter," Ana said, making a point I didn't want to hear.

The room went silent, not knowing how I would react. "Listen, if it happens, it happens. If not, then as Aslynn said, it wasn't meant to be. Something is telling me the clock is ticking."

I also started thinking about the hourglass Metatron had given me.

Just then, the smooth, silky voice of Gabriella cut through the entrance, walking in. Yes, this was indeed my de facto girlfriend. "Hey, sweetie. Been awhile," she purred, turning to the group. "The clock is very much ticking. We found one of these creatures trying to enter Salt City. Why? I don't know. But it is very much communicating with something."

She walked up, planting a peck on my cheek. With her new role as mayor of Salt City and after taking over the remnants of several Vampire Courts, we hadn't spent much time together since I got back. It was the typical meeting every two to three weeks, leading to us both saying we needed more time together.

Aslynn sneered at the woman. They didn't like each other, and it was as clear as clean glass.

"Right. Do you know where or who they are communicating with?" Ed asked while everyone turned to Gabby.

"It's outside of the Plane, from what we gather thanks to Mags-Tech giving us access to their etho-satellites," Gabby concluded. That was the length of her knowledge.

"Get to it," Mouth grumbled as Carvel nodded in agreement. The ogre had started getting more involved in these types of conversations. The bone he had across his forehead, taking the place of his eyebrows, shuffled.

"Yes, please do," Carvel's nasally voice cut through the meeting.

Ana took charge of the meeting. "Yes, we are aware of the recent uptick in communications we can't track. That is why we are all gathered here. Effective immediately, we are activating Max and Ed's team to full duty under the direct guidance of the Supreme Council. Max"—she turned to me—"you are to use the Timegate and retrieve the last part of the table."

I opened my mouth, only to close it once again. Gabby nudged me with her elbow. "There's no such thing as a dumb question."

Mouth, hearing this, chimed in. "With him, there always is."

"The thing is, I don't know how to use the Timegate. I mean, not fully," I said as Aslynn and Jamison both cleared their throats.

"We have recently been given access to Titania's archives. She asked us to provide you with this, free of obligation," Aslynn said, walking over and handing me a book similar to the one Lilith had given me. She hesitated for a second too long, letting her hand sweep over mine.

Gabby, seeing this, cut a glare through her. I didn't understand Aslynn's new attitude toward me. Had I done something? Or . . . I had questions for Gabby.

Petro dropped down, sniffing the book. "It's one of those magic book things. You know, like the Fountain of Youth journal. It's more than a book, boss."

"Yeah, I figured as much. So, what's the plan?" I asked. The others in the room looked at me blankly before Ana again spoke up.

"The plan is for you, effective immediately, to put all your resources into this. You will have the full backing of this Council." She turned to Goolsby.

"Yeah, I'm in," he rumbled.

"Great," Ana declared with finality. "It's settled. You will need to keep the team you take small to avoid any unneeded issues while traveling."

As the words passed her lips, an alarm sounded, followed by several red flashing lights.

"What's going on, boss?" Petro howled.

"Good question."

Angel ran out of the room they were using to talk with Tristen. "We have reports of another of these creatures in Chicago."

Ana nodded at Two. "Send the team."

Several Night Stalkers ran out of the back room, motioning for Angel to join them. Ana nodded her head. "Go," she directed Angel.

I started to turn, only to have Ana directly in my face. "No. You have other obligations. It's time for someone else to worry about this."

Gabby put her arm through mine, and they exchanged a genuine smile. "I'll make sure he gets to it," Gabby assured her.

Ana let out an honest-to-God chuckle. "I know you will."

Mouth, not having a show of affection from Gabby, let out a loud, "Hmph."

"What's up there, big guy?" I asked.

"I don't want to be the one to say this," he grumbled, "but out of all these knobs, you might just be the one to do it. No one else would be stupid enough to handle it."

Carvel snickered. I turned to Mouth as Gabby let go of my arm. "That's the nicest thing you've ever said to me. You want to come along?"

"No," was all he said, pointing at Phil and Petro.

"Yeah, I agree. You'd make us look bad, you know. Too much firepower would make us stand out. You hold the fort down here."

Mouth actually smiled.

"All right," Gabby interjected. "I think we have work to do."

"I need to talk with Aslynn and Jamison before we go," I said, motioning to the room Tristen was still in.

"Right. We'll be at the Atheneum. Once you're done, Max, come see us," Ed said, also turning to leave.

Phil eyed me skeptically as Petro and Gabby followed behind me.

CHAPTER 8

How Have Things Been?

Tristen stood up, but I motioned for him to sit back down. "This involves you," I said as Petro landed on Phil's shoulder. I turned to Aslynn and Gabby. "You two good?" I asked as Jamison let out a little whistle.

Gabby spoke first. While this was a losing tactic for some, for others, it was a chance to take accountability. "My family—" Gabby paused. "What's left of them caused a lot of issues with their family."

"*Issues*?" Aslynn hissed. "Your father once tried to have the both of us killed."

"My father is dead. I do not condone all of the business he was involved in, but let's be honest with each other here: What did your father try to do to him?"

Aslynn took a deep breath before letting it out. "I see your point. But . . ." Jamison walked over to Gabby, reaching out his hand to shake.

Gabby reluctantly took it. "None of us can be held accountable for the actions of our fathers," Jamison said, letting a wicked grin slip. "I mean, look at Max's grandfather."

Petro screwed his face up to argue, only to cock his head, agreeing.

"I guess you're right." Gabby smiled as Aslynn rolled her eyes, finally reaching out a hand. "I promise to uphold and repay any pain my family may have brought upon yours."

Aslynn spoke next, glancing at Max. "I see why you like her."

"All right. With that out of the way, I need to ask for a favor," I started, pulling out the book Lilith gave me. "This is clearly Fae made. What can you tell me about it?"

"Well, it's similar to the one we gave you. Like Petro said earlier, this, too, is a key. It just needs a little special magic poured into it," Aslynn explained as I placed it on the table.

"Okay. Point taken. How am I supposed to know what type?"

She shrugged. "Listen, Max. There are some things I just don't know about. Titania was very vague when she gave us the other book," Aslynn said, genuinely not knowing.

I chewed my bottom lip in thought as Phil walked over to pick it up.

"Well, all this bullshite has me thinking. If I were a betting man, I would say each book is a key to a certain time, and so there are only so many of these books."

We all turned to Phil. Even Tristen was taken aback by his intuition.

"Phil," I said, exhaling his name. "I think you are onto something. The book of King Arthur goes to where we need to get the table. This book?" I pulled out the one the siblings had given me, holding it up and opening it to the title page, slowly reading it out loud. "The Crusades . . ." I let the words roll around in my mouth. "That's not ominous."

"Well," Phil spoke up again, "we studied all that poppycock in the Guild. The Order Society came from those snots. And no, before any of you asks, I haven't a clue what that means."

"It was a trying time for everyone," Jamison said, nodding. We were onto something. "It was a time where several artifacts were rounded up by the regulars in an attempt to keep the Ethereals at bay."

"Oh shit," I huffed. "I give Goolsby's family one of those

notes. I bet I use this book to do it."

"Hey, boss," Petro chirped, smoothing out his mustache in thought. It was as if everyone's brain was about to explode. "Maybe we are meant to go to both places?"

"Maybe. But here is the favor I need." I turned to the two Fae. "We have a stop to make on this *quest* . . ." I drawled out. Petro and Phil smiled. "And we're taking Tristen with us."

"Really?" he burst out, excitement cutting through his voice.

"Yeah. But what I need to do is tell everyone he is with you. We've learned our lesson about playing all our cards," I continued as Jamison and Aslynn glanced at each other.

"Of course." Jamison smiled. "Anything for you, guys. No one will even know if we say we took him to the Plane."

"Precisely," I replied.

"It's settled, then," Aslynn said. "When are you leaving?"

I cocked my head. "Soon. If you two are good, I'd like to get things moving."

"Very well," Jamison said as Aslynn walked up to me. Gabby fluttered her eyes at me.

"I'd not screw this one up." Aslynn smiled, planting a peck on my cheek before smiling at Gabby. It wasn't a show of disrespect but rather her telling me in real time not to screw things up with Gabby.

"I won't. At least, I'll try not to," I replied before the siblings walked out, letting the door click shut.

Petro, having a book's worth of things to say, started jabbering, even with Gabby in the room. "Damn, boss! The ladies were fighting over you, and Gabby was all like *hiss*, and Aslynn was all like, 'Hey, big guy.'"

"Okay, okay," I stammered as even Gabby let out a snort.

"I like her; I see why you are all friends. I'd never met them before," Gabby said, picking up one of the books.

By this time, I was blushing. "It's not like that."

"Oh," Gabby guffawed. "It's just like that. She likes you, but in a siblings kind of way. I could tell as soon as she touched you. They are both protective of you. Well, of all of you."

"They are good people," Phil added. "You both have more in common than a bird in a tree."

I screwed my face up. "Like what?"

"Well, bruther, you were kinda, sorta with both their old chaps when they died."

The sobriety of the statement rang true.

"Honey," Gabby whispered, seeing my expression. She lifted my head with her strong fingers. "Don't let the ghosts keep you up at night. You've done more for her family and, in many ways, mine than we can ever repay. It's the price of responsibility."

"I didn't do enough." The weight of my words cut through the room. Petro buzzed over to stand on my shoulder.

"Boss, think of how many people wouldn't be here if not for you. You're a hero. Or at least, you're trying to be."

Petro was right, as always. Gabby cared for me, as well as everyone else I surrounded myself with. Even Mouth and Carvel had started showing some modicum of respect for me.

"I know. I just hate how everything has gone. Think about it. I mean, Tom, Destiny. Who's next? We have to finish this. And when I say finish this, I mean it. We're going to get that table, visit the Crusaders, and if we have to take the fight to the Old Gods . . . we will."

"Aye, bruther!" Phil bellowed as Tristen, Gabby, and Petro all walked closer to me, holding their hands out.

In a show of teamwork, we all piled our hands on top of each other as Petro spoke up, misquoting *The Three Musketeers*.

"All for one, and one for everybody!"

CHAPTER 9

The Timegate

After our meeting, I met Ed and let him know we were going dark for the time being. Much to my surprise, he didn't push back. It was a testament to the amount of trust I had gained over the past several years.

He understood, and even more, would be there if needed. As always, there was a plan B. But that was for us to know and for everybody else to find out. Yes, Tristen would go with us, and with that, give us more time to figure out why he was so important.

Tristen stood at the table in the middle of the Postern, going through a stack of charms the girls had put together for us. Even Casey had suggested that she and the girls could come along, only to have Neil get in trouble at a movie theater, proving he still needed adult supervision, so they would remain behind.

Gabby, Phil, Petro, and I would be the ones to take on this mission. While I didn't want her to join us for her safety, it was more of a good-luck-leaving-me-behind type of situation. That, and she had threatened to drain me of all my blood if we left her. In all fairness, we hadn't truly taken her with us before, and I, for one, was looking forward to the extra firepower. Since neither book took us to the Plane, it was safe to assume she would be safe.

Going into the unknown was always a mixed bag. Things could go as planned or, as we had found out more times than not, everything could go to shit as soon as we exited the gate.

"Hey, boss," Petro said, landing on the table. I had laid out all the clocks and Tom's journal on the Timegate. "You think they had Pixies back then?"

"That's the thing. Besides the Crusader's bit, who says we aren't going into the future?"

Phil smacked his hands on his head, acting as if it was exploding. "Diabolical, bruther."

"I'm just saying. Who knows. I'm not sure what this whole King Arthur thing is about. Gabby and I read the book last night —"

Petro cut me off. "I'm sure you did." He was doing the hip gyration, a time-honored tradition of Pixies.

Gabby grinned. "Maybe."

"Enough," I huffed. "We just need to understand we are there on a mission. We don't go straying off." My eyes locked onto Tristen. "That means you especially. That's another thing." I pulled out the hourglass full of sand. "I'm thinking we need to pay Hades a little visit first."

While we hadn't told Tristen about his parents yet, it went without saying that Hades might have some wisdom to impart on us. Plus, he needed to know about his son, which I was sure by now he had more than one.

"Aye. Way to use your nogging. I forgot about that time doohickey," Phil explained, reaching for the weapons cabinet as I walked over, pushing it shut. "Waah?"

"No future weapons. Just us and what we can take that doesn't stand out," I informed the group while Phil frowned. "We don't need to take a bunch of guns into the past."

"That's poppycock."

"Yeah, poppy socks," Petro followed.

I smacked my hand on the table, getting everyone's

attention. "This isn't the time, gents." I turned to Gabby. "And gentesses. We need to be focused. First, we go see Hades, then we get the gate working."

Tristen spoke up first. "*The* Hades? He is real?"

"Yeah, kid. Very much so. Look, I'm going to lay it out. He is . . ." I hesitated, getting a knowing look from Phil and Petro. They cared about his feelings.

"Ah, just say it, bruther. He's your old man," Phil blurted out. Tristen simply nodded.

Petro flew to Tristen's shoulder, slowly landing. "It's okay. My dad used to fart in the main offices of the Fae High Court and leave. Let me tell you, son. We all have our skeletons."

"Tristen," I said, seeing the truth landing on his face.

"I know. I mean, I didn't know, but I knew I was different, even from the other kids. I knew there was more. What else do you know?" Tristen asked.

Again, glances were exchanged around the room.

"It's complicated," I sighed, seeing his face.

"What?" he asked. It wasn't that he was aggravated or even surprised. He just wanted to know.

"Your mother—"

Petro cut me off. "Your mom is Titania. The Fae queen."

Tristen looked confused before controlling his emotions. "Okay. What does that mean?"

"That means, bruther, that you are sort of a demigod. You know. All powerful," Phil blurted out.

Gabby walked over, scratching Tristen's back as only a mother could, smiling at him before talking. "It means you are important. Everyone is important, but you . . . you are truly important."

I sighed, knowing the feeling of learning life-changing news. "Kid, it ain't half bad having a famous family, but it doesn't need to leave this room. If certain people knew, it could cause issues. Issues you don't want to deal with."

"Okay." Tristen nodded. There was relief from knowing who his family was showing on his face.

"Well," I started, opening the box with the two clocks I had secured from the part of the table we'd retrieved from Salt City. "Here is what I'm thinking. We have two books and two clocks. I'm not sure who planted the pictures, but it's clear someone did so long ago. I shouldn't have burned them. All we have are these drawings I made of them when we got back."

Gabby picked up one of the clocks and the drawing of them sitting beside each other. "You notice something about the hands?"

I leaned over her shoulder. "They're still in the clocks?"

Gabby then picked up another drawing showing the back of the clocks. "Yes, and there seems to be a keyhole in the back."

She pulled the winding dial out of the clock. At the same time, the dials shifted to a set time by design. Smiling, Gabby pointed at the clear opening for a key where she had removed the dial.

"Hmph," I blew out. "You're saying that the books are keys, and we put them in the clocks. Then . . ."

"Then we activate the gate with one of the clocks. We take the key from the face of the clock and use that one. If I were to guess, there are more than just these two clocks, even though they are similar down to the cracked fronts," Gabby finished.

I bobbled my head. "Not to mention there are three that I saw in the pictures."

"Hey," Petro started. "How do we figure out which clock goes with which book?"

Again, Gabby smiled, opening Lilith's book. On the bottom of the first page was a date. She turned the clock around, showing a matching number. "It's genius if you think about it. Like one of the nuclear code things. You have to have both parts of the key to use the gate."

"Okay, so like the last book we got a key from, we just need to . . ." I licked my lips, grabbing the book and taking several steps back. Pushing my will into my hand, I let energy flow from my body as hellfire danced from my hands.

This time, the book started pulling from me as hellfire encircled it.

"Wow," Phil mouthed, backing up not to get his beard burnt.

Red flame flowed around the book as I set it down, still letting energy flow into it. The metal engravings on the front of the book started flowing together, forming a key. In less than a minute, it was over.

"Hand me the other book," I said as Gabby chucked it at me.

This time, however, instead of hellfire, blueish water magic started the same process. Again, I set the book down, and another key emerged from the book's cover.

"See, boss." Petro winked. "All you needed was a pretty lady."

Gabby grinned. "Prince Petro, if only we had met sooner."

I smiled at the interaction as I picked up the keys, placing them on the table next to the hourglass and clocks. "You know something about this time stuff? I'm fairly certain I take those pictures and put them in that table at some point. I must not have put the rest of the pieces together to prevent us from using the gates early."

"Bruther, I need you to bring it down to a first-grade level," Phil blew out.

"We are supposed to be doing this right here, right now. No sooner, no later. Now, I say we head over to see Tristen's pops. Listen, man, I wouldn't set my expectations too high here. I'm not even sure we are supposed to do this, but something is telling me it's important. He might be able to help you out."

"In what way?" Tristen asked. His energy was contagious; he was excited.

"He will know how to get whatever is tracking you to stop. You guys are blood. He will know," I explained while everyone nodded. "In addition, if everyone thinks you are on the Plane with Aslynn, and whatever shows up there, we will know it's something different. Plus, Titania will handle it."

"Let's go see the old underworld bag of bones!" Petro exclaimed. "Don't forget I had to go see him last time to come save you in the Under. He owes me a favor."

"Favor?" I asked as he did the hip gyration.

CHAPTER 10

Dear Old Dad

The cup hit the wall before I could get a word out. Lana, Elf warrior and guardian of the Everwhere's version of the Atheneum, was clearly distraught. Small speckles floated in the room, as was the norm in this version of the Atheneum. The usual cool breeze of the in-between added to the familiarity of the room we were now standing in.

Petro dusted as he flew behind me, being the target.

"She's got rabies, boss!" Petro exclaimed as I held my hands out. Gabby, for her part, was leaning against the doorframe of the vault leading to the gate to Hades Keep, grinning while lighting a smoke.

"Now, just wait," I said as she pulled out a dagger.

"Lass!" Phil interjected.

Gabby had seen enough.

Moving at lightning-quick speed, Gabby shifted off the door, grabbed the knife, and raised her hand. Lana froze. Gabby had a way of doing that. The look on her face was calm yet definitive in its meaning.

"Enough. I can see somethings got you upset. Let's see if we can sort it out," Gabby proposed.

Lana let her shoulders slump before realizing she was, in

fact, acting crazy, and we were her friends. "Alright. Petro," she huffed as Gabby handed her knife back. "Why don't you tell everyone about your brother breaking up with me?"

I glanced at Gabby, seeing her holding in a laugh. Shaking my head, she quickly realized the seriousness of the situation.

"What do you mean he broke up with you?" Petro guffawed, flying out from behind his cover—that cover being me.

"He was here, then said he had to go and wouldn't be back for a few days."

"So?" Petro followed, screwing up his face.

"That was eight months ago. He has another Elf—I know it!" Lana proclaimed.

Petro let out a snort, only to get a death stare. "No. I talked to Gran a few months ago. The old fart box Gaseous and Gran got in some trouble and were given community service. That means no leaving town. He wanted me to get a message to you." Petro's face dropped.

"Petro?" Lana asked as he dusted lightly.

"Oh, yeah. My bro has a message for you. He is stuck on the Plane for the next ten months; he got in some trouble. He misses you, and something about his baby boo-boo," Petro spit out.

"Really?" Lana asked, her mood shifting.

Phil spoke up this time. "What did the little turd do?"

"Yeah, he and the gas man got caught tooting in the queen's guards' ride when they came to town. They may have gotten drunk and drawn a naked scimitar on Titania's windshield. It had a huge wien—"

"Okay, we get the picture," I interrupted before Petro could finish. He continued.

"With the new Pixie alliance, instead of having them killed, she just has them cleaning up the embassy's garden. You know, getting rid of the bugs."

"I'm so confused," Tristen added, not wanting anything to do with an angry, scorned Elf.

"Lana and Petro's brother have been dating for a couple of years," I explained as Lana shifted, grabbing her bag. "Where are you going?"

"The Plane. My little lover needs me." Lana turned on her heels and headed toward the Everstern, leaving us alone.

"You guys never disappoint," Gabby said. "What's next?"

"Let's get moving. Petro, activate the gate," I instructed as he zipped into the dark room.

Tristen shrugged, following as Phil motioned him into the room. This was the only known gate to Hades Keep. Fortunately for us, Hades had cranked down the shrinking tunnel of doom, leaving us a nice long pathway to his main chamber halls.

Gabby and Tristen, not being familiar with Hades other than the usual stories, walked several feet behind us.

"Old grumpy pants ain't that bad," Petro finally spoke, his small voice echoing.

"The Lord of the Underworld," Gabby said. This was the first time I could remember hearing hesitation in her voice.

Tristen, on the other hand, was full of nervous energy. "Where is he?" Tristen asked as Petro darted to the large door which led to Hades's main throne room.

Petro started knocking on the door with the hilt of his dagger. "Open up. I won that bet, and you owe me!"

Silence greeted us before the sound of something shuffling inside eventually made itself known. "Who is it?" a booming voice echoed from behind the door.

"You know who it is; you're Lord of the Underworld! It's Prince Petro, and you lost the bet. Time to pay up!"

I swatted at Petro. "What the hell is that all about?"

"Yeah, we made a bet when I came through here to save your skinny ass."

Gabby snorted. "It *is* rather skinny."

"What was the bet?" I asked, ignoring the comment.

"Well, he bet we wouldn't make it back. I bet we would," Petro replied, knocking on the door again.

"Bruther, what did you bet?" Phil inquired.

"Well, if we didn't make it," Petro started, "he would get my DVD collection. And if we did, I could pick something from his treasure room. He was showing it off, and there was a kickass set of silver wing braces and armor in there. He didn't want me even looking at it."

"You mean Orion's armor?" Tristen spoke up.

Even I had heard of it. It was celestial armor worn during the Great War by the king of the Pixies, given to him by Gabriel himself—an angel I also happened to have met. Believe it or not, I had read some of the books on artifacts Jenny had recommended after Ed was put in charge of the Artifact Retrieval Team.

"Yeah, that's the one," Petro replied.

"Hold on, bruther. You bet your"—Phil lowered his voice —"*grown-up* DVD collection?"

Petro dusted. "Yup. There was no way I was going to let him get his hands on those; they're collector's items."

"Sure. I'm sure Casey wouldn't mind," Gabby drawled, walking over and knocking on the door.

"I'm busy," Hades boomed.

"My name is Gabriella. I am Barnabas's daughter, and we are here with your son."

More silence greeted us before the door slid open after another minute. There, standing in all his glorious shining armor, was Hades. It was evident he didn't like losing bets. Or, as *I* was betting, he never actually did.

"I see," Hades said before shifting to a welcoming smile. "Well, come in, please. You are my guests. Food and drink!" he bellowed, clapping his hands. Several small ghouls came running out with full trays.

"Hey, what happened to all the Pixies?" Petro asked as Hades motioned for us to sit at the large table in front of his massive throne. He was, of course, several feet taller than the rest of us.

Tristen was the last one to enter and sit down. Hades cleared his throat. "Barnabas was a good man. He kept me very busy back in the day. I know who you are, Gabriella. My condolences to you and your remaining family. He visited me once—him and Vlad."

Hades was avoiding the main topic sitting at the far end of the table.

"Thank you for the hospitality." Gabby turned to us. "Again, you all never fail to disappoint. I thought you all were joking."

"Joking?" Phil guffawed, already two glasses of wine and a turkey leg deep. "Wait till you see his collection." He motioned to all the figures encased in the walls while Gabby's face went blank.

I cleared my throat. "Hades, it's always a pleasure." The Lord of the Underworld nodded. "I need you to meet someone. Tristen." I motioned for him to come closer.

In a show of courage, Tristen walked directly up to Hades's gleaming shin braces. The room stilled as Hades leaned forward, his steel-gray eyes locking onto Tristen's. He was clearly doing something. Both men stayed completely still, locked in place.

Petro dusted slightly, setting his cap down. "It's a soul gaze, boss. It will take a few minutes."

I leaned forward. "Petro, what did you do when you came through here last time? He seems a little different."

"Well, we had a party," Petro said, picking up his drink.

"Let me get this straight. While you were on your way to the Under to save me, you stopped and had a party with Hades?"

"Yeah, boss. Told you it was a crazy trip. It got nuts! There were imps, and I had to call Casey to tell her about the ghouls. Then Cerberus showed up, and the party really started." Petro stopped, realizing I was just staring at him.

"Cerberus?" Gabby asked.

"Aye, lass. He's real, and he's such a good doggy. All three of his heads," Phil said in a gushing voice only fit for describing a dog.

Gabby opened her mouth, only to snap it shut again before finally speaking. "Everything you said wasn't bullshit. You know, Max, I don't think people realize just how crazy you truly are."

"Yup," I replied while Tristen slowly started to move.

"He's moving, guys," Petro said as Hades shifted his eyes to us.

Tristen let out a gasp, turning to the table. "I . . . I . . ."

"Have a seat. It will be okay," I instructed, motioning beside me.

Hades stood up with a concerned look on his face before grabbing a goblet full of wine and downing it in one long gulp. I glanced around the room, seeing Maman Brigitte encased in the resin prison, on display for everyone to see.

"I find myself at a loss for words for once," Hades said softly, walking to Tristen and patting him on the shoulder with his massive hand. "If I'd known Tristen was there all this time . . ."

"You would have what?" I asked, taking everyone off guard.

"I would have helped," Hades finished, unfazed. "Does Titania know?"

"Not yet," I replied.

Hades motioned for the ghouls to leave. "Why are you truly here, Max Abaddon Sand?"

"Besides introducing you two? To get the last piece of the round table."

Hades paced around the table, looking at his trophies, flinging his arms behind his back while walking. He was waiting for me to continue.

"It's in another time. The time of King Arthur. We're taking the Timegate and Tristen with us."

Pausing by the angry figure of Mengele, Hades took in a

longer-than-needed breath, almost sucking all the air out of the room.

"So, it's time," he exhaled.

"Time for what?" I asked as he went back to his throne, sitting down.

"I have it on good authority that when the table is brought back together, the Old Gods will come," Hades said, his words heavy.

Phil leaned forward. "Then why don't we just not get it and all that nonsense?"

"What has already happened will happen," Hades replied, taking another sip of his goblet. It seemed to be filling itself. "They already know where we are. It's just the when they are missing. You see, Max, regardless of what anyone does, you eventually go through that gate. You are thinking about things like humans. The table must be brought together. You see, it never truly was."

"I don't understand?" I said as Petro chimed in.

"Yeah, I don't underman either," the Warrior of the Freeze huffed.

Hades sighed. "It is no coincidence you are here. It's no coincidence Tristen, my son, is here." He was affirming their relationship, to Tristen's pleasure. "The gods themselves have brought us together. We knew this time would come." Hades held up a hand, signaling to let him continue.

"Max, everyone knows this has been coming, the question is when. You think we know, but as with everything, there are some of us gods who don't. You don't believe that Metatron getting involved with you was a coincidence? Remember, he knows everything all the time, everywhere, at any time."

"Oh Jesus," Gabby huffed.

"What, lass?" Phil asked.

"So, the Metatron stuff was also real," she breathed out, smiling.

"Yeah, I wasn't dreaming that stuff," I replied, turning my attention back to Hades. Gabby was still trying to process everything I had told her. While she believed it, hearing it out loud and being discussed by the Lord of the Underworld was another level of truth she was still becoming accustomed to.

"Max, what will be will be, and what has been, has been," Hades said, snapping his finger. A ghoul materialized out of thin air. "Please open the vault door."

"The vault!" Petro exclaimed. "You actually paying off the bet?"

Hades nodded. "And maybe a little more. It is my understanding you have the hourglass, speaking of Metatron?"

"I almost forgot," I said, pulling it from my trench coat and setting it in front of Hades.

"Yes. I have wanted this back for some time. But for now, it will remain in your possession. Do you know what this does? What this truly does?" he asked.

"It tells us when our time is up," I answered. Hades smirked.

"True, but it also has the ability to fix something that has been broken. It's a one-time thing, but if you ever break the glass and pour the sand on whatever has been broken, it will be fixed. Also, know that if you break something that was once mine or taken from me, you owe me."

There was a reason he was telling me this, but I couldn't figure out what would be so important to fix. From what I'd gathered, the hourglass alone could tell you when your time was up in any situation, something so valuable in itself that it would be hard to justify using its other power.

And I finally noticed the sand in the hourglass was quickly draining.

"I can see by the look on your face that you truly value time. Good," Hades said, motioning us to the vault door. "Now, time for me to break a few rules." He rubbed his hands together.

"Right on, bruther!" Phil said as Hades wiggled his eyebrows with a wicked grin.

The Lord of the Underworld paused in front of the amber cases embedded in his walls, pointing. "The Green Knight. I may know your story better than you understand the real story of King Arthur." He shifted his focus. "Petro, the armor is yours, of course. For the rest of you, please acquire one item. Max, you have yours. Please walk with me for a moment."

"How will we know what we can take and what it does?" Tristen asked.

"You will know," Hades replied.

We walked through his main chambers into the stone entranceway, where the sounds of a thumping tail vibrated the ground.

"What's up?" I asked as he looked down at his feet. The Lord of the Underworld was nervous.

"I, uh, I don't ask for much from anyone or anything," he stammered before composing himself. "Or tell of things that may not be. I owe you a great debt for bringing my son here. I am, I am afraid, at your leisure."

"You don't owe me anything," I said as Hades took a knee, getting eye level with me.

"Most men would say differently, but you—you, Max, are not a man. Why do you think you are here?"

"I don't know. My charming personality?"

"I would tear most men to shreds in an eternal hell before they reached my doors. You come here and ask for nothing, yet bring me much. The first time we met, you brought me something I had once lost.

"The mighty Prince Petro brings me knowledge of a music wizard named Phil Collins, and let's be real, one hell of a party. I am told not to allow Casey to know. She is, apparently, a spirit of love and pain—two things I don't do well unless I am handing out the pain." Hades paused for a moment, then started back up.

"What I am trying to say, Max, is that you can take the

hourglass, though I cannot let others know I am so soft. But there is more."

Nodding, I leaned against the cool stone wall. "What's up, man? You can talk to me."

"I knew of my son, Tristen. I even knew where he was. He knows how long he has been gone; I told him when we were having our private conversation. You have to understand what you are about to take part in."

"What's that? Another shit show?"

Hades chuckled. "Yes. I would expect nothing else. Just remember what has happened already happened. As long as you know this, you will be fine. I know you are taking Tristen with you, and I think it is a good thing."

"Why?" I asked.

"History knows," Hades replied, standing up as the vault doors opened back up.

Phil's voice boomed from inside the hall. "Bruther! You got to see this!"

"You know, Hades, this isn't the group to let go wild in there."

Hades smiled. "I know. That's the point."

We turned to see Phil, but we were not really seeing him.

"Ah," Hades exhaled. "I see you found the cloak of shadow."

"An invisibility cloak?" I grinned, thinking of all the wizard movies I had ever watched.

"Oy, I can sneak into the movies, go to the bar, hear what everyone's saying about me, and do all kinds of shenanigans."

"Yeah." Petro flew out wearing his newly acquired suit of gleaming armor. "Then we can sneak into the lady's locker—"

"Enough, guys," I called out as Phil slid off the cloak.

Gabby walked out holding a necklace in her hand. "And that is?" I asked just as Hades said, "She has a keen eye, that one. Yes, the necklace of knowing."

Having no clue what that was, I walked over to Gabby,

looking at the jewel-adorned necklace. Gabby filled in the blanks. "I know this from an old fairy tale. Anyone who wears this can see if someone is telling the truth."

I flattened my lips. "Yeah, maybe you can get something else."

She quickly put on the necklace, turning toward me. "Do you love me?" she asked as I stepped back.

"Yeah, of course I do!" I exclaimed. Even Hades let out a laugh at my nervous shuffling. "What's so funny?" I asked while Gabby smiled.

"I guess you are telling the truth," she stated confidently.

"You have to be touching the other person. She was messing with you, boss!" Petro exclaimed.

"Really?" I asked as she smiled, putting her hand on my shoulder.

"Again. Do you—"

I stepped back as she let out a laugh.

"I think it's safe to say he likes you," Hades guffawed. "Wise choices. I approve. But there is something all of you need to know about your final destination. Gabby, you must tread lightly in the land of King Arthur and the knights. You read the story, correct? The one you got the key from?"

I nodded, looking around for Tristen. "Yeah, we did. Hey, where's Tristen?"

"He's fine. Goble the ghoul is showing him around. He has yet to decide what to take with him. I have a feeling he will know soon enough." Hades shifted his tone. "Do you remember reading about the Lady of the Lake?"

"Yes," Gabby replied, remembering the story. "She was also called Viviane. What does that have to do with me?"

"That name in Latin means alive. Her full name was Olim Viviane," Hades said, walking back to his main chambers.

"Once alive?" Petro said as his armor shifted to a midnight black. Lines of gold flowed through his wings.

"What else was said about the Lady of the Lake? Hmm? No one?" Hades continued. "Some of the stories note that she was an enchantress with amazing powers. Powers very similar to those of a Vampire. Or an Elemental."

"She gave Arthur the sword out of the lake," I stated. Hades nodded.

"Yes, a very powerful sword. I'm just saying that you need to be careful with your journey. Now." Clapping his hands, several ghouls brought out more food and drink. "Where else are you going?"

CHAPTER 11

As with Everything

The next stop on our journey was to go see good ole Gooley pants. Tristen's face was buried in the book he'd taken from Hades. It told the story of the Crystal King and, more importantly, of the time he was born. The book was the same as the other two, clearly with a key to that time; unfortunately, he didn't have another clock to accompany it. Marlow Goolsby pulled up an old map on the main screen of his office computer in Riverplace Tower. Nora the accountant stood by the door, going through several files on a tablet. For once in Goolsby's miserable life, he seemed legitimately excited to see us.

"I knew you would be back," he growled, motioning for Petro to grab a notepad. "But all this, Tristen, that's a new level of messed up, even for you."

I shrugged. "I have to keep up with appearances. So, what are we looking at?"

"My family was from a long line of Crusaders. More specifically, from the first Crusades into the second," Goolsby started as Phil cleared his throat.

"A history lesson, mate?"

"You went to the Guild. You know this better than anyone. Yes, my family was a key part of the Crusades, but not for the normal reasons. You know, religious zeal, wealth, status." He paused. "Well, maybe status, but my family was there to collect artifacts to prevent certain entities from gaining too much power."

I looked at the map, which showed the Champagne region of France, near a small village named Troyes. "Is this where your family is from?" I asked. Goolsby nodded.

"Very good," he said. "Yes, what I know is that my relative to whom you gave that note lived in this town. We also have a copy of the book you sent me the photos of. It's digital but a copy, nonetheless. I would say the gate will take you here if you use that key."

Goolsby pointed at a church surrounded by a large graveyard. "This is not a safe time or place to be. Especially you lot."

"Let me ask you a question. Why would we go there? I mean, it's clear that we do, and it's clear we do so as part of this."

Goolsby walked over, pulling out a bottle of Elf juice from his desk, as well as grabbing several cups with his chubby fingers. "That is the million-dollar question. Max, it's nice to see you have a brain. Mouth and I have been making bets on that."

Gabby stepped forward. "What are we going there to get?"

"I don't know the answer directly, but you do realize what the Knights Templar spent most of their time doing?" Goolsby asked.

"Sniffing butts?" Petro answered. The room went silent, waiting for Goolsby's response.

"Prince Petro," Goolsby grunted, "it's not always about sniffing butts. No, they spent most of their time gathering artifacts. More specifically, celestial artifacts. If I were to guess, that would be the place to start." The once upon a time and possibly still crime lord of Jacksonville pulled an old envelope out of his pocket, slamming it on the table.

"What's this?" Gabby asked before I could spit the words out. She was fully vested and was quickly becoming a full-time member of the team.

"When I inherited that old note from Max, this was also in that same container."

Goolsby motioned for me to pick up the envelope. Carefully picking up the ancient document, I pulled out a browned piece of paper covered in meticulous handwriting. Clearing my throat, I read it out loud.

With this note, I share my findings after our visit from the one known as Max. We discussed many things, but one thing in particular did not become clear until later.

Max told of a wild story about King Arthur. While out on our travels, we came into possession of a great sword several months before our meeting. A sword that, to our understanding, is the very one given to the great king before we wiped him from the true history of the world and put him into fairy tales.

If you are reading this, enclosed is the location of this sword. Due to my duties, I cannot give such a valuable possession away.

Phil took a sip of his drink. "That's deep, bruther."

"So . . ." I paused, getting my thoughts in order. "So we go, have a chat knowing about this letter, and get the sword. This is hurting my brain."

"Sounds about right. I have access to the Templar archives, something the Council has always wanted to get their hands on. The sword goes missing around this time. Before you dick this up, listen to me, Max." Goolsby's expression became deadpan serious. "I don't know what you talk to my relative about, but you go, and you get Excalibur, and you take it with you. Don't get my relatives involved."

"So . . ." I paused again, the word *Excalibur* taking hold of me. "We are the reason that Arthur gets the sword?"

Even Nora walked over, getting a drink, realizing the gravity of the events unfolding in the room.

Gabby took an unnecessary breath. "You have got to be kidding me. We are about to make history."

"Or guff it all up," Phil added, finishing off his glass. "This is some heavy shite, bruthers."

"Hey," Petro huffed. "Since when is Gooley pants a bruther?"

Goolsby dropped into a chair. "Prince Petro, if anyone else said that to me, it would be the last breath they ever took. But with you, I can respect your loyalty, something that your types fail to often embrace."

"Your types?" Petro gritted out, screwing up his face and deciding which eye he wanted to take first.

"Magical types, not Pixies in particular. If you haven't figured it out yet, everyone in this room is connected," Goolsby thoughtfully stated.

"What about the accounting lady?"

"Her too," Gabby spoke up. "Mr. Goolsby—" Phil, Petro, and I all jerked our heads in her direction. She quickly corrected course. "Goolsby, I, if anyone, can appreciate living half in the light and half in the dark. My father once told me you were an honorable businessman. I believe that to be true. Max?" She turned to me.

"Yeah, I think we can get this done without wiping you and your family off the map. Thank you. And one last thing: Is there anything else you are keeping from us? You clearly knew about this."

Goolsby raised his hands, showing his palms. "I have no idea where things go from here. All I know is that things are about to get messy. I'm not talking about the small stuff, either. Everyone knows it. The world is watching. I just can't believe it's up to you."

"Me neither," I replied, standing up and taking a picture of the map with my phone.

"It's settled," Goolsby said with finality. "I think it would be good not to see you lot for a while. Max, don't mess this up."

"Me? Never," I replied.

Petro and Phil both groaned.

CHAPTER 12

France

We stood in the Postern, all the pieces of the Timegate sitting on the table. Petro hovered over the keys, looking confused. After all his research and efforts, Tom had made no notes showing if he had ever gotten the gate to work. That didn't mean he hadn't; it just meant he never recorded it if in fact he did. And if that was the case, then he did so for a specific reason.

"What's up?" I asked when he landed.

"Should we take snacks? You know, some chips, a few candy bars, maybe some bugs? They might have old bugs," Petro said. I shook my head.

"No, the less we take, the less chance of us screwing something up." I turned to Gabby. "You have the clothes?"

The one thing we had done was get some clothes situated to blend in. Luckily for us, Gabby had been able to convince a local theater group to lend us some of their costumes. Phil's was my favorite. His overly tight pants flowed into a puffy waist, followed by an obnoxiously flowy shirt.

I was rocking a pair of leather pants and a more moderate shirt. Gabby, as always, looked stunning in a dress. Petro was just plain old Petro. According to the girls, there were Pixies back in the day, so as long as he wasn't out in the open, he would be fine. To the Knights Templar, he would be a known entity, we just needed to keep him away from anyone else involved in the church.

"It's time," I said. For some reason, I was nervous. This gate working meant many things, one of the most important being me seeing my daughter again, if even in the past.

"Tristen, are you good waiting here until we get back? I promise we're taking you with us on the next one. This trip just might not be as simple," I noted.

Phil patted him on the back. "Aye, bruther. We have some thievery to do. There'll be plenty of shenanigans about on our next trip."

With the Postern locked from the inside and several days' worth of food and drink, Tristen would be fine and safe in here. I even gave him the key to the Messengergate and introduced the two of them.

Tristen, even though he wanted to go, nodded. "I'll be fine. Petro gave me a tablet with a bunch of movies on it."

I eyed Petro. He simply shrugged. "PG-13 tops, boss."

"*Rambo*?"

Petro rolled his eyes. "Okay, and *Predator*, and maybe *Risky Business*."

"Eighties R-rated movies?" I prompted, knowing Tristen was over eighteen but ensuring Petro hadn't gone too crazy.

"Scouts honor, boss. Eighties R is like today's PG-13."

"Fair enough. Let's get this party started," I breathed out, picking up the specific key from the Crusades book and the clock that matched its publication date.

"Hold up!" Petro barked. "Casey, Macey, and Lacey brought the voice potion by earlier." Petro dropped what looked to be a small candy in each of our hands. Gabby set hers on the table.

"You know French?" I asked her.

"*Oui . . .*" She smiled, letting the word roll off her tongue.

Phil swallowed his after a few quick chews. "Bruther, this will let us understand French and speak it, right?"

"That's what the ladies said. We should be good for two days. Lacey did say it can be a little off at first," Petro warned, chewing a small piece for himself.

"Go time, folks," I barked in my best military voice. Tristen shook his head, my words clearly coming out in French.

Standing in front of the Timegate, I felt nervous energy wash over my body like a cold shower. This gate had been the center of my life ever since losing Destiny and Gramps. Licking my lips, I pulled the dial out of the back of the clock used to set and wind it. I followed this by placing the key inside and turning it clockwise. The dials began to spin, finally settling on their original time.

"Okay," I whispered to myself. Shifting to the gate, I pulled the key from the slot, placing the clock in the perfectly shaped slot, allowing for a perfect fit. Energy wisped from the gate as I slowly put the key in the keyhole next to it.

The room vibrated, only to settle after a few seconds. We all turned as the door morphed into a purplish glow. We had done it. The gate was active.

"It was a lot more nerve-racking than I thought it would be," Gabby said as we collectively nodded.

Slowly walking through the gate, I felt the immediate sensation of my entire body being pulled apart then quickly put back together. The next sensation I felt was the cold, damp earth greeting my face as the gate shot me onto a dark, dank floor.

Immediately after, the familiar thump of Phil dropping on my back, followed by Gabby, who did so more gracefully, pushed any remaining air out of my lungs. Petro had traveled in the small bag Phil carried over his shoulder.

After several minutes of getting ourselves situated, we quickly realized we were in the basement of what appeared to be a church. Light beamed between the slats of the wooden floor above our heads as the smell of stale dirt and general must permeated the dark room.

Dozens of people shuffled overhead, the smell of food wafting down from the breeze of an outside door being opened. The more we sat in silence, the more the voices overhead started morphing from a mixture of unfamiliar words into clear English.

By now, Petro was out of Phil's bag and zooming around the underground room. I joined his concerned buzzing, noticing no true stairway to the floor above. The room we were in seemed like an afterthought. If it weren't for several lanterns on two old shelves, there would be no sign that anyone had ever been in the room since its construction.

Petro finally landed on my shoulder, motioning Phil and Gabby to come closer.

"Behind the far shelf, there's a tunnel leading off somewhere. I don't smell anyone having been down here in a long time."

I stood up, motioning for Phil and Gabby to inspect the shelf as Petro landed on one of its corners. Keeping my eyes focused above, I noticed several large figures standing directly overhead having a conversation, which would help drown any noise we made down here.

Raising my hand, I pointed to the lamps on the shelf, which Phil slowly started removing and putting on the ground. Gabby joined in as I continued to focus on the shuffling feet above. As if luck for once had decided to join us, the conversation being had directly above us concluded, and the people moved away.

Petro dusted lightly, getting everyone's attention. He pointed at several old marks in the wall, which told us in what direction to push.

Giving a quick thumbs-up, Gabby leaned her shoulder into the shelf and slowly pushed. The sounds of a busy dining room upstairs drowned out the surprisingly silent shuffle of loose earth on the damp floor. A brief puff of wind caused me to jump back, almost making me lose my footing. Phil pointed at the ground, where I had nearly stepped on one of the lamps, as Petro zipped into the dark passageway while we held our collective breaths.

After a brief butt-puckering few seconds, Petro zoomed back in, hovering by Gabby's ear. He was clearly letting her know it was all good. Gabby continued pushing the shelf as Petro motioned for us to enter.

I took one last look at the gate we had just passed through, feeling the weight of the key in my pocket. The small pack hanging off my hip was full of what we always called plan B, better known as weapons.

As the last sliver of light faded into the stone wall, Petro dusted a lantern, lighting it. Shadows danced off the wet stone walls, accompanied by the smell of the undisturbed dirt floor. At the far end of the corridor, a small dot of light was all that gave the room any depth. It was tight, and clearly hidden out of sight and mind.

"I don't think anyone can hear us in here, boss," Petro spoke.

"Old places always have even older secrets," Gabby responded, locking her eyes on the far end of the space.

"What's the score?" I quickly asked.

"Well, the hallway goes on about a hundred feet and comes out in what looks like an old storeroom. I could smell the night air, so it likely heads outside. All I could smell in here is food, and let me tell you . . . good thing we brought some beef sticks with us."

Phil pulled out one of the small maps Goolsby had given us, as well as a map of what we correctly assumed would be the Knights Templar's base, while Gabby pulled out a small flashlight and beamed it on the camp map. "This looks like the building we're in," she pointed. There were only about ten other buildings on the small drawing.

"Yeah," I whispered. "I would think the head cheese is in this building." I pointed to a large, more decorative drawing in the middle of the map. "Then, I would think the main weapons and stores would be . . . ?" I drew out, looking around at the other structures as Petro pointed at the building next to the one we were in.

"It's this one," Petro insisted. Even Gabby leaned forward to see.

"How do you know that, bruther?" Phil asked, scrunching his face up.

"It has one of those Templar symbols on it. Guessing that means it's the most important building here." Petro pushed out his chest.

"Alright, mighty Prince Petro," I exclaimed, leaning over in a small bow. "That will be our main target."

"I'm guessing it's time we do that splitty-uppy thing." Phil rolled his eyes.

"Yup," I said. "We stick to the plan if we split up. Petro and I find this Hugues de Payens guy. Goolsby said the seal on the letters was his. We know La Count Goolsby works with him."

"We got him, boss." Petro saluted.

I stepped back, looking at everyone. "We'll meet back here in one hour. Any longer than that, we still stick to the plan. As soon as you're done with your part, you come here and wait for the others. If anyone is in trouble, activate the comms stone." I pointed to my ear. While we all had them in, we figured it would be a bad idea to walk around talking into the empty air during the Crusades.

"We'll get the sword," Gabby added as Phil nodded.

"You guys sure?" I asked one final time as Gabby smoothed her hands over the curves of her body.

"French men, and well . . . me?" Gabby teased. "Phil will be able to get around with the cloak while I keep everyone distracted. We got this."

"Sheesh," Petro gushed as Gabby planted a peck on my cheek.

"A little peck on the side for me, lass?" Phil grinned, turning his cheek as she looked down at his overly tight pants. I had to get a few pictures of him in them. Gabby had quickly joined the honorable inner circle of shit talking we often participated in.

"I would go ahead and put that cloak on to cover up the monstrosity they call pants you are wearing." Gabby wiggled her eyebrows. It was time to go.

CHAPTER 13

The Ghost of Goolsby Past
France
Max and Petro

Cool, fresh air and a sky so dark it looked as if it had swallowed the night itself, holding patches of eager stars, greeted us as we stepped outside. While I had breathed in the Everwhere, the Under, and the Plane, the fresh French air from a history I was yet to know filled my body with energy.

While the map had made the compound look small, in reality, it was spread out, resembling a village more so than a base of operations. We had taken some time to get a firm grasp on the early years of the Crusades and, more importantly, the Knights Templar.

From what we could gather, and from Goolsby's projection, we were roughly in the year 1090 to 1110 AD. The only thing interrupting the still night was the comradery and food being shared in the church's main hall.

I patted the bag hanging from my hip as Petro peered out. "You smell anything funny out here?" I asked. Petro sniffed.

"No. Other than everyone around here needs to take a shower and clean their butts."

I watched as Gabby sauntered around a far building with a cloaked Phil close by. She was getting into character. "The main building is at the bottom of the hill. I'll let you know when it's game time," I said, walking down the small hill.

Much to no one's surprise, a guard stood in front of the large wooden doors leading into the building. A dull white cape flowed around his neck, followed by a large hand encased in a gauntlet resting on the hilt of a massive sword. The man's face, while stoic, portrayed the typical time-honored expression of a guard who would rather be off drinking with his friends.

Not wanting to hesitate, I walked directly up to the man, who stiffened.

"Halt. State your business," the guard demanded. Upon closer inspection, he was dressed as a full-on knight. While he was being professional, it was clear I didn't look completely out of place, since he hadn't drawn his sword.

"Good evening," I greeted, having the odd feeling of my lips moving differently than the words coming out of my mouth. The translator was working. Using my prior military prowess, plus knowing how much it sucked pulling guard duty, I shifted my tone to a more relaxed cadence. "At least it's a good night to be on duty."

The guard's voice matched the tough exterior. "Much better than last night. I stood in the cold rain for hours. Could be worse." He chuckled. "We could be heading east with the others."

"Right," I joked, figuring he wasn't going to try and skewer me. "I'm here to discuss an artifact."

"Another one of those, I see. That's the third one this week." The guard leaned close. "Better be good this time. The last guy who stopped by to talk about artifacts is in the brig."

"The brig?"

He nodded. "Something about him having one of those flying little people. He was lying." The guard leaned in even closer. He was the gossiping kind of guard—one of my favorite types. "I don't think he was lying. I think the grand master knows the Pixie will show up to help his friend. We'll see. They set up all sorts of traps."

"So, they're looking for a Pixie? Any specific reason?" I asked.

He shrugged. "You ever seen one in a cage? My name's Gaston, by the way. And who are you?" Gaston was getting back into guard mode. The pleasantries were over.

"Max, my name is Max Abaddon. I am here to see the grand master, and I do have a Pixie." I patted my bag.

Gaston's eyes lit up as he pushed off the wall. "Are you for certain?"

"Yeah." I slowly reached into my pouch, pulling Petro out. Having listened to the conversation, he had loosely tied a rope around himself.

Lightly pulling him out, the guard's eyes widened. "I'll get you in to see the grand master immediately."

"Why are you so excited?" I asked, again feeling my mouth make odd shapes as clear French rolled out of my mouth.

"He has wanted a Pixie for months. It will put him in a good mood, and you know what that means," Gaston said.

"Yup, extra rations." I smiled.

"I knew I liked you. You must be with the knights or with the Crusaders," Gaston suggested, pulling out a key and unlocking the door.

"Yes, I am doing fieldwork. That's why I'm here with this prize." I smiled. Gaston even turned his back to me while walking inside.

"Julius." Gaston smiled, walking to another large wooden door with a guard. "Is the grand master taking guests? This one has something I believe he will want to see."

Julius was significantly more skeptical than Gaston. One of his eyes was covered by a leather patch, making him seem even more ominous. The odd thing about it was that I could feel the man scanning me from behind the eye patch. I was betting he had some type of magical abilities.

"I see," Julius replied, looking me up and down. "If they got through the front gates and wards, it must be safe." His voice, while gruff, had intelligence behind it.

"Yes, of course. Max, show him," Gaston urged as I again reached for my bag and pulled out Petro, who by this point was in full acting mode as my captured Pixie.

Julius's eyebrow almost touched his hairline before he lightly knocked on the door.

"Yes," a muffled voice replied.

"We have a live one, sir," Julius talked into the door. I was surprised he didn't need to scream. Another thing that hit my head movie was the mention of wards. Magic was being used, and the more I focused on my surroundings, the more it was making itself known.

Julius snapped on his heels, turning back toward me. "You are free to enter." Before I could take two steps, Julius smacked his index finger in the middle of my chest.

"Is everything okay?" I asked, not pushing the issue.

"Something about you is off—no funny business. I'll have my eye on you." He creepily pointed to his eye patch. I was almost certain his actual eye was sitting on a shelf inside the room.

"It's probably the Pixie dust," I replied. "I got the stuff all over me."

Gaston nodded. "I heard that stuff can mess with you."

Nodding and ready to get back to it without having to fight my way in and out of the situation, I smiled.

Once I entered the room, several things became immediately apparent. Artifacts—some familiar and others more alien than those I had back home—adorned the room's shelves and various glass cases. Books and other magical items sat on a large table next to a fireplace that could heat the entire building. I was starting to sweat just by walking into the room.

Magic was obviously a more open and known phenomenon

in the history of the world than we had been led to believe. I needed to have a long talk with all my past history teachers, especially the ones who'd tried to fail me.

The door clicked shut behind me, the main focal point of the room coming into sharp focus. Unlike his distant future relatives, La Count Goolsby was roughly two hundred pounds lighter and looked more curious than commanding.

"Count Goolsby?" I asked while he nodded.

"Yes, and you are?"

"Max Abaddon," I replied, waiting to see how he reacted to me being there.

The count walked around his desk, lifting the top of a chest. Frosty smoke arose from the well-used chest. He had ice, something I didn't know they had at this time in history.

"I must admit I am at a loss." He grabbed two metal cups and an ice pick, chipping several shards of ice from the block. "You clearly made it through the wards surrounding this camp, and my guards. Plus, I have no clue who you are, but you know of me."

"Yes, about that. I didn't come through the wards." I was starting to think honesty would likely be the best course of action here. The man in front of me was not only curious but intelligent enough to know when something important was happening around him.

"You fooled my guards. And here you are. Plus, you haven't tried to kill me yet," the count continued, walking over to another chest and pulling out a coconut, two bananas, and a pineapple. "So, you've captured a Pixie?" He turned, continuing to make whatever fruity concoction he was wiping up.

It was time to end the charade. "Petro," I said flatly.

He darted out of my bag, hovering between the two of us.

"I see." The count's curious eyes scanned Petro, quickly realizing he wasn't a normal Pixie. It also might have had something to do with his new armor.

"And you are?" the count asked as Petro landed on his table, dusting.

"Prince Petro. Taker of the Eye, Savior of the Max, Warrior of the Freeze, King of 80s Movie Trivia—" I cut him off before he could get truly going.

"Thanks, buddy. I think he gets the point. I am going to tell you something, but I must ask you a question first," I said as Goolsby mixed the ingredients in a large glass bowl with a hand crank on the bottom leading to blades. He was using a medieval blender.

"Proceed," the count prompted, adding the fruit.

"We are from well over a thousand years into the future. For some reason, I leave you with a note that has been passed down through your family."

The count paused, pouring two glasses; he quickly grabbed a small cap from a bottle on his desk. Petro, seeing the drink, scrunched up his face. "Don't you know to add rum to that?"

The count's brow furrowed in thought. "Hmm. An alcoholic drink. I never thought of that. You know, I put this recipe together after a recent trip east. A mixture of ingredients from several locations all in one place at one time."

"Well," I followed, "trust us. Add rum and call it a piña colada. Your legacy will be one of fame and fortune."

"Will it, now," the count hummed, walking over to a shelf and grabbing a bottle marked with an *X*. "Rum. We don't get much of this unless we are on the coast, but . . ." He poured a decent amount into the mix, but not enough to overpower the drink. "Mostly it's wine, but I am afforded certain luxuries due to the nature of my work."

"Your work?" I asked as Petro took the first drink the count poured.

"Look around," he said. "This is the Crusades. There is a fine line between religion and the magical world, which I am very much aware of. Two sides trying to get their hands on the ultimate power. Please make no mistake; I am a believer, Max Abaddon, but the question is . . . are you?"

For the first time since meeting the man, I had the feeling he was more calculating than I had given him credit for. There was an edge in his question. "A believer in God, yes. In magic, also yes. And to be clear, everything in between. What if I told you I have talked to several angels and demons alike?"

"Don't forget the old man downstairs," Petro added, looking down at his small cup.

"The drink is at no obligation to either of you. You are guests in my office." This changed things slightly, as he was doing the dance. "The man downstairs?"

"It's a long story, but the difference between Heaven and Hell is not as much as you would think. Listen, I need to give you a note. With that, I will answer any questions you may have," I proposed as he handed me a glass and held it up to toast.

Taking the first sip of the drink, his eyes widened. He slowly lowered the frozen drink, breathing out, "Rum . . . piña colada . . ."

"You like that?" Petro asked. The count just chuckled.

"I am at your disposal. If I can't make it through this Crusade, I can make my fortune in drink. I am going to ask you again: What are you here for? I know it's not just to give me a letter."

I nodded, taking a sip. The fresh fruit and less-than-smooth rum mixed in what could only be described as the perfect drink. "We're here to find something to help us complete a mission."

"A quest," Petro interjected. "It's a quest."

"Yes, of course," the count replied, motioning for me to continue as he took several more sips from his drink.

"Anyway. In the future, King Arthur's round table is being put back together. There is something here that helps us along that journey. What that is . . . I don't know. Maybe it's even just talking with you."

Count Goolsby walked over to the shelf behind his desk and

picked up the other guard's eye, setting it in a small box. "I was skeptical of you at first. Not many know of such things. We just had a group return from England who were searching for artifacts from that very time. Around certain people, such words will get you killed."

"Do you know what they found?" I asked, already knowing the answer. The count would clearly figure it out after we left.

"We haven't cataloged the items from their journey yet, but no such tables were found. Some weapons and books, but nothing else."

"Count, our time here is brief. Please ask your questions. If we can, we will help you, but I'm afraid I don't have much else to offer."

The count poured more drink into our cups. "Tell me of my family. Am I remembered?"

Of course it would be about him and his footprint on history. In all fairness, I would ask the same question. "Your family is very powerful in the future. You will have a descendant named Marlow Goolsby. He and I have an odd relationship, but it all stems from this conversation we are having right here, right now."

"Don't forget about Mags-Tech, boss," Petro added.

"Yes, and your family creates a company that helps integrate the stuff you have here with technology," I stated as he leaned back.

"Tech . . . nolo . . . gy," he sounded out.

"Show him your phone, boss. The one from the CSA. It's a Mags-Tech phone," Petro said as I reached into my bag, pulling out the honest-to-God flip phone. It was meant to be simple and had the ability not to allow magic interference with its signal. That was unless you were in another time.

I held the phone up, snapping a picture of the count and turning it to him.

"My God," he breathed out, seeing his own reflection. Petro, doing the most Petro thing ever, clicked a few buttons, and round glasses and a mustache appeared on his picture. "What type of wizardry is this?"

"Technology. This isn't magic—it's science. Well, maybe some magic," I replied as he reached for it.

I handed it to him, and he pulled it greedily to his chest. "Can I have this?"

Petro and I glanced at each other. "Tell you what. I need to erase a few things on there, but if you promise to get this letter and anything else that might be important to Marlow Goolsby in the future, I will leave this with you. But I will not explain how it works or what happens when it loses power."

"Power?" The count set the phone on the table. I grabbed it and started clicking buttons.

"Electricity," I replied as he screwed his face up.

"Magic," he concluded. I was forgetting how things were at this time, and much like the items in this room, magic was likely often used when making things happen.

"Any other questions?" I asked, snapping a quick selfie with the count and the two of us before handing him the phone.

"Yes. How long will these Crusades go on?"

The expression on my face was enough to deflate Count Goolsby.

"A long time, two to three hundred years. There are breaks, but just know that Pope Urban the Second does reclaim Jerusalem."

"The year is 1096. The primary forces are already moving toward Jerusalem. This is welcome news."

"Listen. It's not pretty, and things get worse before they get better. The world is about to go through some of the most trying, darkest times it will ever see. You know about magic, and this should be enough to help you see things through. But I can tell you, most don't. If I can give you one piece of advice: stay here. Don't chase fool's gold. Chase what you have here." I was almost preaching at this point.

The count set the phone down. "Julius!" he called the guard, who opened the door, seeing the small box with his eye on the table. Reaching down, the count poured the remaining piña colada into a small cup and handed it to the man.

"Sir." Julius smiled, taking a drink, after which he slowly pulled the cup from his lips, an expression of pure joy taking hold. "This is amazing, sir."

The count reached out for the cup as a loud slink and thump rattled the guard. The room stilled as Petro wrinkled his nose, flying to my shoulder.

"What just happened?" I asked as the count turned around.

A one-foot-long blade shot back into the sleeve of his shirt. He quickly shook his hand, blood flecking the floor. Julius's one eye started to cloud over as he slowly dropped to his knees. The move was ruthless, swift, and life ending.

"Yeah, what the hell?! He had a future, you know!" Petro exclaimed.

"To start an empire is to keep one's secrets. I would prefer to keep this meeting out of the history books. Julius had no family and was injured during a battle, ensuring he could not bear children. His lineage ended here."

I stepped forward, letting hellfire dance through my eyes. "That was uncalled for, but as with everything here and now, it was supposed to happen. What about Gaston? The other guard?"

"He will meet the same fate, as well as anyone else who you have crossed paths with," the count promised, running his hand over the cell phone. I noticed his uncomfortable shifting, and I let the hellfire flicker out of my eyes.

"Tell you what. Petro here can pix the other guard. He'll not remember the last hour or so—plenty of time. And before you go destroying your own camp, we haven't talked with anyone else. I will state, this is your best course of action," I said with finality.

The count nodded. "Very well." He pulled out a bag of silver dust and spread it over Julius's body. Within seconds, the lifeless figure started dissolving into nothing.

"Oh, and count," Petro started, "it might be a good thing not to be such a dick all the time." His words echoed in my ears in an odd language. "*Ça pourrait être une bonne idée de ne pas être un connard tout le temps.*" The translation potion was wearing off early.

"We have to go," I stated, feeling my lips match my words.

Count Goolsby nodded, speaking in heavily accented English. "Yes, it is that time. I have much to do. Please, write your letter. I give you my word."

Prior to leaving the count's office, Petro made it a point to fart. Anyone familiar with the harrowing history of Pixie flatulence knew the count would not be using his office until morning once the odor set in.

Petro and I now stood in front of Gaston. "Game time, buddy."

Before Gaston could react, Petro dusted him with a flurry of clicking wings. The guard slid down the wall before he could compute what was happening.

"Why did you fart in the man's office?" I asked as we walked into the dark.

"Why not? Plus, he didn't have to kill that guy," Petro replied as the sound of the door opening behind us reached us.

Dropping behind a row of bushes out of sight, we both smiled as the count bent over, gagging in the cool night air.

CHAPTER 14

Shopping Spree
France
Gabby and Phil

The tall, lean Frenchman stood lazily reading a book as Gabby entered the storeroom. Food and other provisions sat on shelves, while swords leaned on racks at the far end of the room. To each side, locked doors secured what was likely the very thing they were there to find.

Looking bored, the man at the small standing desk sensed Gabby before he looked up at her. There was a time in every man or woman's life when they met what was likely the most drop-dead gorgeous person they had ever stood in front of. For the young man at the makeshift check-in counter, this was such a time.

Phil stood in the shadows of the entrance under the cloak, smirking at the scene that was quickly unfolding.

"Uh, um, uh, ma'am?" the guard stammered, his jaw literally opening and shutting without saying anything. His eyes were clearly trying to lock onto anything other than Gabby.

"Hello, what's your name?" Gabby asked, letting every ounce of Vampiress ooze from her.

"I, uh, my name," the young man stammered. He wasn't a day

over twenty. "My name is Jean Paul."

"Jean Paul," Gabby let his name roll off her tongue. Stepping closer, she placed her hand on the rough wooden counter. The night's shadows lent to her already striking beauty. "I am here to see if you have any bath soap?"

"Soap?" Jean asked the air itself.

"Yes. Between the cooling nights and dry air, I am in desperate need of a bath," Gabby purred. She was laying it on so thick that even Phil was standing completely still, watching the utter breakdown of a young man in the face of true, deadly beauty. Gabby was a hunter, and John Paul was the prey in this environment.

Gabby walked to the young man's side, opening a path for Phil to walk around the counter. "Should I be talking with someone else? Are you not the storekeeper?" Gabby asked.

"I-I," John stammered. "Yes. The rest of the storekeepers are away for the night. I am in charge here."

"Oh. The man in charge," Gabby purred, running her fingernail up his forearm.

"Yes," Jean's face shifted as he quickly reconsidered his position in life. To him, this was something that only happened in stories he heard from knights. The love of a mysterious, beautiful woman late at night. With this thought, he resolved himself. "I am the only one here. I can help you. What's your name, my lady?"

"My name is Gabriella." Gabby stepped within inches of the young man.

He froze, not knowing how to command his body. Phil again didn't move. It was like watching art. A Vampire, when they were enthralling a human, was something of legend. The pheromones they released mixed with whatever power they controlled to pursue their unknowing victim. One thing the movies got right.

The young man closed his eyes as Gabby leaned in. But

instead of kissing him, Gabby, not an inch from the man's mouth, took a deep breath, pulling in some of Jean's. The effect was immediate, as the man's body became rigid.

Jean's eyes shot open, the blank gaze of someone under a spell all telling. Gabby turned to Phil, letting every bit of the sauce she had laid on the poor young man drain from her body. It took Phil off guard just how quickly she shifted.

"Lass, you could have at least warned me to turn my head," Phil's disembodied voice floated.

"He's sweet. Naive but sweet," Gabby replied. "The keys are under that desk. We have about fifteen minutes."

"Then what?" Phil asked, pulling off the cloak.

"I'll have to try something a bit more aggressive to keep him still. I would rather not have to put anyone under the fang. Plus, sugar buns might not approve."

"Sugar buns?" Phil asked, puckering his face.

Gabby giggled. "I probably shouldn't have said that, but now you know."

"I've seen those buns, lass. There's nothing sugary about them."

Gabby grabbed the keys. "Are we really having this conversation?"

"Oh, we better not keep sugar buns waiting." Phil winked.

They both quickly moved, checking doors and keys until they finally landed on the metal door in the back of the building. Phil stood in front of the lock, taking a deep breath. "You smell that?"

"Magic," Gabby replied while Phil nodded. Magic was oozing from the locked room.

The door groaned as if not wanting to give up its secrets. What lay before Phil and Gabby was a room full of wonders which would make even Ed, Jenny, and Dr. Freeman drool.

Jewel-encrusted goblets, gleaming armor, and artifacts of unknown origin and value sat on shelves, waiting to be cataloged. The two were unaware that these items had not yet been vetted. The items which had already been deemed truly valuable had been taken to the church's vault hundreds of miles away. That was the point of this outpost. Items secured during the Crusaders' travels were brought to outposts such as this to be identified.

"Holy shite," Phil breathed out.

"Is that . . . ?" Gabby pointed to a familiar-looking clock.

"Aye, another clock. That's coming with us." Phil picked it up before pointing at a stack of swords.

"Which one do you think it is?" Gabby asked as Phil started sorting through them, pulling out his phone.

He held up a picture of Excalibur. "That one." He pointed.

Wrapped in leather, a sword longer than the rest of them had the same ornate hilt as the one in the picture. Phil quickly unwrapped the blade, and an almost blinding, gleaming light beamed from the sword. It was reacting to the magic coming from Phil.

"You feel that, lass?"

Gabby nodded. "Yes. It's like . . ." She hesitated. "It's like it's alive."

"It's giving me the willies. Let's take it and go."

Gabby scanned the room. "Should we take anything else?"

"No. I don't reckon we should. But . . . if we take anything else, it was meant to be," Phil thoughtfully replied.

"Look." Gabby pointed at a necklace similar to the one Gabriel had given Max.

"No. Those are meant for a specific reason. Plus, sugar buns already has one. I'll see if the others are ready to go."

The two walked past a still enthralled Jean Paul, slowly sitting him in a chair before leaving the building as if they had never been there.

Phil activated the communicator in his ear. "Hello, sugar buns? Are you all ready to go?"

Max's ear started burning, notifying him that someone was calling.

CHAPTER 15

What's Next?

T he empty calm of the Postern settled my nerves as we all stepped back into the present time. Besides being called "sugar buns" no less than ten times, our retreat from camp had gone well, as if we had never existed. There had been no alarms, no guards, or any notion from Count Goolsby that the base had been infiltrated.

"Did it work, bruther?" Phil asked as Petro sniffed the room.

"Hold on," I replied, pulling out my backup phone. I had watched *Back to the Future*. I quickly shuffled to the picture I had taken of Marlow Goolsby's letter. "Yeah, I think it did," I concluded, seeing the picture of the old letter I had just written.

"What are you sniffing for?" Gabby asked Petro before we all quickly realized Tristen was no longer in the Postern.

"Welp . . ."—sniff—"it seems"—sniff—"Tristen is with the Messenger," Petro concluded.

With the short few moments of disorientation, I hadn't even noticed him not being there.

"We'll get him in a minute. Let's see that sword," I prompted as Phil clunked it on the table—followed by a familiar clock. But there would be time for that later.

My hands buzzed with energy as I pulled back the cloth covering. An almost blinding light beamed from the sword, making it hard to look at the blade directly. To my eyes, the silver-and-gold wisp of a celestial artifact wept from every fiber of the weapon.

"What do you see, bruther?" Phil asked, walking to the weapons cabinet to grab his actual pants. "No peeking."

"Thanks," Gabby joked, to which Phil blew a raspberry.

"Yeah, I could see your meat and potatoes through those nut smugglers," Petro added.

"It's celestial—no doubt about it. I can't believe it. I mean, you said the picture matched, but are we sure?" I asked, refocusing on the fact that we had Excalibur sitting in front of us.

"We need to show that to the others," Phil suggested as the snap of his skintight pants signaled that the nightmare of Phil's tight pants was over. "Oh, and let the lass tell you about her little shoe show with the guard."

I raised an eyebrow as she just shrugged. "Someone had to make a sacrifice," Gabby stated, running her fingers over the hilt of the sword. She looked at Phil as he walked back to the table. "You're not changing that shirt?"

"I think it's right proper. Reminds me of Bobo's. I might wear it for a few," Phil proclaimed.

"You didn't just ruin a young man's life, did you?" I smiled.

"Maybe a little. But when he wakes up, it will all have been a dream," Gabby said

I picked up the sword and held it at the ready. To my surprise, it had next to no weight for a sword of its size. "Amazing." I paused. "Do we think it's a good idea to let the others know we have this?"

"Well," Gabby unnecessarily cleared her throat. "After our meeting with Goolsby, we knew this was the main reason we were going, so why not?"

"All right. Let's check in with Tristen."

I put the sword away in the weapons cabinet, but as I did, I could swear a distant, ancient voice echoed for a brief second in my mind. *"The end . . ."*

"You guys hear that?" I asked, but everyone shook their heads.

"Yeah, you going crazy, boss," Petro exclaimed, opening the Messengergate.

Entering the Messengergate always brought back memories of my first time in the Postern. More importantly, it brought back memories of the trouble I had gotten into with Carvel when Phil and I had visited him drunk. For those who forgot, it was the whole ICUP note situation.

There, sitting at his desk with Tristen and a pile of pizza boxes, was the Messenger. Having been busy lately, the ancient entity was no longer a dust-covered mess and had even graduated to moving around.

"Hi, honey, we're home!" Phil bellowed as Tristen ran to us. His face was full of wonder and questions. He was clearly one for a quest, as the others would call it. Truth be told, I was also starting to consider it a quest—an epic journey back in time to save history.

"Hey, guys, you've been gone for a while, so the Messenger popped out and got us some food," Tristen said. The Messenger nodded. If I wasn't mistaken, he had pizza sauce on his robe. He had clearly also indulged in the late-night delicacy.

"We were only gone for an hour or so," I noted.

"More like a day," Tristen corrected.

"Well, that explains that. When we use the Timegate, an hour equals what? A day?" I guessed as the Messenger spoke up.

"That is correct. Time flows as time passes."

"You knew about this?"

"You never asked."

Note to self: Ask him about the other gates. I'd never thought about asking him. The more I pondered the thought, the more I wondered if he had been around during King Arthur's time.

Petro cut through my thoughts. "Hey, can I have some of that pizza? You know Pixies and fairies love pizza."

"Yeah, I heard from some crazy wizard in Chicago. He swears by it." I turned to the Messenger. "Were you around during the time of King Arthur?"

He flattened his ancient lips, sitting back down behind his table. The massive cavern stilled as we all gave the Messenger our undivided attention. He had a story to tell.

Reaching down, the Messenger slowly pulled open a drawer. The sound of dust on the wooden track crackled as he pulled out a gauntlet matching the one I had used in the Under. The shiny yet battle-worn gauntlet clanked on the table as he cocked his head. "Yes. I was. I have been here since the time before time."

"That means before the Great War, boss."

"Thanks, Petro. We're all ears," I followed as the Messenger ran his time-worn hand over the massive piece of armor.

"I used a gauntlet just like that in the Under," I said. He nodded.

"Yes, he used to make his rounds. This piece of armor and the one you used belonged to Lord Lancelot, or as you know him, Sir Lancelot."

"Didn't that wanker bump uglies with the king's old lady and cause all kinds of trouble?" Phil interjected. We all stared at him while he shrugged. "Whaa, I read that book thingy before we turned it into a key."

"Since when did you start reading?" Petro asked as Phil grabbed a piece of pizza, joining Petro.

"Sheyla said it would be good for my noggin. Plus, I've been studying the Everwhere."

The Messenger cleared his throat. "Yes, that Lancelot. Make no mistake—he was one of the greatest warriors ever to grace the Earth realm. We all have faults in our hearts. Regardless, Tristen filled me in on things. Did you get what you were looking for?"

"Yes," I replied, acting like I had a sword in my hand.

"I see . . ." the Messenger breathed out. "Why do you think King Arthur, the table, the sword, and everything is so important? Or maybe the question is more about that specific time. A reason for that time to be known and be so important."

I pondered the question, a mix of thoughtful and thought-provoking. The sound of Phil assaulting the pizza filled the space while I thought.

"The round table. It is a weapon and shield against the Old Gods," I replied.

The Messenger grumbled. "Yes, true. But the reign of King Arthur was only so long."

I raised my hand. "I was sorta thinking he was like a Mage. You know, ages super slow, or hell, maybe an immortal."

He shook his head. "He was just a man. An extraordinary man, but a man nonetheless. It was the items and knowledge he possessed that gave him such great power. As for the wizards of that day, things were very different. Often ruthless, unyielding, and small in numbers. In those days, people traveled more freely between the realms. The Vampires stayed in the shadows, and many an immortal walked the Earth."

"Merlin," Gabby interjected. The mention of Vampires had gained her attention.

"Yes . . ." the Messenger drawled out. "It was a time of transition and change. The Postern started soon after the fall of Camelot. My realm was but a part of it. When Camelot fell, Mordred sought to activate the round table. If he had succeeded and not used its offensive capabilities but rather opened a portal, we would not be here right now."

"When you put it that way, I guess it was an important time." I turned, seeing Petro and Phil no longer eating pizza but fully locked in on the story.

He continued. "Either way, Arthur never had to truly activate it. He had Excalibur and the knights, not to mention Merlin, to do his bidding. But I digress. The Knights of the Round Table were some of the fiercest warriors ever to exist. You all remind me of them in certain ways."

The Messenger again rubbed his hand over the gauntlet. "I once was able to leave this place." He motioned with his hands around the massive room. "When Camelot fell, I was forced here in perpetuity."

"Purple-blueity?" Petro quickly asked.

"I was forced here, no longer able to leave. I had a duty, even millennia before that time, but as I stated, it was a time of change. Before you ask, I never met you during those times, but if what I believe is to be true, you all have a part to play." The Messenger held up the gauntlet. "This gauntlet is the opposite of its brother. The other protects, this one destroys."

"Wow," Petro gasped. To be fair, the Messenger was just that good at telling a story, even if it was short. He had a way to draw you in.

"Max, I want you to take this with you," the Messenger offered.

I held the weight of the gauntlet in my hand as memories of the other melding with my body resurfaced. It wasn't that the other piece of armor I had used in the Under was a shield. It just kept me from feeling pain. Pain that I very much suffered.

"We take much more with us, and we're going to have to move into Camelot." I tucked the gauntlet under my arm, knowing we had to go soon.

"Oh, no, you are not going to the golden years of Camelot. By the date Tristen gave me, you will go to the beginning of that story. The round table was built, but Camelot was not completed yet. No, you will be arriving at a time of turmoil." The Messenger stood up.

"You know why we're going." I took a breath, thinking through his story. He knew more, but what did it matter? A thought started tickling a corner of my mind. "You said Mordred, Arthur's son, almost activated the round table. How could that be if we get the piece we need?"

The Messenger chuckled as if he was about to throw on a red suit and give out Christmas presents. "Almost."

"Almost?" Phil repeated.

"I guess he didn't have all the pieces." He was trying to be funny. Like a surgical comedian, he had taken all that time to set up that very joke, hoping someone would ask.

Petro buzzed over to the ancient man, high-fiving him for the pizza. "Thanks, bro! All the pieces . . ." Petro winked at him. "Good one."

"Thanks again." It was time to leave. "We'll talk to you soon and let you know if we have any more questions."

The Messenger simply nodded. Before I stepped through the gate, I could hear the shuffle of a pizza box behind me.

CHAPTER 16

The Last Supper. Before Dessert, That Is

T he Atheneum's dining room was buzzing. I couldn't remember the last time everyone had been in the room actually eating a meal. Scents of rich food and hot bread wrapped around my brain like a warm blanket on a cold night. It was nostalgic in a way that felt more like déjà vu.

Doctor Freeman sat with several books open in front of him, revealing the different versions of King Arthur's stories. While we had done this before, with Excalibur sitting in the middle of the table, it was good to give them one more look.

Ed, Jenny, and Frank were all watching Phil eat a plate of baked chicken with contempt on their faces. He was, like always, making a show of eating.

Casey, Lacey, Macey, Neil, and Petro all sat at the small Pixie table next to the sword.

"When does Angel get back?" Gabby asked.

Freeman slid a piece of paper in front of me without telling me why. Glancing down, I saw an image of the Lady of the Lake with Excalibur, followed by a few paragraphs.

Frank snapped out of watching the Phil show. "It might be a few days. She didn't get into any details, but they are sure it was another one of the knights of the Old Gods types. She was saying that the others think the same thing we do. None of this timing is a coincidence."

"Right." Ed also dragged his attention away from Phil's violent eating. "Ana sent the rest of the retrieval braces. All you should have to do is attach them to the corners of the table, and like the gate rope, it will come back with you."

"I still don't get how it works. So, it doesn't matter if we can't get it through the gate door, as long as we pull these through with us, it will be rerouted," I said, regurgitating what I had been told they had done with the others.

"That's correct. Our job is not to ask the why or the how." Ed grinned. "So, you plan on taking both the sword and the gauntlet?"

Scratching my stubbled chin, I clicked my teeth. "Not sure. We don't need to take too much with us. We find the table. We stay out of trouble. We leave."

"Sounds"—slurp—"about"—slurp—"right, bruther," Phil chimed in, taking the final bite from a ravaged chicken carcass.

"Right, I see. There are so many what-ifs with this, I'm starting to second-guess things," Ed cautiously said.

"All we can do is go. We stay here, and things could be fine while we figure out the situation with Tristen—"

Frank interrupted me. "Yeah, stay here, and they're likely to put you on those recent OTN murder cases. Another one last night. A regular killed a sensitive."

"There will be time for that later. Ed." I shifted my focus on him as Jenny continued tapping on her laptop. She was researching the digital files, looking for anything about the sword. "Don't overthink it. We're in and out. No side quests. I had enough of those to last a lifetime."

"Right, but you may be involved and not know it yet," Doctor Freeman interrupted Ed. "Look." He turned one of the older books around. An intricate picture showed a man who seemed to be wielding fire—hellfire, to be precise.

"Could be anyone back then." I slapped my hands on the table.

"Yeah, guilty until proven innocent!" Petro added as his son, Neil, tapped him on the shoulder, whispering in his ear. "While I meant to correct myself, Neil said I'm right. If it smells like a Pixie's butt, it's a Pixie's butt until you see the bog skunk."

"The man on the picture is wearing a trench coat," Gabby pointed out.

"That could be armor," I tried to deflect, to everyone's deadpan gazes. "Okay, point taken," I huffed. "Doctor Freeman, what does it say about that picture? And is there anything else in that book that seems different to the others?"

"Well," Freeman started, "this is the sword, without a doubt. It's the only image that I see truly matches. It's a short passage." He cleared his throat. *"On the Eve of the blood moon, Arthur found the sword and, with it, was given the power of the Old Gods."*

He paused at that statement. I cocked my head. "Is this the only book which mentions that?"

"Yes, I believe so. We wouldn't have found it if we hadn't been looking up the sword itself. Let me continue. *'On the Eve of battle, Excalibur made itself known to the true king of Camelot. Given as a gift to protect the lands by the one they call the Lady of the Lake.'"*

"Well, if that doesn't give you the willies," Phil blew out.

I held the picture up. "Sounds like we may be walking into a hornets' nest. So, I get that Arthur already had power, but I always thought he pulled the sword from the stone or something as well."

Jenny turned another picture around. "I believe he did, but that doesn't mean it's the same sword. Does this look familiar?"

I squinted my eyes, seeing an all too familiar weapon. It was Durundle. "Well, shit," I grumbled.

"Right, none of this is a coincidence. I don't think it's happenstance you have that sword, Max."

While in the Under, the sword had separated itself from me, but in the real world, it was still very much a part of me. Since then, I tended to use the hellfire whip my body manifested instead of the sword.

"I have a bad feeling about this," I said while Phil and Petro groaned.

"Boss, you aren't allowed to say that," Petro complained.

"I know, I know. Let's just keep focused on the task at hand. So, we know two things. One, we give this sword away—"

Freeman cut in. "Maybe not. He could get it either way. You might just have it for the long term; it was listed as lost in history."

"Only on the history the Mage community knows. No, I think we give this sword to him, or someone else. I think Durundle is another mystery to solve. Just remember, the decisions we make here and now affect everything," I reminded them, refocusing my thoughts on the gauntlet.

If it was indeed a powerful weapon, taking it with us could also be problematic, causing additional issues. I was starting to believe that we would just be bringing duplicates of items that were already there.

"Right, everything has led you to those two items," Ed stated, taking a sip of coffee. "I suggest taking them. That being said, if the situation arises where you lose either of them, it will more than likely be for a reason."

"I agree," Doctor Freeman added. He had stopped ruffling through papers and books and was now snacking on a plate of French fries. "The sword makes total sense. The gauntlet might just be a tool for you to use. You'll know if you see Sir Lancelot. Do you think it will do that dissolving into your body thing, like the other one did at the Under?"

"I'm not sure. Everything seemed to be backward down there," I replied, snagging one of Doctor Freeman's fries. "I'll try it on before we go."

Tristen had sat quietly throughout the entire conversation, eating a plate of food. In all fairness, all he had done was drink sodas and eat since we had been around each other.

Seeing my eyes shift to the young man, Ed turned to him.

"Right. Tristen, are you ready to go with Jamison?"

The young man hesitated, not having been addressed directly until now. He knew he was going with us, but we had also told him it was imperative not to let the others know. He glanced nervously over at me as I shook my head slightly.

"Yeah, I suppose so," the young man replied, looking back down at his plate of food. He didn't feel comfortable lying. Though the more I thought about his words, the more I figured he wasn't really lying but simply answering the question with a generic answer. He seemed to know how to play the game, just like me. Words meant things in the magical community.

"Very good. He will be here in the morning to get you," Ed finished, slapping his hands on the table before standing up. "It looks like there's nothing else we can do. I'm going to call Ana Vlad one more time to make sure there are no changes before you all leave tomorrow."

Like any time we were going to do something that was likely to get us killed or cause significant emotional damage, we were leaving as soon as we left the room.

Gabby, knowing what I was thinking, smiled at me before speaking up. "I think we all need to get some rest. I need to check in with a few people." She stood up.

Petro stood up as well and started doing the hip gyration. "I'm pretty sure they're going to go bump uglies tonight."

The thing about Pixies was that once one of them started doing the hip gyration, any Pixie within eyeshot of the originator of the obscene gesture started doing the same thing. This was the first time I had ever witnessed Casey, Lacey, and Macey joining in on Petro's ever-famous dance of seduction.

"Really? You guys too?" I asked, watching as Neil started as well.

Not to be outdone, Phil stood up and joined in the celebration at my expense. Gabby winked at me. "I think Phil just killed the mood. Sorry, honey."

The rest of the room burst out laughing, as even Tristen found himself almost choking on the chicken he was trying to eat. The reality of the situation was that Phil had a significant lack of coordination when trying to do things such as walking and other fashionable dance moves.

CHAPTER 17

The Time Bandits

O ver the years, the Postern had become more of a clubhouse rather than the pristine room I had inherited. Between the weapons cabinet, chairs, and table, the space was cozy. Work had been done here, and I felt as if I had spent more time in this room than I had on my own.

Backpacks from old trips to other realms and even an empty Vamp Amber sat on the large table in the middle of the room. A Planes Drifter T-shirt sat on a small set of shelves by the weapons, and directly beside that was Phil's wannabe Thor hammer. He was a fan.

Doctor Freeman had raided the vaults at the Atheneum for more period-accurate clothes. Instead of the overly tight pants Phil had donned before, Freeman had thankfully located a light set of leather pants with tall boots and matching chest armor.

Not as tempting as she had been before, Gabby was now wearing a black suit with a leather belt and strap over her chest. A large gray cloak with a hood finished off the outfit. She looked like a character in a medieval video game.

Petro sported his new armor, while I was in a similar outfit to Phil. The small armor-plated vest I wore had a lion's head engraved in the center. Leather shoulder pads and a strap around the waist finished off the look. The star of the show, however, was Excalibur hanging off my hip. The good old doc had even found a large enough scabbard for the blade.

We all took one final look around the Postern as I activated the gate. The familiar rumbling started while I opened the infinity pouch, motioning for Petro to fly in.

After a light dusting and a snap of the bag closed, I walked through the gate. Just as before, the gate spit me out like a rotten egg, but unlike in our previous trip, instead of loose dirt, cold hard stone greeted me. Quickly rolling onto my side, the rest of the group started coming out one by one, also hitting the hard ground. Tristen was the last to come through, actually staying on his feet.

Standing, I took in the oddity of our surroundings, backing up several feet from the massive hole in the wall. Gabby walked beside me while the others continued to sort themselves.

"What a view," Gabby breathed out as we both took in the scene.

We had come out inside a tall tower atop a massive, abandoned castle. The hole in the stone wall faced the ocean, while a slit in the wall on the other side of the room overlooked a massive forest seemingly taking over the entrance of the castle.

"Yeah, this place is old, and we are already on old times," I replied, opening my bag so Petro could zoom out.

"Well, bruthers, there's no going back now," Phil huffed, also taking in the view.

"This place smells funny," Petro noted, zooming to small stairs leading down into the castle.

"My hair has been standing on end since I hit the ground. This place is buzzing with energy. Anyone has an idea where we are?" I asked the group.

Tristen was the first to speak. "I spent a lot of time in England. This area looks like a place called Golden Cap. At least the beach area. It would line up with where we believe Camelot is."

"That would mean it's north of here. So, what's this place?" Gabby asked as I pulled out my phone. We had downloaded as many maps and notes as we could from Doctor Freeman.

Gabby leaned over my shoulder. "That place Tristen mentioned is a mountain on the ocean. So that would be here." I clicked a marker on the digital map. "That would mean we need to head in this direction." I drew a line to the location we had marked before leaving.

"Northeast," Gabby followed, taking a step back. "Petro, do you smell anything down there?"

Petro was still hovering next to the stairs with Phil, discussing something. "I don't think we're alone in here. I smell . . ."—he sniffed the air again—"food, and maybe a troll. I can't tell."

"Are they dangerous?" Tristen asked.

"Bruther, trolls are a tricky business. They might try to eat us or eat all our snacks," Phil said, pulling out his wannabe Thor hammer. He had nicknamed it the mule, saying it had a "wicked kick."

"Might not be a troll." Petro continued to sniff. "We just need to be careful." He pulled out his Elven sword. The green blade glowed as Pixie dust floated over it, reacting with the weapon.

The typical dreary English skies in combination with the light breeze from the ocean sent a shiver through my body. Something was absolutely not sitting right with me.

"Everyone, keep quiet. We stay in line and work our way to the bottom floor. It's later in the day, so I'm not sure it's a good idea to leave the castle till morning," I said as Phil screwed his face up.

"What does that mean, bruther?"

Petro smiled. "That means we are going to pee on someone's march."

"Pee on someone's parade, buddy," I corrected the Warrior of the Freeze.

The plan, as always, was fairly straightforward. Petro would take the lead, while I would follow behind in case we ran into any problems. While Vampires also had a keen sense of smell and overall danger, Pixies were in a league of their own.

The stairs spiraled for several stories before finally ending on a floor with several doors. A secondary set of stone stairs led to a separate area. To our right, the main staircase led further into the building's guts.

"Petro," I whispered. "Anything?"

Petro flew around the main room, finally stopping in front of one door and motioning for the rest of us to get closer. Petro dropped on my shoulder. "The rest of the rooms are empty, but there's a bunch of stuff in there. No people."

Slowly pushing the door open, the hinges creaked, lighting up every nerve ending in my body. Knowing it was easier to just rip off the Band-Aid, I swung the door open. For once, the move worked.

Finally letting out the breath I had been holding, I slowly entered the room. Large books sat in piles, while chests full of what appeared to be clothes lined the walls. But what truly got my attention was the pair of modern hiking boots sitting on the floor. We weren't the first ones to use the gate.

I reached into my infinity bag, pulling out one of my favorite charms: a silencer. While it was called several different things, I liked to call it what it was: a device that would make whomever was inside the bubble able to talk without anyone hearing.

After a light pop of ozone, a light blue bubble expanded all the way into the hallway as I pulled the door shut.

"We can talk," I said, picking up the boots.

"Who do you think they belong to, boss?" Petro asked as Gabby and Tristen started looking at the books and other items in the room.

"Well, according to the tag, they're from the sixties," I replied, setting them back down.

"Here," Gabby almost barked. "It's a journal."

Concern had taken a hold of her face. She recognized something. "What is it?" I motioned for the book, which she chucked at me. Running my hand over the leather cover, I opened it to the unmistakable handwriting of Gramps. Tom had been here. My grandfather had been here, and I had questions.

"It's Tom's," I trailed off.

Phil let out a whistle. "That old dodger was here. Go figure."

"Yeah, it's a journal about King Arthur as a kid. It was like he was studying him." I flipped to the last page. There, in all its glory, was a picture of a sword encased in stone. "Here." I pointed to the last page.

"That key looks different to the one we used with the clock," Petro noted.

I shrugged. "Who knows? All I know is he was here in this castle." I froze, thinking of the implications. He could very well be here now. While he wouldn't know me if he was younger, there was a chance.

"Who's Tom?" Tristen asked, setting down a small red book labeled *Spells*.

"It's Max's grandpa," Petro explained, looking at the journal.

Tristen scrunched up his face in concentration. "So, he used the same gate?"

I shrugged. "Perhaps. We would be naive to think the Timegate is the only way to travel through time. All I know is that we need to keep an eye out for other signs of him being here. This may be all tied together."

"We better get moving," Gabby suggested as I tucked the journal away, snapping the silencer off.

Again, we started our journey into the ravaged castle. The next floor was blocked by crumbled sections of ceiling, as well as several massive holes leading into the main room below.

We made our way by several more blocked floors before Petro came to a screeching halt. He held his hand to his lips as he zoomed down the hall, only to return several seconds later. He buzzed as close to my ear as he could, making me shiver slightly. "There's someone on the next floor down. It's the main hall."

I pulled out my phone and typed a message. *What are they doing?*

"Whistling while they work," Petro replied, shrugging.

I turned to the others, motioning for them to stay put. I nodded at Petro as he landed on my shoulder. We were about to make our presence in the past known.

Glowing yellow light from a fire flickered on the final turn into the main hall, the sound of whistling filling the massive room. The clinking and clanking of various items accompanied the tune as the person on the other side of the wall happily worked on something.

Petro took off, hovering a few inches overhead. Stepping out of the shadows, I held my hands up. "Hello? I come in peace." Of course I would say something stupid like that.

The man continued to whistle, his back turned to me, as he held up a finger, telling me to wait. He was laser focused on whatever he was doing.

I glanced at Petro, who pointed at his head. The man was wearing a gleaming silver skull cap and a large cape. The thought lasted for only a second before a puff of purple smoke snapped in front of the man, distracting me.

"Well, at least I can use the leftover potion," the man huffed, finally turning around.

Standing roughly five feet tall and clearly a wizard of some type, the eccentric man in front of us was not the least bit concerned that we were standing in front of him. He was bald under the silver skull cap he wore, and several pouches hung off his belt, as did a large dagger.

"Well," the man said, picking up a large silver staff that matched his skull cap. "Get to it. Who are you, and why are you here? The villagers talk you into coming into the haunted castle?"

He was clearly not concerned with Petro. That is, until he squinted his eyes and saw the armor he was wearing; then his expression shifted to one of caution.

"My name is Max, and this is Petro," I replied as Petro pushed his chest out.

"Prince Petro," the Warrior of the Freeze added.

"I see," the man drawled out. "Oh, and you can tell your other friends they can get out of that stairwell. It's bound to cave in."

I looked at Petro, who zoomed off down the hallway. "And you are?"

"Most others know me as Merlin."

"Of course," I huffed.

"Is there a problem?" Merlin asked, taking a few steps closer and taking a large sniff.

"I don't think so. It's just . . ." I drawled out as the others walked around the corner.

Merlin was staring at me as if trying to figure something out, but he shifted his focus as Phil made his presence known.

"Hello." Phil raised his hand. "What's this all about?"

Merlin nodded. "Making a potion. I'm calling it . . . the fog of war. It makes the battlefield rather hard to navigate."

"Well, bruther, sorry to disturb you."

Gabby nodded as Merlin perked up, walking over and taking her hand. "My lady. You are?"

"Gabby. I'm here to ensure this crew stays out of trouble." She beamed a smile at Merlin, who took another breath, quickly figuring out what she was.

"I see. Well, I'm surprised someone such as yourself is out in the daylight," Merlin said, shifting his focus to Tristen.

"How did you know?" Gabby asked as he smiled. Since the development of Syntho-V, and taking into account her heritage as a third-generation Vampire, she could be out in the sunlight, something Vs of the past clearly could not do.

"Just a hunch. My lady, I would recommend keeping your secret to yourself here. Young man"—Merlin shifted—"who are you?"

"My name is Tristen. I'm here to . . ." Tristen trailed off as I cut in.

"He's here to stay out of trouble. He is also the son of Hades and Titania."

Merlin took a step back, hesitating before speaking once more. "Who are you all, and why are you here?"

I figured it was time to lay all the cards on the table.

"Guys, I'd like to introduce you to Merlin."

The amount of air that got sucked out of the room with that statement hit even me.

Phil's eyes opened as wide as I had yet to see. "*Waahhh*," he exhaled.

"Yup," I simply responded, turning to Merlin. It was time to get to the point. "My name is Max Abaddon Sand. We have come back in time in an effort to secure a piece from the round table."

If a legendary wizard could have all the blood drained from their face, Merlin was doing so in spectacular fashion. He swayed lightly, leaning on his staff. I reached over, grabbing his elbow, feeling the raw power flowing through his body. "Hey, sit down. You need a drink?" I asked. He nodded, pointing at a large growler of ale.

"Oy, I got it," Phil said, taking a sniff of the liquid before handing it to the wizard. "That smells proper.

Merlin waved his hands in the air, slamming the bottle to his mouth while ale poured from the edges of his mouth. After four large gulps, he smacked the remaining drink on the table.

He let out a sigh before looking up. "Everyone, please sit. Max, you said your last name is Sand. Are you sure?"

"I'm pretty sure. It's a family name passed down from my maternal grandfather. My father assumed her family's name.

They made a big deal about it," I said, taking a seat in front of the old wizard.

Merlin leaned forward again, looking at me with an odd intensity. "Who is your grandfather?"

My stomach started to get that feeling, as if I had eaten too many cheap tacos. Something important was about to happen. "Tom . . . Thomas Gabriel Sand."

Merlin slumped back in his chair, letting out a full-on belly laugh. After several seconds of us exchanging confused glances, he sat up straight once more. "What do you think my name is?"

"Merlin," I replied. The sound of Petro messing with something clanked in the background.

"True. But that's not my real name. At least not my surname. Can you guess what that is?" Merlin asked.

"Sand. Your last name, or your family name, is Sand," I slowly pieced together.

"Oh shite," Phil let out.

I leaned back, realizing I was, in fact, related to Merlin. The gears in my head started to take their final turn as I formed a singular thought. "Tom is what to you?"

"Hmph." Merlin slapped his legs, standing up. "He's my wayward son."

Petro landed on my shoulder, dusting lightly as I started processing what I was hearing. "That was his stuff in the room upstairs." Merlin nodded. "I don't understand," I admitted.

"Everyone, relax," Merlin spoke up. "There is much to catch up on. Tom is my son, and he spent most of his time . . ." He paused. "Time was something he spent a good bit of his effort on, as I am sure you are aware. That and talking to the dead."

I let out a whistle. "I don't think I've ever been fully aware of anything Tom ever did. Do you have any more of that ale?" I asked.

CHAPTER 18

Those Were the Days

The early morning dampness of a non-air-conditioned stone room lay on my face like an unwanted hangover, which I also had after a night of drinking with Merlin the Great. After a quick stretch, the unnatural warmth of Gabby stretching her arms around me grounded me into remembering the rest of the night, when I was preoccupied with Gabby.

One thing about Vampires was that after certain physical activities, their bodies became extremely warm to the touch. It wouldn't last, but considering I was an oven myself, the mix of our body heat was offsetting the cool British morning.

The other side of the castle was in much better shape than the path we'd followed down the tower. Several rooms had been saved from the ravages of time, not to mention Merlin's use of magic. He had restored a livable section of the castle.

Phil and Tristen had their own rooms, while Petro had effectively passed out in front of the fireplace. Old ornate wooden furniture filled the space as tapestries hung from the walls. The fireplace at the far end of the room had fizzled out overnight. It was cozy and, in many ways, resembled a medieval high-end hotel room at some boutique establishment.

"Morning." Gabby smiled.

"Hey, babe," I yawned. She pointed at the fireplace.

Still in my birthday suit, I grabbed one of the robes sitting on a chair next to the bed. Merlin was a good host. I had honestly fully expected to wake up missing my liver or a kidney.

Tossing a log in the fireplace, I pointed my ever-trusty hellfire finger gun, letting a spatter of the good stuff bring the fire back to life. If there was one thing I would go to my grave having perfected, it would be starting a charcoal grill on the first try.

Jumping back in the bed, Gabby again wrapped her arms around me. "Did last night really happen?" she asked.

"I tried my best," I smirked, snickering when she smacked my chest.

"You wish; though I'm not complaining. No, Merlin, and what he said about Tom. He could be lying."

I sighed. "Perhaps, but I don't think so. It's hard to explain, but I feel that it's true. I know he's a strong wizard, but as Lilith always said: Blood is blood. Plus, your type always knows. Hell, I can't get around a V without them grinning at me for smelling you on me."

"True. He seems honest enough. Why didn't you show him the sword?" Gabby asked.

"I wanted to be sure before playing my full hand, but hell, the old timer probably knows we have it. I want to see what he has to say this morning. If everything passes the smell test and we get down to business, I'll let him know. I mean, last night, all we talked about was his potion, which we interrupted, and the castle."

Gabby sat up. "You're right. It was like we didn't even care to talk about anything else. You think it was the ale?"

"Yeah, I do. As much as Phil drank, he's not even likely to remember last night. Him and Petro were going at it. I think they drank that barrel dry." I planted a kiss on her cheek. "When Merlin wants to have drinks and talk about his potion, I think that's what you do."

Just as we were about to get out from under the covers, Petro flew out from behind a bookshelf. He was clearly not fully recovered from the night, letting out a belch while not so gracefully landing.

"Morning, you two," Petro started, not realizing the state Gabby was in. I at least had a robe on. His eyes widened once he noticed, and he turned away, only to turn back, then back away again. "Jeez, guys, you could warn a Pixie. I almost saw the goods." He paused. "Hey, you guys been bumping uglies?" Without facing us, I could tell he was about to start giving us a hard time.

I yawned, standing up in my robe. "First, you've seen my goods. Second, what is number two of the bro code?"

Petro paused, thinking through the rules I had laid down with him. "Always knock on the door unless it's an emergency."

"Well?" I followed.

"It's an emergency! Merlin is making pancakes, and they smell great! I think he's even cooking real, old-timey bacon. It's an official food emergency."

"I find your reasoning acceptable," Gabby spoke up. "Now, can you give us a few minutes?"

Petro turned around, saluting, only to see Gabby getting up. He quickly turned around again. He was, for the first time I could remember, blushing. The Warrior of the Freeze took off, not looking back this time.

"That never gets old," I said quickly, getting my clothes on.

"He doesn't want to disappoint you," Gabby observed. "And he doesn't want the food to get cold."

"That and if Casey found out he saw you in the buff, which you know he would not be able to not tell her, she would likely blame me and pix my underwear drawer."

"How many times is that?" Gabby asked.

"I think we are up to fifteen at this point."

From the hallway, a crushingly hungover Phil bellowed,

"Pancakes!"

As we walked into the kitchen, we saw a Merlin covered in flour, talking with Phil and Petro. Tristen was already eating.

"Pancakes?" Merlin asked.

"Yeah," Petro started. "They're cakes you make in a pan. You got any syrup?"

"Syrup?"

"Like maple syrup from a maple tree, bruther," Phil explained.

"Hmm," Merlin pondered. He quickly ran into the other room, coming back with a solid amber ball. Holding it over a bowl, he blew into it, and it dissolved into a rich syrup.

"We call these flour biscuits. But pancakes sound much more appetizing," Merlin said as Gabby and I sat down.

Merlin rolled up one of the pancakes before dipping it in the syrup, which dribbled down his gray beard as he took a bite. The old wizard's eyes rolled back in his head as he let out a smooth, "*Ahhh*. Yes. I hereby proclaim these to forever be known as pancakes."

"We totally just invented pancakes," Petro boasted, pulling out a piece of paper he kept to add to his many titles.

"So, what's the latest addition, Petro?" I asked as he licked his lips.

"Inventor of the Pancake. It will go right after Taker of the Eye, I think."

"Sounds good, bruther," Phil said, diving into a violent assault of his food.

Filling my plate with half-an-inch-thick bacon and a stack of perfectly done pancakes, I ate away the previous night's drinking. No words were spoken for several minutes, and even Gabby had syrup dripping from the edges of her mouth by the time it was all said and done.

Merlin smiled, patting his stomach. "The syrup completely changes the food. Very well done. Now that we have the first meal out of the way, I believe it's time we get down to business."

I quickly realized where I had gotten my straight-and-to-the-point attitude from. Great-grandpa. Thinking about Merlin like that, I started to understand we weren't that far removed from each other.

"Yes," I agreed. "We appreciate the hospitality. Maybe we can offer you something in return, besides inventing pancakes." I pulled the side of my cloak to the side, revealing the hilt of Excalibur for the first time.

Merlin's eyes went wide, and he wiped his hands off, walking around the knotted wooden table.

"It's truly time," he whispered. It almost seemed like he was speaking to someone else in the room.

"I see you know the sword. Listen, last night, we didn't talk about much of anything. What does this mean to you?" I pulled the sword from the infinity scabbard. It was the same type I used with Durundle, allowing the blade to disappear magically, only leaving the hilt.

"About last night. The potion had some lingering effects in the air. It is supposed to preoccupy you from the task at hand. Think about it; the fog of war doesn't mean a literal fog. As for the sword and your quest, this means everything," Merlin breathed out.

"Mate, when in the history of Camelot and King Arthur are we?" Phil asked. The food had his brain firing on all cylinders. To be fair to Phil, he had grown as much as I had over the past several years.

Merlin smiled. "I knew I liked you. A brute with a brain."

"I wouldn't go that far," Petro chimed in. Phil, of course, made the fake fly-swatting gesture we all used when Petro was poking fun at us, which was the majority of the time.

"You are here at a critical time. The sword from the stone was damaged, and the Saxons pose a great threat to the throne. I knew you would come—not you all specifically, but she told me you would."

"Who?" I asked, taking a sip of hot tea.

"The Lady of the Lake. Powerful old magic. She told me you would come and bring Excalibur."

"How do you know the sword's name?" I followed. It wasn't that I was trying to poke holes in what he was saying; I was genuinely curious.

Merlin grinned. "She told me. Something is missing, however, and she has it. The scabbard."

"That's right," Phil again spoke up. He did make a point of letting us know they taught the history of Camelot at the Guild. "It is more powerful than that shiny sword. It provides total protection from useless knobs."

"Correct again. I am happy to hear our strife does not go forgotten in the winds of time. Yes, we must go to the Lady of the Lake and give her the sword."

I turned to Gabby. "Guess we can strike that one off the list. It's not you in that lake."

"Good. I'm not a big fan of swimming," Gabby replied, pushing back from the table. We were talking about the conversation we'd had with Hades.

"She's an Elemental," I said. Merlin bobbled his head.

"And who told you this?" he asked, finally wiping the syrup out of his beard.

"Hades."

Tristen, hearing his father's name, looked up momentarily, only to go back to eating the last pancake before Phil could.

"You did say this was his offspring. So, you truly know Hades? Who else do you know?" Merlin asked, still running his hand over Excalibur's blade.

The old wizard would be surprised. Hades, Trish, who was probably in Egypt or something, and Davros, who would absolutely be roaming the countryside, as would be Vlad, not to mention his sister Ana. Come to think of it, Lilith, Bo, and even

Belm were possibly running amok.

"What is it, boss?" Petro asked, seeing my expression go blank while thinking.

"Just thinking about everyone else we know who's running around. I never thought about it. Merlin, to answer your question, it ranges from demons to gods. We've been busy—the Old Gods are coming."

"Yes, the Old Gods. They're always coming." Merlin flailed his hands. "The last time Tom came here, he told me the same thing."

While I wanted to ask how long ago that was, I knew it didn't matter. Time was of no consequence at this point. But I did want to know what happened. "What happened to Tom?"

"One day, he just stopped coming back. He was having issues with someone in another time. The future, I believe, and was afraid he was going to lose his way back. I don't fully understand it, but he went through that same gate in the tower and never returned. How is he?"

The room stilled. "He . . ." I took in a deep breath. "He was gravely injured in a fight and was eventually stabbed with a soul sword next to one of the Pillars. He dissolved into it. Do you know about those?" I knew how crazy I sounded.

Merlin shrugged. "Hmph. Using a soul sword to gate yourself by having your essence absorbed into one of the Great Pillars. That's my boy. He must have been listening to me all those years."

I shook my head, not wanting to go further down that rabbit hole. "Back to what I was saying. We need to get to the round table. If you agree to help us, the blade is yours."

It was clear he was fully aware of what was going to happen either way. "Okay. But you need to be aware this journey will not be easy. There are parts of the story you know that have been lost in the winds of time. The journey will be perilous, but we will make it."

"Can't we just use a gate?" I asked.

He snickered. "No. In these times, using a gate attracts a certain amount of attention—attention neither you nor I want to deal with."

Gabby cocked her head. "Didn't we use a gate to get here?"

Merlin's lips flattened. In all the excitement, even he had not thought through the current situation. He eventually spoke up. "True."

"What about Tom when he gated?" I asked.

"He did something to ensure it wasn't an issue; I'm not completely sure what. Morgan le Fay, Arthur's half sister, has been somehow tracking the gates for years." Merlin grabbed his staff. "If we gate from here to Camelot, we may end up on the bottom of the ocean or in stone. The Fae can still get away with it, but Tristen is likely the closest thing to a Fae that has been seen in these lands in a long time. They are fighting a war on their Plane with the Dark Elves and have mostly just ignored us."

"Well, when can we start?" I was ready to get the party started, aware that time back home was moving at a faster rate.

"We leave today; it will take us five moons to get there. We will consult with the Lady of the Lake on the way. My vision is not clear on our journey, nor on what happens once we get to Camelot. Arthur may not be so giving."

"Let us handle that. We came prepared to negotiate," I followed.

He nodded. "I'm sure you did. We have much to prepare and discuss. We leave at midday."

CHAPTER 19

The Forest of Folly

We continued talking with Merlin about the way of things in the future. While he was eager to learn, he was also spending a good amount of time telling us how dangerous of a time this was. Oh, and then he mentioned the dragons.

Much to our surprise, the old wizard had just enough horses for all of us. He had definitely been using divination, but while it was clear he was aware of things to come, it also appeared it wasn't an exact science, though his power was evident. Walking out the main entrance, he waved his hand, and any signs that he had been there turned into dust.

One of the most surprising things was his keen interest in Tristen and his power. He had yet to ask about mine, though I was certain he already knew about it. We eventually discussed Lilith, but again, he acted as if he was unconcerned. In many ways, I felt as if he was already aware of everything. Divination had been used in the past to explain and lay out prophecies. Tom had once explained that some diviners could see decades, if not centuries, into the future. While less detailed than near future divination, it was to be taken seriously.

Tristen trotted his horse between Merlin's and mine. "In the future, this forest isn't here. These trees are huge."

He was absolutely right. The trees reminded me of the large redwoods in Northern California. The massive canopy kept the sun hidden, creating a dark, shadowed forest. The singular path we rode on was more of a cleared path than a road, with brambles and bushes lining its sides. One could easily get lost in its vast embrace.

"Yes, I see. This forest is alive. Not with villain nor Saxon, but rather the deceit of Morgan le Fey—Arthur's half-sister and scourge of this land. You know the lore," Merlin grumbled.

Petro, now sitting on my shoulder, glanced at me, sharing the same thought. I turned to the old wizard. "So you're saying it's not safe?"

"Precisely that." His words were muted. The sound of ruffling leaves in front of us was a timed omen. Something was watching and listening to us.

We rode for an hour before any sign of trouble presented itself.

In the middle of the rail was a massive dead deer, its antlers almost too many to count. From where I sat, it was as large as my horse. Weeks of decay gave the animal a zombielike vibe, the stench of death hitting us with force. Petro, ready for these types of occasions, pulled a small bandana over his nose. Merlin looked over cautiously.

"Pull your swords—all of you. Be ready for folly," Merlin instructed, reaching for his staff.

"We'll have to get the carcass out of the way; the brush is too thick to go around. I could burn us a path," I suggested just as Merlin held up his hand, indicating us to be quiet.

"No, to burn the forest would be too dangerous. The lords of the forest, even though enchanted by Morgana, would not let us leave without a fight." Merlin dismounted his horse, his cape fluttering in the breeze from his swift jump. While he was old, he was quick.

I jumped down, motioning for Phil, Gabby, and Tristen to

stay put. "Petro, you smell anything?"

"I'm trying not to, boss; that thing stinks. It totally reeks of magic, and not the good stuff."

Merlin pulled out a small pouch of dust and tossed it into the air. The sparkling material hovered as if unaffected by gravity as the old wizard held his hand up, manipulating the dust.

"Ogov, berum, revelos," Merlin whispered into the wind itself. His words hung in my mind. I could feel the magic pouring from him.

The dust shifted into a column, slowly engulfing the deer and covering its body. This was old magic. Luckily for us, we had also brought along several enchanted items and potions the girls had put together for us. Pixies were at times even better than the best witch.

Merlin smacked his staff on the forest floor, the earth ringing like a bell. The dust immediately shot toward him as he sucked it into his lungs, only to blow it back out. The dust again flowed onto the deer, which started to twitch.

"Be ready," Merlin exclaimed as I let the full might of Excalibur shine in the dull light. It needed no sun or source of light. The weapon oozed with power, and as Merlin and the story went, was a source of light unto itself.

The deer started moving while Merlin slowly walked backward, finally stopping beside me while Petro zoomed over to Gabby. The sound of Phil flexing his hand on the leather handle of his hammer was a familiar comfort.

After several seconds, the deer started getting to its feet. I stepped forward, but Merlin held his hand to stop me. "It must be a fair fight."

"Nah, not my thing. *Ignis!*" I barked. Instead of manifesting Durundle, I let my hellfire whip snap into existence, crackling on the damp soil. Merlin looked surprised as I walked forward with Excalibur in my other hand. Its featherweight allowed me to use both weapons.

"Wait," Merlin drawled as if he were bored, rolling his eyes.

"Yeah, bruther. His noggin is hard as stone," Phil huffed, knowing I was probably making a bad choice.

The deer lurched to life, a purple haze oozing from its eyes. I stopped moving forward when I saw its antlers turn to blades, instead snapping my whip, but the deer shook its head, deflecting my blow.

"Use Excalibur, you fool," Merlin barked.

Before I could take his advice, the deer from hell charged. Even though I was fast, the deer was faster, reminding me of Onyx, the foulmouthed unicorn. I shifted right as it swung its majestic head, catching the edge of Excalibur. Sparks flew as I flung my hellfire whip overhead, snapping it at the tail end of the deer, forcing the creature to buck and stand on its two hind feet.

"Should we help?" Gabby asked, but Merlin shook his head. "No."

"Why didn't the sword cut through that creature?" Gabby followed. Tristen shifted in his saddle. He wanted to join the fight.

"He didn't want a fair fight, and the sword knew it. I told him." Merlin didn't move, standing stoically as he watched the fight unfold.

Hellfire from my whip smoldered the brush on the side of the trail as the deer let out a flurry of kicks. Shifting right, I saw my opportunity when it swung its head in an attempt to behead me. Pulling up with Excalibur in hand, the deer's two front rotted legs flew into the woods with a snick-snack of the blade, forcing the zombie deer to stagger backward. Again, seeing an opening, I snapped my whip at its exposed belly, ripping into it.

The creature, knowing its end was near, let out a guttural howl, every tree around us shaking with the force. As a final "kiss my ass" from the deer, every antler on its head shot out like a dozen razor blades.

I pushed my body to the ground, pulling in my whip as

several blades smacked into my armor. "Look out!" I yelled just as the sound of metal on armor rang from behind me. What I didn't expect was turning back to see Merlin holding up his staff while the blades dissolved into it before hitting anyone else.

I froze on the ground while the deer slumped over in what I could only assume was its version of the second death. In reality, I was likely doing it a favor, releasing it from whatever enchantment it had been under. I slowly stood, realizing one of the smaller antlers had lodged itself in my chest armor. Under the metal and leather, I could feel the light trickle of blood.

"I think we're good," I huffed. The entire fight had lasted less than a minute.

"No, we should leave," Merlin replied just as the loud thump of something heavy slammed into the ground, followed by the sounds of roots being yanked out of the earth like a tooth being pulled out with a pair of pliers. Something big was coming. I glanced back at the deer, only to see a purple haze replacing its rotted body. It had already dissipated into the air.

Hey, even I wouldn't go around killing innocent deer. This one had had blades for antlers and was basically a possessed zombie. PETA would have to cut me some slack.

An ominous groan emanated from every direction. It was like Mother Nature herself was trying to tell us we had just made a mistake. A haze of smoke started building from the hellfire, burning the undergrowth and adding to the list of issues I had just created. Yes, the forest was now on fire, and it was my fault.

Merlin leapt onto his horse, grabbing mine by the bridle and bringing it to me. "When I say now, I mean the present time. We are in grave danger. We now have the forest to answer to."

Jumping on my horse, my chest burned. I was betting the antler was poisoned or spelled. I didn't have time to check, however, just pulling the blade from my armor, feeling the slink of metal from my chest.

The old wizard watched me. Once he saw the injury, he shook

his head, loosening the reins of his horse so it launched forward, slinging loose dirt. I glanced back, only to see the others charging forward. We rode for another five minutes before finally reaching a large clearing. Merlin, obviously knowing this wasn't good, pointed down.

"Look at the ground," he said.

Scanning the dark forest, the signs of freshly turned dirt and the smell of fresh earth became apparent. Something had just turned the ground up. The rest of our merry band of misfits all came to a halt on the outskirts of the large opening.

Petro zipped forward. "Something smells funny, boss." He sniffed, taking in the scents of the forest before pulling out his sword.

"Prepare yourselves," Merlin instructed, throwing a ball of light into the massive tree canopy. Light erupted, showing us what was waiting for us on the other side.

On the far end of the opening, dozens of glowing green eyes stared back at us. Topping it off were the two large trees that had, for some reason, decided to sprout arms and root legs. Angry, twisted faces etched into their bark looked back at us, not wanting us to proceed.

"What happens if we turn back?" I asked as Merlin cocked his head.

"More of the same, I'm afraid. I haven't worked with these woods for some time. They are rotten with Morgana's stench. We would be good not to die here today."

He was referring to the forest as a living, breathing thing, almost describing an Elemental. I knew better than to piss those things off, telling me this was something different.

"You heard the man. How do you want to play this?" I asked the group.

Gabby pulled out two katanas. I was starting to notice a pattern with Vs and ancient Japanese swords. Phil again pushed power into his wannabe Thor hammer, while Tristen's hands started glowing. Merlin stared at the young man, seeing him focus his powers.

"Well, it looks like you all have done this before." Merlin jumped off his horse, picking up a clump of dirt and smelling it. "Max, I see you wield the power of hellfire. I have yet to see it used in true battle. The earth is fouled with Morgana's magic. There is no recourse. I said to use restraint earlier, but that is no longer necessary."

"Oh shit, boss. He wants to see the juice!" Petro exclaimed.

"What is the juice?" Merlin asked as I smiled a wicked smile I only reserved for when I was about to let all literal hell break loose.

"He's going to show off like a popper, isn't he," Phil asked while Gabby nodded.

I turned, seeing the smaller creatures start to run toward us. "*Ignis!*" I barked, letting Durundle spring to life. With Excalibur in one hand and my hellfire blade in the other, I slid off my horse. Without moving, I shot a beam of hellfire directly at the closest of the large trees. Tree ogres, I thought to myself. These were now known as tree ogres.

Hellfire spattered the massive tree, immediately catching it on fire. This created another set of problems, and the tree was now a pissed-off flaming tree. I started moving toward it as the thundering hooves of Phil and Gabby on horseback blew by me, slamming into the smaller tree monsters. They looked like the Swamp Thing, out of the old comic books.

"It's time to toss some salad. Charge!" Petro yelled, zooming by. His new armor was muted in the dark forest. He was a lethal dart of death.

"What is 'toss some salad'?" Merlin asked.

"It's . . . It's complicated. It's an issue with phrasing. Let's get this done," I replied, taking off at a full-on sprint, finally leaping toward the massive, clearly pissed-off burning tree ogre. Merlin's lack of interest in getting involved in the fight was surprising.

Two massive limbs crashed down while I jumped several feet out of the way. Glancing toward the others, I saw Phil hammering away on the heads of the bush monsters as Gabby followed behind, taking off their heads while they were dazed. They made a good team, pulling a smile from me. The thump of a branch inches from my head brought me back into the fight.

By this time, I had garnered the attention of the second tree ogre. Excalibur whistled down the branch as it smoothly cut through the flaming tree's appendage. Swinging a follow-up swipe of my hellfire blade, I set the stump ablaze before the tree could pull it back.

Red flame now flickered, creating shadows, making the situation look more ominous. Petro flew by with a branch, caching some of the flames. He was going to spread the fire.

"Petro, get the other one!" I yelled as he changed directions toward the other lumbering figure.

"It's just you and me, big boy," I growled while another limb slammed down directly on top of me. Ready for the move, I held both my hellfire blade and Excalibur over my head, and the limb splintered to pieces. Unfortunately, I wasn't looking at its roots skimming the ground, and I went ass over tea kettle. "Graaaah!" I yelled, feeling the root coil around me like a snake.

While not ready for the smack, I knew precisely what to do. Pulling my hellfire blade in, I hypercharged my hand, pushing my will into it, making it glow like a furnace. The root turned to ashes in my hand as the tree let out a tooth-rattling wail. It recoiled, pulling back what was left of its limb, as I noticed Phil and Gabby still fighting headless hedges. Tristen was holding back, eyeing the other tree.

"Go for their roots! Or legs, or whatever the hell they're walking on!" I yelled, also pushing the message into their thoughts. They immediately shifted course, the two of them jumping from their horses.

Getting to my feet, I again charged the tree ogre, slashing as it dropped its massive heavy limbs on me with several sweeping attacks. At this rate, it would be out of limbs soon. Finally seeing my opening, I launched a pillar of hellfire directly into its roots.

Again, the tree wailed as it started swaying. "Watch out!" I shouted as the flaming tree slammed to the ground. Its leaves were now on fire, catching the forest ablaze.

The other tree ogre, seeing this, charged in an all-out assault on me, but a pillar of silvery light shattered its trunk, wood splintering into a thousand pieces as Tristen finally made his calculated move. I finished it off by launching another pillar of hellfire into its roots.

Petro zoomed by with the branch again, catching several of the brush monsters on fire as Gabby and Phil made quick work of the final group. I coughed as smoke and flame filled the once dark forest. "We have to go," I said, jogging back to Merlin.

We all converged on the old wizard, only to see him leaning against a tree, eating an apple. Petro landed on my shoulder. "You've been here eating an apple the whole time?" the Warrior of the Freeze asked.

Merlin nodded. "Yes. I wanted to see what you all were capable of. The road ahead is just as treacherous. We can talk when we exit the forest, which is now fully on fire," Merlin said as he mounted his horse while we all watched.

Phil made the universal symbol for crazy, spinning his finger next to his head. We all nodded. Even Tristen agreed. "Thanks for jumping in." I nodded at the young man, who smiled.

Again, Merlin took off at a brisk pace. This time, Petro rode with me. Cupping my hand, I pulled him in front of me.

"Hey, buddy. That whole 'tossing salad' thing? Really?"

Petro rolled his eyes. "I was in the moment, boss. You won't tell Casey I tossed some salad, will you?"

"No, buddy. Just promise not to use that one again . . ."

Petro agreed as the glow of the burning forest shone over my shoulders.

CHAPTER 20

A Knight Like No Other

T he forest burned like a volcano in the distance. Red and orange colors pulsed in an otherworldly glow as a blazing inferno raged while we sat next to a small yet comforting fire.

After exiting the forest, Merlin had steered us toward a small cluster of hills facing the spectacle. Activating one of his charms, a hazy bubble had erupted around us, opening toward the burning forest. According to the old wizard, no one could see us or our fire as it crackled while we were inside.

"I never liked that forest anyway. It was always giving me trouble," Merlin reflected.

"How was the forest an arse?" Phil asked, chewing on the leg of some unidentified cooked bird.

Merlin flattened his lips. "The usual. It would open up spots when it was raining. One time, I needed some firewood, so I cut up a tree that had fallen over. I woke up the next morning, and my cart was in pieces, nothing but a bunch of leaves lying around. I can go on."

I finished my mouthful of food. "Well, it won't be a problem anymore."

"Unless it tells any other enchanted forests, though I take it that's not a thing in the future." Merlin raised an eyebrow.

"Nah, only on the Plane," Petro said, warming his wings by the fire.

"Max," Merlin paused. "I have to ask you about that other sword. May I see it?"

While it was a strange request, the old wizard was interested, so I obliged, bringing my hellfire blade to life.

"Very impressive." Merlin reached over, making a grab for the glowing blade as I froze.

"You might not want to do that," I warned, but he just shook his head, putting his hands around the blade.

The glow of hellfire immediately fizzled out, the weight of the sword in my hand taking me by surprise. He had somehow pulled the sword that had melded with my body away from me.

"What the hell?" I asked, handing it over. The familiar weight of its hilt gracefully slid from my hand. I hadn't felt the sword this way since returning from the Under.

"Precisely." He winked at me. "Yes, yes. I see. How did you come to have this?"

"Gramps left it to me."

"Gramps?"

"That's what the big bag of bones calls Tom," Petro explained.

Merlin stood, walking over to Excalibur, pointing out just how similar the swords were. "This was the sword that Arthur pulled from the stone. It was destroyed. But . . . here it is in all its glory."

"It's called Durundle. It had been in the hands of several great warriors over the years. Probably the reason I'm still alive," I said, reflecting on just how many times the sword had, in fact, saved my ass.

"I don't know how Tom did all this, but here we are." Merlin chuckled.

"Here we are," I repeated.

Merlin shifted his focus to Tristen as Gabby scooted close beside me. Unlike this morning, her body was cool to the touch.

While she could eat regular food, she still needed to take Syntho-V, and she had only brought a limited supply. She was saving it for when she needed it. While one dose the size of a shot could last for weeks, she had already commented that something with time travel was cutting that time down.

"Young man, you are indeed special. So, I must ask: What is your full name?"

"Tristen Ban."

While the name hadn't immediately meant anything to me or the others when we had asked previously, something was tickling the back of my thoughts now. Merlin again flattened his lips, something I had noticed he did when thinking.

"I see. Even with parents such as yours, it's a very interesting name. I wonder how it came to be?" Merlin asked.

Tristen looked thoughtfully at the fire burning in the distance. "It is a given name. I'm not sure from there."

Phil cleared his throat; I had heard the spiel from him before. This was something he'd studied at the Guild. "There's a certain type of diviner who does it. It's all the rage," Phil started. Merlin scrunched his face, trying to keep up with his slang. "They go into some drooly trance and out spits the name."

"What?" Merlin finally asked after a long pause.

"They use a special enchantment that calls on the power of time and space, or some poppycock like that. Back home, there's an entire section of books about it and what the names could or do mean. It's not an exact hole in one, but like I said, all the cool kids are doing it," Phil summed up.

"Yes, I see. Young man, you have a very powerful name. You see, there is a man alive today, a king. His name is King Ban of Benwick."

"Great, another coincidon't," Petro said.

"Coincidence," Gabby corrected.

"That's what I said, a coincidon't," Petro asserted. Besides cuss words and generally flowery language, Petro often had trouble with s's.

I watched as Merlin scanned the group. He wasn't going to tell us the whole truth.

"This is no coincidence. You are all in here and now for a reason, all coming together for a purpose. Maybe—" Merlin was cut off by the sounds of a horse and the clank of armor.

Phil, Gabby, Petro, and I all shifted as Merlin slapped the top of his legs, standing up. "Ah, he's here."

"Who's here?" I asked. A dark figure appeared in the opening of the bubble, facing the burning forest.

"Sir Rose. He's a Knight of the Round Table."

"No shit," Petro got out first as we all stood.

"Why so excited all of a sudden?" Merlin asked as the knight stepped into the bubble, allowing the light from the fire to illuminate his face.

There, in the dark of night, was the spitting image, if not a little more worn, of Ed. For a few seconds, I almost thought it was the man himself, until the slight differences took shape. A horizontal scar crossed his face, topped off with a missing ear. But even more interesting was his armor. Unlike my perception of the Knights of the Round Table, his armor was pitted and scarred, dull from years of battle and use. He didn't resemble the stories of shining metal and chiseled features.

Merlin turned. "You have recognition on your faces," he noted before turning to Sir Rose. "My good man, just in time."

Sir Rose nodded. "Merlin, I can see you finally handled that pesky forest. Right. I headed this way as soon as your message arrived."

"Ha," Phil barked out. "He said it!"

"Said what?" Sir Rose asked.

I motioned for Phil to stop. Now wasn't the time. Merlin stepped forward.

"I would like to introduce you to some important people; people who have a part to play."

"I see." Sir Rose relaxed his posture. "I am Sir Rose of Camelot, Knight of the Round Table and slayer of night shades."

It was then that Gabby and I noticed the unicorn horn tied to his scabbard. When he said night shadows, he meant Vampires. I glanced at Gabby. Unlike Merlin, he probably wouldn't be able to tell.

"Awesome, you have a title! I'm Prince Petro, Warrior of the Freeze, Slayer of the Eye, Inventor of the Piña—" I cut him off.

"Keep it short. We need to get some sleep tonight," I said.

"I'm Petro. From the Plane. I hang out with these big lugs."

Sir Rose lightly bowed. "A prince, I see." He genuinely smiled. While I could address the Vampire hunter thing later, his clear acceptance of Pixies was enough for me. Plus, he was also directly related to Ed. "You have my sword as long as we are in the company of each other."

"My name is Max Abaddon," I started as Merlin topped it off.

"Sand. His last name is Sand."

This got a reaction out of the knight, whose eyebrows shot up. "I see. I don't see, but I see."

Merlin wasn't letting him know all the details, and his explaining it this way was sending us a message: only talk about what is needed. While the old wizard obviously trusted the man, he didn't want to spill all the proverbial beans at once. For all I knew, he already understood we knew Ed in the future, and Sir Rose being here and being trusted was not a coincidence.

"My name is Gabby." Instead of shaking his hand, she bowed. Sir Rose returned the gesture.

"And you, young man?" the knight asked Tristen, who straightened his posture.

"My name is Tristen."

"Tristen." He let the word roll off his tongue. "That's a fine name. It is an honor to meet you. Maybe one day you can be a knight."

Tristen let out a smile. "That would be cool."

"Cool? It's rather hot at times in all this armor during the sun season." He turned to Phil.

"Always saving the best vittles for last. Name's Phil. I keep this lot out of trouble."

"It's my honor to meet you all. I come bearing news," Sir Rose started before Petro interrupted to add some flavor to Phil's introduction.

"Yeah, he's usually the one getting into trouble. Eats all the food and drinks all the booze. One time, we were at Walmart chasing a ghoul, and he was all like, 'Throw up your wiener warmers,' wanting to fight, then—" Petro rambled before I stopped him.

"Enough, Prince. It sounds like Sir Rose has some important news."

Using his title made him push out his chest. "Proceed, brave knight," Petro graciously allowed as Sir Rose cracked an actual smile, looking out of place with his battle-worn appearance.

"Thank you, my prince. You will have to tell me of this Walmart at a later time," Sir Rose said. Petro pushed his chest out even farther. "I bring word of King Arthur and his main army. They, as you may be aware, are across the lands taking on a rogue army sieging the lord of the Gale's castle. King Ban is back at Camelot with an arsenal of his men. Word has come of Morgana sending an army of the undead to Camelot."

"Troubling," Merlin pondered. "How long till he returns?"

"Not in time. I was tasked with seeking your help. Your message about heading to Camelot and meeting you here was timely," Sir Rose advised.

Merlin handed Sir Rose a cup of ale, waving his hand over the ground behind the knight. Roots started rising from the ground, forming a chair as the knight sat down. He had done this before.

"You will stay here for the knight." Merlin stood, bringing his horse inside the bubble. Pulling out a small jar, he rubbed its contents on the animal's forehead, which shrunk to the size of a small house cat. Again, Sir Rose didn't act concerned.

Following this show of magic, Merlin waved his arms around the bubble, and rock formed around us. Roots sprouted from the roof and sides of the large enclosure. He had effectively created a small cave for us to stay in overnight.

Note to self: learn that little trick at all costs.

"Wow. I haven't seen magic like that since I was a kid!" Petro exclaimed.

"Aye. That was some of the old top shelf," Phil added, also impressed. I turned to Gabby, seeing her mouth open. I held my finger to her chin, closing it.

"Yeah, he's something else," I whispered before focusing on Merlin and Sir Rose. "So, what's the plan?"

"The way I see it, there will be a trade for what you seek. Other than the offer you bring." Merlin turned to the others. "For now, we drink and make merry."

CHAPTER 21

The Frozen Forest

T he plan was relatively simple. At least, it sounded easy after the gallons of ale Merlin somehow had on his person. I was betting he was using special magic and had an entire house in his bag.

On our way to Camelot, we would leave the sword with the Lady of the Lake—to be taken by King Arthur—before we went off to fight an apparent army of zombies. Merlin had made the point of telling us we were stronger than we even realized, and that the world had yet to see such a powerful group.

This, of course, had gained Sir Rose's attention. While Merlin had explained that we were from another time, he'd left out the rest of the details. More specifically, the part about us stealing a part of the round table. I took it as a point not to tell a knight of said table our plans.

We also learned Sir Rose had two boys, and due to his position, both were no longer under his watchful care. We decided it was best to keep our assumptions about him and his future family to ourselves. If the opportunity presented itself, we would tell him, though Merlin had made it clear that the less we discussed the future, the better.

The morning dawn yawned awake as Merlin dispelled the small protective cave. Smoke layered the countryside, mixing with the usual English morning fog, creating a bowl of soup for us to travel through.

"The smoke is getting all in my mustache, boss," Petro complained, taking his place on my shoulder.

"You can fly up and get out of it. I'm thinking it might work in our favor and give us some cover," I suggested, getting a nod from Merlin.

Sir Rose mounted his horse. "The trip will be perilous after the lake of wandering tides. We can make it before nightfall. As Max suggested, it is better for us to travel under cover until reaching the forest of frost."

"The forest of frost?" Tristen asked. The young man was captivated by the knight.

"Ah yes, you are not from here. It is safe, but as noted, a forest that was frozen after a great battle." We were on the move as he started telling the story. "Two great wizards fought for love. Love of the Lady of the Lake. Merlin can tell you more, but in a fit of rage, one of the wizards froze the lake in an attempt to keep the other from ever having the love they both longed for."

Merlin cackled. "They went mad with their lust for power and love. Do you know what that power was?" Merlin glanced at the hilt of Excalibur peeking out of my cloak before starting back up. "Not happy about the situation, the Lady of the Lake froze them both as a punishment for freezing her home. As it is written, they turned into the forest itself, freezing along with it . . ." Merlin paused. "It is also said that once she is reunited with what was taken and the wizards were also looking for, the forest will thaw."

"Fairy tales in a land of fairy tales," I huffed as Sir Rose nodded.

"Yes, but true, mark my words. There is something great in the air. I can smell it on the lot of you. I wouldn't doubt you are all somehow tied to this land. To the Lady of the Lake and to my king. Yes, I see the sword you carry."

Luckily, after getting my sword back from Merlin, it had melded back with my body. Sir Rose, while halfway through the bottomless pit of ale, had told the story about the time he'd tried to pull the sword from the stone in an effort to become king.

"Well, now that that's out of the way, we should talk about these undead. What have you heard?" I asked.

Sir Rose nodded as the rest of the group steered their horses closer to hear. "Just that. They are the bodies of the dead raised from the grave. Mindless beasts with one focus: To take away the life taken from them."

"Zombies. He's totally talking about zombies," Petro pointed out.

"*Zombies.* Interesting word." Sir Rose flattened his lips. "Camelot is still new. He is a young king, and this a test of his strength."

"Yes," Merlin spoke up. "Arthur is still a young king. We are lucky you are all here."

Sir Rose shook his head. "Merlin, you talk as if these are great warriors."

"They are. When we get to the castle, you will see. I was given the chance to see already, and they are not that different from me. They have the gift."

Sir Rose turned to us, looking at us through different eyes. "Three wizards, including Merlin. We may just have a chance."

"Four," I spoke up. "Petro is one of the fiercest warriors I've ever had the pleasure of knowing."

"Yeah," Petro chuffed.

"I see." Sir Rose nodded. "My apologies, Prince. I have known other fierce Pixies, but I must admit, you are all special."

Petro scooted closer to my ear. "You mean that, boss?" He was blushing.

"Hell yeah!" I exclaimed. "Sir Rose, I can assure you, you have our support."

"I believe you. I don't know if I should, but I do." Sir Rose held up his hand, pointing at the clearing fog and smoke as the crystalized outline of a forest came into view. "We're here. Stay close, and don't touch the trees. If we see any creatures, they should stay away."

We continued in silence as the gray sky morphed into a midnight haze of dark blue. Like the other forest, the trees' canopies covered the gray sky, not allowing true daylight to pass through, giving the entire space a dreamlike vibe. Flakes of freezing mist hung in the air, looking for a place to settle.

A purplish glow radiated from above as we entered the forest. This path, unlike the last one, was wide, allowing us to ride next to each other. My breath huffed out like a steam engine, forcing Petro to bury himself under my cloak.

The muffling effect of the frozen ground made it quiet, like being in a library. I was just waiting for the screaming librarian to come out and greet us.

"How far to the lake?" I asked as Merlin shrugged.

"Not far. Once there, we will need your power."

After the brief conversation, we rode in silence for what felt like an eternity until we came to an opening in the trees. While still covered by the forest, a large frozen pond sat several feet off the path. In my mind, I'd imagined a large lake. Some things the story just got wrong. Or, as it was with most history, it had been changed for various reasons.

"We're here," Merlin proclaimed, dismounting his horse. "Everyone, be sharp. Do not react to anything you see. We are guests here." The old wizard paused. "I hope. Everyone wait."

Arriving in front of the frozen lake, Merlin stood in a trance with his eyes closed. He was trying to communicate with the Lady of the Lake.

Meanwhile, Gabby pulled me closer. Doing what I did best, I let my body heat up. It wasn't that Vs got cold; they simply liked the warmth.

"You okay?" I asked. She nodded. I often forgot just how

lethal she was. Love could do that to you. Yes, I was in love with a Vampire. Don't judge me until you've met one.

Merlin slowly turned. "You can melt the ice. Be gentle."

I nodded, taking off my gloves and handing Petro to Gabby, who tucked him under her cloak. Sir Rose shuffled, the crunch of snow under his feet echoing. I dropped to one knee, placing my hand on the frozen water. Being roughly the size of an Olympic pool but round, I would need to slowly heat the water without boiling it.

My hand started glowing as I pushed hellfire into my hand, being careful not to release it into the water. I would keep my hand on the surface.

As the red glow of hellfire engulfed my hand, Sir Rose gasped. "Hellfire. He is a demon."

The slink of his blade being pulled from its sheath was cut short when Merlin smacked his hand. "Don't be a fool. He's neither demon nor man. He is caught between worlds, and that includes the world above."

"A Fallen Angel," Sir Rose whispered into the frigid air.

"If that works for you. But yes, he is something this world has never seen," Merlin replied.

The crackle of thawing ice started sounding across the pond. It was working.

"My apologies," Sir Rose conceded. "The mystery of this group grows." His words trailed off as I stood up.

"It's done. The rest will melt. That's about as gentle as it gets," I assured, stepping back. "Now what?"

"Now," Merlin drawled out. "Now we wait."

CHAPTER 22

The Not So Lady of the Lake

Seeing snow always had a way of calming my nerves, even while being from Florida. The eerie dark silence of the frozen forest, like something out of a gothic fairy tale, was, in fact, something out of a gothic fairy tale.

We stood silent for more than an hour, waiting for Merlin to say something. He was again in some type of trance. Thoughts of the trip and everything that had led me to be here had started weighing heavy on me.

I'd always thought I would spend my time after being introduced to the world of magic doing cool things, like . . . That was the thing; I didn't know what else I would be doing. I was almost certain that if it wasn't me, it would be someone else saving the world or whatever it was I was truly doing. Once again, there was too much going on. Why had I decided to bring Tristen with us? Why had I brought Gabby? More importantly, why wasn't I looking for my daughter, Destiny?

Gabby broke the silence. "Hey. You okay, babe?"

"Yeah. Just thinking about things," I whispered back. She had noticed the lost look on my face.

"Well, if it makes you feel any better, so is everyone else," she whispered back.

Looking around, it became evident why everyone had been

so quiet. Phil, as well as Tristen and Sir Rose, all stood with the same expression I'd probably had on my face before Gabby talked to me.

"What's going on?" I asked.

She shrugged. "Something that's not got my panties in a wad."

I quickly pushed the mental image of her in her delicates out of my mind. "I think it's time we wake everyone up. I'm guessing Petro is in the same boat?"

"He was dry humping the air. I put him in your pocket." Gabby giggled.

Quickly grabbing the Pixie prince out of my pocket, I shook him like a literal saltshaker as he started grumbling.

"Boss, I'm awake, I'm awake. Stop shaking me, or I might start enjoying it."

"I see you're okay," I huffed, pointing toward the others. "Some type of mind magic or trance. Time to wake up the boys."

"Man . . . I was having some great trance time. Me and Casey —" I stopped him.

"I get it, buddy. Wake them up."

Petro, before flying off, lightly dusted me, and the fog that was lying thick in my mind lifted immediately. After dusting everyone, minus Merlin, the group started coming around.

"Holy shite." Phil stretched. "What the hell was that?"

"Mind magic," Gabby informed Phil as Tristen and Sir Rose also came around.

"Him too," Sir Rose finally said after scanning the tree line, referring to Merlin.

Merlin slowly opened his eyes, looking at everyone before frowning. "Everyone keep moving, if even in place." He let out a sigh. "She isn't going to make this easy." He shifted his focus to the now thawed pond. "Okay, enough. Let us in."

With those words, the water in front of our feet started parting, exposing a walkway into the water. Dark, uninviting, and generally not looking friendly, the water held steady as if held up by glass walls.

"Ah, she's ready to see us now," Merlin said, matter-of-factly. The old wizard stepped forward, leading the group as we all glanced at each other.

Phil shrugged, following behind Merlin. The rest of the group walked in a single file into a large corridor covered in ice. Smacking his metal staff on the ground, light radiated, filling the dark cavern. Frozen skeletons and discarded weapons lay strewn around, along with what appeared to be long since dead Pixies.

Petro's anger took hold as he took in the scene. He wasn't too happy about seeing that Pixies had died here.

A large set of doors stood at the end of the corridor. Merlin motioned for me to help him push them open. Unlike the rest of the space, they were completely thawed out.

Decades of unuse made the doors moan, protesting. Glowing yellow light from a fire pushed warm air onto my face as we walked into a massive, ornate living area.

A massive chandelier hung overhead with lit candles, and a fireplace large enough to walk into sat at the far end of the room. Tapestries and various pieces of old yet ornate furniture fit for a king sat in a large pit in the middle of the floor. A table covered in exotic fruits and clear jars full of unknown items sat next to another filled with fresh food and drink. This was a place of power.

"Hello, Merlin," a woman's lofty, ghostly voice echoed off the walls.

Everyone turned, looking for the source, only to hear her words float into their ears like she was whispering in their ears. A shiver went down my spine as an empty glass vase on the table started filling with red wine.

"You have left me here for a very long time, Merlin, the great wizard of Camelot. Yes, I know of the current day . . ." She had more of a hiss in her voice this time.

Merlin stood resolute, taking in a deep breath before speaking. "Don't be so dramatic. You told me to let you lie here until the sword made itself known."

The lofty voice again flowed through the room. "You and your friends may end up in my entrance hall if you are wearing a false face."

Merlin shook his head. "For the love of the gods, you're older than time itself. You just took a little nap in the grand scheme of things. Stop being a bad host and show yourself."

Out of the far corner of the room, a shadow moved. Instead of the lofty, ethereal voice from before, a significantly sturdier voice boomed. It absolutely had the feel of a scorned lover who still tolerated her ex talking because she actually liked them in some sick way.

"You look older. Age hasn't treated you well."

"Nice to see you again, Nimue. Beautiful as always."

"Hah, last I remember, you called me a wretched scourge and then told someone I was an evil witch," she retorted.

Gabby and I glanced at each other as Petro flew out, landing on my shoulder. This caught her attention.

"You heard all of that?" Merlin asked, cocking his head.

"I hear everything."

Petro interjected. "Oh yeah. She's an Elemental for sure."

Nimue turned her full attention to Petro and I. Walking over, her finger traced across my chest. I could feel Gabby tense.

"Calm down, my night shade. I'm not going to suck him dry," Nimue stated. Phil, Petro, and even Tristen started laughing, Phil even letting out a full-on snort.

"What is so funny?" the Lady of the Lake asked, turning.

"Lass, where we come from, that means . . ." He paused, gathering himself. "That means something else."

"I see." She paused, closing her eyes briefly before snapping them back open. "Or *when*." Again, Nimue turned her attention to Petro. "I know this armor. How did you acquire it? It was lost on the field of battle."

Petro, in the most Petro way, rolled his mustache between his fingers. "Hades gave it to me."

"I see," she huffed. "Well, Merlin, you brought a group of interesting people with you. Did you tell them about the others they saw on the way in?"

"The dead ones?" Gabby asked. After the night shade comment, I noticed Sir Rose looking at her.

"Very much so. Merlin?" Nimue prodded.

Sucking in a deep breath, Merlin walked over to the wine, grabbed a goblet, and poured it full. Before taking a sip, he nodded at Nimue.

"You are dumb as a stone. It's at no obligation to any of you. Your Pixie friend is right about me, but not entirely." She huffed again.

After a long sip, he turned to us. "I have come down here before, but couldn't open the door. Those are the bodies of others I have brought down here, though not for the reason we are here today. The Pixies were an ambush that followed us in."

I cleared my throat. "So, you brought people down here for whatever, and since our host didn't want to see them, she just killed them."

Merlin simply nodded.

Getting back to my roots, I continued by pulling out Excalibur. "I believe this is why we are still alive." I knew a good bit about Elementals. After spending time with Black River, I'd learned they were also part of the Old Gods' world.

She walked over, holding out both her hands as I held the sword out. "To be fair," I again spoke up, "I don't think you could have frozen me."

"Perhaps; perhaps not," Nimue replied, scanning every molecule of the sword. Snapping her finger after holding the sword in one hand, a matching scabbard appeared in her other. Without taking her eyes off the sword, she deposited the weapon in its home. The tang of the hilt hitting the scabbard echoed like a massive bell.

"I am sure you know the story," she proclaimed. "The sheath is in many ways more powerful than the sword itself. Merlin, you have indeed outdone yourself." She walked over to the old wizard, placing the palm of her hand on his face. "You were such a good lover."

"Yuck," Petro mumbled. Nimue turned to him with laser eyes, and he quickly corrected himself. "I mean him. Not you, my lady." He turned to me. "Don't tell Casey I said that."

"Scouts honor," I replied as she motioned us to the table.

"It's safe," Merlin confirmed, picking up a peach and taking a bite out of it.

I walked up to Sir Rose, who was still looking at Gabby. "Hey. Let's talk for a second."

He nodded, and we walked to a corner of the room. Merlin turned back, motioning us to go while Nimue started telling stories about Merlin to the others.

"Are you okay?" I asked as he turned to me with the focus of a hunter.

"She is a Vampire. She must not leave this place."

Knowing he was going to say this, I nodded. It was actually a method I'd read in a book about how to make people agree with you. You had to love self-help books in the future.

"You heard what she said earlier," I started, figuring I would lay it all out. "We're from the future. When I say future, I mean hundreds and hundreds of years from now, and all of this—what we're doing here, Camelot, this whole time—is all part of fairy tales we are told as kids."

Sir Rose nodded, returning the gesture. "I figured something was off about the lot of you. I do know Tom, Merlin's son, was said to travel in such a way."

"Yes, with that being said, I am Tom's grandson." This took the knight off guard. "He was stuck in the future, hundreds of years from now."

"So you are related to Merlin. But that still doesn't solve what I, as a Knight of the Round Table, have been tasked with."

"What's that?" I slowly asked.

"Purging this land of the curse of the night shades."

"What if I told you we know your distant relatives, and your bloodline carries on? Even more, Vampires and humans live side by side."

Sir Rose froze at those words, but not at the part about Vampires; rather, at the part about his bloodline.

"I-I," he stuttered. From the story he had told us earlier, he was absolutely worried about his family name carrying on. "My sons survive this land?"

"And they flourish. I don't know how many generations have passed, but Edward Rose, *our* friend"—I emphasized the word *our*, pointing at Gabby directly, who was obviously hearing the entire conversation—"is a great man and mentor to not only me but everyone in this room. He went to great lengths to save her life and, if I'm being completely honest with you, all of ours. And we have also saved his. He is a great man."

Tears welled in the stoic knight's eyes as he pulled them back with all the might of an entire army. The internal weight he had been carrying with him since leaving his boys had been raging inside of him, looking for a way out. A path I had just given him.

"You must believe me. She is a good woman, and . . ." I paused. "I love her dearly. She means a lot to all of us and to Ed."

"I believe you, Max. Even though I don't always see the way, I can see lies. It is something I have been gifted with." Of course, he was a sensitive, I thought to myself. "Your words ring true."

I placed my hand on the man's shoulder. You could tell he wasn't used to compassion or another person laying a hand on him. In an odd show of respect, Sir Rose dropped to one knee, pulling out his sword and holding it up to me in one fluid motion. I glanced around the room, seeing everyone watching.

"Take the sword, fool, and give him his new charge. Younglings," Nimue scoffed, taking down an entire goblet of wine.

"I don't understand," I said as Merlin walked beside me. Sir Rose didn't move.

"If he breaks his vow to hunt the Vampire, he must be given a new charge. The fact that he is not doing so for the king means he has pledged his allegiance to you," Merlin explained as Sir Rose continued to look at the ground.

He'd agreed to break his vow after learning his sons would survive and his bloodline would live on. Flattening my lips, I came up with the perfect solution. I wasn't always a knucklehead.

"Sir Rose, I am charging you with carrying out your duties as a Knight of the Round Table under the rule of King Arthur. You will continue to be his knight with no obligation other than protecting your king and his honor."

Not knowing what to do next. I tapped each of his shoulders with the sword before he finally stood. A smile radiated from the man as I handed him back his sword.

Phil, Tristen, Gabby, and even Nimue exploded in applause. I had actually done something right.

"Thank you. Thank all of you. Not only for being here but also for bringing the tools with which my king will thrive. Not many men would give away the hand of a knight so quickly. You are an honorable man."

"Well," I chuckled, lightening the mood, "I'm not much of anything but a little of everything."

Even Sir Rose let out a laugh. Nimue spoke up, handing the knight a full goblet. "Max, we have much to discuss. I can smell much on you, and you are wise, considering your lineage."

Merlin shook his head. "What does that mean?"

"A fool and his folly, my dear Merlin. Let us dine, lover."

"She's not your great-great-grandma, is she?" Petro asked. He always had a way with words.

"Oh no." Nimue smiled. "That is another story I'm sure Merlin will tell you when the time is right."

Roasted quail, an honest-to-goodness bowl of mashed potatoes, and various vegetables and breads lay strewn on the table at the perfect temperature. Petro and Phil had already made a mockery of the bounty, an odd brown gravy streaking Phil's beard while Petro acted like he was dueling a large chicken leg on his oversize plate.

The fire crackled in the background, loudly echoing off the rock walls. The clink of glasses and shuffle of plates made this a proper meal. Merlin, sitting on one side of Nimue, and I on the other, had taken an entire rack of lamb and was deconstructing it as if he were a surgeon.

Gabby and Sir Rose found themselves in a conversation about Vampires. He was clearly avoiding the subject of how many he had dispatched over the years. Tristen, as was the norm, was outdoing Phil on the sheer amount of food he was eating. Nimue, after squinting her eyes at the young man, had walked back into the room with a sugar drink, the equivalent of Southern iced tea.

After letting out a burp worthy of Phil, Nimue turned to me. She was not so much of a proper lady but rather a construct of one. "So, Max, I know what you are. The pieces that bind you. I also sense you have been around someone I know. Have you met Black River?"

"Yup. It's a long story, but he is on the Plane guarding a path to a keep and some mountains. I figure he is there as we speak. Wise and strong. He did me a favor—well, a few."

"Yes, he can be very dramatic, all high and mighty. He is indeed strong, very strong. I see you understand what I am—at least as much as you can. So, tell me of your powers?"

"Well, I can use hellfire and water. The cool thing is, I can use magic that's been used on me. It's not nearly as strong, but I can use it. Recently, it's started sticking, if that makes sense."

"You're getting older," Nimue again belched. She didn't apologize before getting back to her point. "You are going to Camelot. I see danger. I also see that you are going to come face-to-face with a truth. Yes, I know why you're here. That is one of my gifts."

"So you know what we must do. The Old Gods are finally making their move." I didn't mention our task in case Sir Rose overheard us. Nimue seemed to understand this.

"I do, and I see fog. I wish I could tell you more, but strong magic is at play. Magic that will seem familiar to you."

I took a deep breath again, glancing at Gabby, who nodded at me. "So, you're saying I'm going to run into someone I know?" I asked, taking a sip of ale.

"Perhaps." Nimue smacked Merlin on the back of the head as he slurped on a bone from the rack of lamb. "I don't miss that," she followed while Merlin rolled his eyes. They had a love-hate relationship that was as deep as the ocean. They had been through something together, something hard that pulled them together yet kept them at a distance.

"Where was I?" She refocused. "You must succeed on this task. You know who the sword will go to, but there is another sacrifice to be given."

"Sacrifice." I set the small spoonful of roasted potatoes down. "Are you saying we all don't make it?"

"Make it? Yes. In the way you think? No." She was being genuine. Her face was one of concern, her eyebrows furrowing. "Can I ask you a favor? One that I would like you to keep to yourself."

"I don't see why not," I promised.

She nodded, leaning in closely. The smell of freshly cut grass emanated from her; she smelled like a forest. "Do you think you can find this place in your time?"

"Yes, I think so. Tristen was certain about the area we gated in through. It seems fairly simple."

She chuckled. "You would think. I want you to come see me during your time. I see darkness, a long dark trail that seems to go on for a long time. My one gift is foresight. Many Elementals have this same gift—Well, maybe not Black River, but he is a bit of a horsehead at times, all bite and no bark."

"I can do that," I responded. "Can I ask you a question? When you mentioned about us not making it how we think we are going to, what precisely do you see?"

"All I can say is that not all of you will leave this place. That is all," she said before she again smacked Merlin on the back of the head.

CHAPTER 23

The Road to the Castle

We stayed in small rooms that looked more like caves. With candles hanging from the roof, ornate furniture, and a fire raging, the carved-out room radiated heat through the natural stone. After walking to our quarters for the night, it became evident that the sheer size of the compound Nimue had was staggering. And to think this might still be there in the future.

We frequently visited Davros's keep, and any chance of another place to lie low was tempting. I was curious about seeing her in the future.

After another meal to send us off, we left the Lady of the Lake behind, only to find the forest a thriving green. Rabbits scurried around the mossy ground, no sign of ice or snow to be found. Overnight, all the ice and snow had melted, and the forest had transformed to its former glory.

As the lake closed back in on itself, Merlin turned to Sir Rose, rolling his head around as his bones cracked. "Sir Rose, I feel much is in our favor today. We ride until we reach the fields. From there, we see just what we are dealing with before going into the castle."

Sir Rose nodded as he kicked his heels, pushing his horse to take off at a steady trot. Petro, riding on my shoulder, watched as

Gabby and Sir Rose rode in front of us, still talking. His life work had been put into question, and Gabby was more than willing to talk to him. It was her superpower. She was an amazing listener and what I liked to call a silent leader.

"So Boss," Petro started, "you got a bad feeling about this?"

"Oh yeah, for sure. No doubt," I forewarned. "Nimue told me something that I can't get out of my mind. I told Gabby last night."

"I bet you did." Petro smirked.

"Gods and graves, is that all you think about?"

Petro paused, deep in thought. "Yeah, I think so. I also think about being a prince and keeping all my bros and broettes safe. I think about Golden Grahams." He stopped when he saw me smirking.

"Anyway, she said that not all of us are going to go back the way we think, or something like that."

Petro clicked his now armored wings—something he did when thinking. "Maybe she just means we all don't gate home the same way."

"No, it seemed more ominous. She told me not to worry, but it didn't make any sense. Listen, I want you to keep close. You know, keep an eye on everyone. Look for anything that's not normal."

Petro shook his head. "Boss, I hate to break it to you, but we're heading to Camelot and just gave the Lady of the Lake Excalibur. Oh, and Ed's relative is with us, and Merlin is kind of a crabby old jerk. Am I about right? Oh, and don't get me started on that lady's burps. I could smell them at the far end of the table."

"I guess you're right. I'm just asking you to keep an eye even on me. Make sure we're not getting into anything we can't get out of. You have a nose for it." I smiled as Petro poked his chest out. Truth be told, I was right in what I was saying.

The forest finally opened up into rolling hills. Green pastures and random groups of farms lay miles apart as the countryside melded into a scene worthy of the greatest classical painting. Gabby was now riding beside me, having taken a dose of Syntho-V.

It was at these quiet times that things always decided to ruin the pristine mood that had set in. A small fire billowed smoke into the gray sky on the other side of the next hill. Merlin and Sir Rose had noted that the fields would not be manned for another two months to start prepping the crop. We had only passed a handful of people on the trail, most of them hunters heading off into the woods.

Sir Rose held up a hand, telling us to stop. Turning his horse to face us, he motioned for us to come closer. "No one should be in these fields; the hunters don't stop and set up camp or a fire, and all the knights are either at the castle or with the king. Be ready. I'm going to ride up and see if there is any danger," he informed us, grabbing his sword and pulling it from its home.

Petro sniffed the air. "Hold up, I can check it out; they won't even know I'm there."

Sir Rose glanced around the group for approval. I smiled. "Yeah, he's got this."

Petro saluted. The helmet built into his armor formed over his head as he darted into the countryside.

"Bruther, should we go to the tree line and wait?" Phil asked, making a good point.

Merlin shook his head. "No. It's likely there are eyes already on us. We are good to press forward." He squinted his eyes, scanning the trees in the distance.

"How will we know if it's safe?" Gabby asked as I huffed.

"Give it a few seconds. If he comes darting back, cursing, get ready for a fight," I cautioned. For some reason, I already knew what would happen. The trail of dust heading back to us at maximum speed was all the confirmation I needed. Everyone rustled in their saddles.

"Boss!" Petro barked before reaching us.

"Spill it," I instructed once Petro landed on my shoulder. His chest heaved as he finally caught his breath. From what I could tell, the hill crested roughly a mile ahead.

"Okay, it's a mess. There're about ten rough-looking *hombres* by the fire. They have a couple tied up. They look rough, boss. The couple smelled like poop."

Sir Rose cut in. "Those are farmers; they've been collecting fertilizer for the fields. That's not out of the ordinary, but them being bound is. As a knight of this kingdom, I must help."

"Oh, and there's like two ogres and what I am pretty sure is a witch," Petro concluded.

Shaking my head, I set my jaw. "Maybe start with that next time. Merlin, is there anything we should know?"

"A witch? Hmm," he contemplated. "What did she look like?"

"I didn't get a good look, but she smelled like sugar."

"How do you know all this, Prince?" Sir Rose asked. Phil already had his wannabe Thor hammer out, and Gabby was pulling out her katana. The knight curiously glared at the unfamiliar type of sword.

"The nose knows." Petro rolled his shoulders back, pulling out his green blade.

"Merlin might be right; you all might be a force to be reckoned with," Sir Rose proclaimed.

At those words, I patted the back of my horse's neck. "You ready, girl?" The horse reared on its rear legs as if about to lead the greatest cavalry charge in history, then launched forward. Two seconds later, the rest of the group shot into motion.

Fire Breeze was a horse with its own personality. Over the past two days, I had grown fond of the animal. I never steered her or gave her direction, and when fighting in the forest, she had jumped into the battle as if knowing my thoughts. White with large brown patches of fur, she was a thing of beauty.

Gabby's horse was known as Night Wind. Sleek, black, and completely complementing, the noble steed had a cadence that would make the proudest show horse envious.

Tristen rode a younger horse known as Thunder, named after the thumping of his hooves when he ran. Youthful and full of spirit, the two were a fitting match.

As for Phil, his horse was simply known as Brick. A large gray male horse, Brick was as thick as a mountain and had made it his mission to give Phil a hard time. It seemed like a love-hate relationship while casually riding, but as soon as the situation dictated, Brick charged into action, using his massive weight to cut down the tree creatures.

Merlin had roughly a dozen horses and had taken an annoyingly long time picking out one for each of us. As for the old wizard, his was lean and strong. Spotted like a Dalmatian, the horse was known as Gash, named after the large scar that traced her side from the blade of a sword at some point.

Sir Rose hadn't said much about his horse. One thing was evident, however: his horse loved him as much as he loved it. They were dependent on each other. A horse bred for battle, he was an extension of the man who rode him.

Hearing us coming, the first spell cast shot overhead just as I crested the hill. Petro had failed to mention not only how large the bad guys were but also the fact they wore pitch-black armor, many of them wielding large double-sided axes.

Petro launched from my shoulder and Fire Breeze broke to the left as the witch launched another spell toward us. Green and spitting sparks, the spell was definitely meant to kill.

Leaning forward, I slung a ball of dripping hellfire directly into the now moving group. This not only caught their attention but also hit the shoulder of one of the dark knights, spinning it around.

I immediately noticed that while its shoulder was melting, it was still moving as if nothing had happened. Petro was in the air —drawing the witch's attention—when a swarm of previously hidden Pixies launched from a bush. He had a fight on his hands.

Galloping at full speed, the group turned when Phil, Gabby, and Sir Rose literally jumped over the small hill's crest several meters away, cutting to the right. Confused, half of the group shifted their focus just as Phil's hammer slammed into one of the dark knight's chests. He had fully charged the blow, sending the knight flying dozens of feet.

Staying focused, I immediately noticed the witch wasn't taking her eyes off me; she saw me as the primary threat. Behind the off-putting woman, Sir Rose launched from his horse, running his sword through one of the two ogres now in the fight. He was literally going head-to-head with an ogre.

Gabby joined the fight while Merlin, as was becoming the norm, just sat on his horse watching while eating an apple. His long staff was in front of Tristen, stopping him from joining. I needed to have a chat with him.

The thought disappeared when something slammed into my side, knocking me off the horse. Stunned, I stood, bringing my hellfire whip to life and slinging it overhead. Like mindless drones, the knights seemed unfazed, but the witch hesitated. She didn't like what she was seeing. Even more, she had now noticed Merlin.

"Go," I huffed at Fire Breeze, who whinnied before trotting out of the line of fire. She was making a large circle around the fight.

The witch launched another spell while I held out my hand, sending my own ball of force, a little trick I had improved on. Slamming into her spell, it immediately dropped to the ground, and a massive chunk of earth ripped into the air, the chunks of wet dirt thumping the ground around me. I cracked my whip at the first knight, wrapping it around its head while I superheated the lasso, effectively burning its head from its body.

One down, four more to go.

In the distance, it was clear the others were in full fight mode. Glancing up just before two more of the black knights reached me, Petro was flying in circles, slicing through the lesser

Pixies. While he was a bit of a goober at times, he was, at the end of the day, a lethal warrior.

"Go get'em, buddy," I growled again, cracking my whip.

With a ball of hellfire in my other hand, I leaned into the fight. Slamming the ball in the face of one of the knights, I was only able to tag the other. I immediately paid for this when he swung his axe, kicking me back several feet.

The only reason it didn't finish its blow was because the axe bounced off me and was now lodged in its head. The gauntlet I had let meld with my body had done this; I could feel it as my hand tingled.

But I didn't have more time to think about it. The knight whose face was basically melting swung its axe just as another spell zipped by. This time, I was ready to push my body forward. Little known fact that I'd learned in judo: Always lean into the fight and use your opponent's momentum as a tool.

Ramming my hellfire blade through the black knight's body, I used my forward motion to turn, cutting it in half. My immediate fight was over. The top section of its body stilled before folding over on the ground.

Turning to focus on the witch, I glanced at Merlin, who was slowly walking down the hill toward us. She launched several more spells while I slung a small ball of hellfire at her feet, knocking her down.

Before I could speak, a heaving Petro darted out of the sky, stopping only a hair's breadth away from her black eyes. Blood and gore dripped from his blade, purple blood spattering his armor. He had won his fight.

"Listen, lady, don't move. I can pluck out an eye faster than you can fart," Petro ordered.

Turning back to the others, Merlin was shockingly now standing behind me with Tristen. He leveled his staff at the witch. "Go help your friends," he instructed, not taking his eyes off the woman.

One ogre sat on the ground, picking up its arm and trying to put it back on. This clearly wasn't going to work. Phil was now also on the ground, going toe to toe with the last of the black knights. Behind them, the other knights lay in pieces. Gabby had gone to work while Phil kept them busy. Sir Rose had clearly spent his time focusing on the ogres. Of course he would go after the biggest thing on the battlefield. *Typical Knight of the Round Table*, I thought as the ogre slammed into him.

Gabby, meanwhile, sliced off the other ogre's head as if it was made of butter, her sword blazing hot. This was a testament to her weapon of choice.

"Sir Rose!" I barked as Gabby got the message. Putting her head down, Night Wind, her horse, rocketed forward just as the ogre was about to smash Sir Rose.

While he might have moved if given the time, Gabby didn't give him a chance. Flying by, she drew her other katana, launching from the horse while cutting the massive beast's head off like she had a pair of scissors. When fighting an ogre, it was good practice to take off its head, as cutting off its body parts generally just pissed them off.

Unfortunately for Sir Rose, the ogre stammered before falling on his legs with a thud I could feel in my feet. The fight was over.

A wet nose nudged my back. It was Fire Breeze. After a quick once-over, she turned back to Sir Rose as his horse trotted forward, nosing the stuck knight.

Sir Rose looked up as Gabby walked up to him. The two paused, looking at each other. No more words would be said. Gabby had earned not only his trust but also his respect. It was the type of look that didn't need any words.

"Phil!" I yelled, and he jogged over. Black goo was spread over his armor, a smile sitting on his face. He had enjoyed the fight.

"Lookee here," Phil blew out. "That's a fat one, that is." He was referring to the ogre.

"Give me a hand," I asked, heaving the headless beast off Sir Rose with Phil's enhanced strength.

"I hate ogres," Sir Rose grumbled. "Can one of you untie the farmers? Figure out what happened."

"I got it," Gabby volunteered.

Turning, I saw Merlin and Petro were still in a stalemate with the witch, waiting for the rest of us. Walking through the mess of bodies, I finally reached our prisoner.

"What's up?" I asked while Petro stayed laser focused.

"She is one of Morgana's; she would rather die than talk. Or she doesn't have the choice. As soon as we start pushing her, she will die. Nasty bit of magic."

The witch was oddly unassuming. Wearing a light set of dull leathers, if it weren't for her pitch-black teeth and eyes, she would look like the farmer's wife they had tied up.

"Yeah," Petro added. "She's not twitching, but sure seems to like her eyes."

I noticed light marks on his armor. It was true how strong it was. In most cases, Petro would have at least broken a wing by now. "You good?" I asked him as he continued to hover.

"Yeah, those were sprites—aggravating little things, but not too smart. I think a few got away. At least they weren't Pixies."

I turned to Merlin. "So she won't talk. Do you have a spell or something?"

"Strong enough to counter Morgana's magic? Likely not."

A thought traced the edges of my mind as the item Gabby had taken from Hades came into focus. "We might just have something. Gabby!"

She trotted over on Night Wind. "Sir Rose is fine. A little sore, but everything's good. The farmers are talking with Phil. What's up?"

"That charm you got from Hades. Didn't he say it can tell if someone is telling the truth or something like that?"

"That's right. It can also convince someone to tell the truth by not letting them know they are. You just have to place it on them."

Merlin reached for the necklace after Gabby pulled it from her neck, then the old wizard held it to his lips, breathing it in. It was the second time I had watched him do this.

"This will do. Very strong magic. Familiar and strong." Merlin motioned for Petro to back off before he draped it over her neck.

Turning to Tristen, I could see the excitement in his eyes. "Are you okay, kid?"

He nodded, lips flattening. "You know I can fight."

"Yeah, but you need a sword. You know, just in case." I looked at the closest black knight who was clearly not getting up, considering its body was in ashes. "That one has a sword—go grab it. Be careful, and don't touch anything else. Use your gloves. Petro can dust it to make sure it's not got anything nasty on it." I pointed at the leather gloves tucked in his waist.

The witch erupted in a gurgling cough as dark spittle flew from her wretched mouth. Instead of staring at me, she was now looking up at the sky, swaying.

"Hmph," Merlin huffed. "This may just work." He kneeled by the witch, waving a hand in front of her face. Her expression was one of being in another place. "Why are you here?" the old wizard started.

She breathed out in several steady heaves, "To gather . . . the eyes . . . of the fields."

"What the hell does that mean?" Petro asked, landing on my shoulder.

Merlin held up his hand. "Who sent you?" While he clearly knew the answer, he wanted to know who else might have sent her or who else they may be dealing with. I would ask the same question.

The witch started shaking violently. She was under an enchantment not to talk, and the power of the necklace was pushing her. Gabby shifted uncomfortably.

Merlin, seeing this out of the corner of his eye, turned. "She's been dead for weeks, possibly longer. This is just a husk, a life taken to do the unspeakable. We are doing her a favor by letting her pass on to the Everwhere."

Gabby nodded for him to continue.

"Who sent you?" he asked more forcefully.

"The Lady . . . of the Shadows," she breathed out again, her chest continuing to heave.

"Did she send you directly?"

The witch spasmed before settling again.

"The Anger of the Grove."

Merlin leaned back, looking back at me before turning to her for what I guessed would be the last time. Quickly pulling out a pouch, he grabbed a fistful of dust and blew it in her face.

"What was your name?" Merlin asked.

A small, sad smile swept over the woman's face. Her eyes started hazing over as the dark black pools once there began softening.

"Gale. I'm so cold. Where am I?" she asked.

"You are home. You are at peace." Merlin swept his hand over her face. Cupping his arm around her, he slowly lowered the once living woman to the ground, carefully placing her head on the ground.

We all watched as Sir Rose walked over. "Merlin, do you need the bag?"

"Yes." Merlin stood, looking down at the woman. Digging his hands into the small bag, Merlin pulled out a handful of seeds. Sprinkling them onto the woman, he waved his hand again over her while a green glow radiated around her body. Within seconds, flowers and small garden plants started sprouting from the body, and within a minute, she was nothing more than a small mound of plants.

"From nature we come, to nature we go," Merlin finally spoke as the two farmers stared in shock.

"You're Merlin," the man barked louder than needed.

"I am he." He turned to Tristen. "Come with me, young man. I'll take a look at that sword."

Sir Rose took over the conversation while Merlin walked back to his horse. "How many others have you seen?"

The man pointed into the distance. "More."

The woman, whom I immediately liked, slapped the man on the back of the head. "You nob; they want to know if they're riding into trouble." She smiled, winking at Sir Rose. "These here are knights. That one is one of the Table."

"Sorry, my lord." The man bowed his head. "Hundreds. They were heading to the castle."

"Why did they take you prisoner?" I asked. They both looked at me like I was stupid, the dirt caked on their faces contrasting with their piercing blue eyes.

"To eat us, of course, and to not tell others of their numbers," the man replied, more focused.

"Yeah, that witch said something about eyes and stuff. Pretty sure that was about what he said," Petro added.

"Thank you, Prince," Sir Rose said. I started to notice that any time Petro got on a roll or Sir Rose didn't understand Petro's jargon, he began with a "Thank you, Prince."

"I suggest you head home," I told them, and they both nodded and bowed.

"Yes, thank you," they stammered, shuffling off toward the tree line. Phil pointed at a bag full of food the black knights and ogre had left.

After several minutes of getting situated, we watched them head toward a distant clump of trees.

"Right," Sir Rose started. We all froze in place, turning toward him. "What?"

"Nothing." I smiled. "It's just . . . You keep being you."

"Nothing!" Phil exclaimed. "He gabbed it out of his smackers!"

Petro buzzed to the knight's shoulders, landing on him for the first time. "Yeah, you said it. It must be in the blood."

"What did I say?" Sir Rose asked, shrugging like a kid in a candy store with only a dollar. Hey, inflation . . .

Gabby smiled. "Your future offspring says that very thing before about every sentence. 'Right.'" She made a poor impression of Ed.

"Right," Sir Rose repeated, shaking his head and realizing he'd done it again. In all fairness, I hadn't heard him say it till now.

CHAPTER 24

The Field of Ashes and Bone

T hat night, we stayed in a patch of trees surrounded by a rock ledge. The terrain was becoming rocky, with taller hills and less farmland. While the kingdom was surrounded by fields to gather crops, it also felt more ominous.

The fire crackled as Merlin once again pulled out an entire feast for us to enjoy. Before settling down, Sir Rose had spent a couple of hours teaching Tristen how to handle his new sword. The young man was enjoying himself.

"So, what about the Anger of the Grove?" I started, chewing on a piece of bread. "They sound like bad news."

"Yes, it is a scourge this land has yet to see. If Morgana has partnered with the Anger, then it explains the army of the undead," Merlin lamented in a wistful voice.

"It sounds like you've run into this nutter before," Phil noted, already making a mockery of the meal.

"No. But I know a few things about the Anger of the Grove. Word has it that they are a demon straight from the bowels of hell," Merlin stated, using a more ominous tone. Wine dribbled from the edges of his mouth as he took a long drink.

"The boss and I know all about that place. We were there fighting dragons and dealing with angels. It was crazy, and don't get me started on the Ford Escort," Petro added with a smile. He cut himself off before he got going.

"Really?" Merlin's eyebrows almost touched his shiny metal cap. The old wizard's face went from one of not believing us to understanding we were telling the truth.

"You fought a dragon and survived?"

I smiled. Petro, of course, couldn't keep his mouth shut. "Fought? More like fell in love." He snickered. "The dragon totally had a crush on the big bag of bones. Even Gabby saw the humor after hearing the story."

Letting out a long sigh, Merlin leaned back on a rock. "Why am I not surprised? Well, this means we might just survive this mess. I do know one thing: The king finds the sword, and I become part of this story that has yet to happen. In the morning, we ride to the forest of hope."

"Why do they call it that?" I asked as Sir Rose took a seat, explaining.

"It's a small forest that oversees the castle. There is also an underground passageway to the castle from there, but the door can only be opened from the inside."

Not liking the sound of that, I rubbed my mechanical calf. "So, we have to get one person inside while the army of the undead is surrounding the castle."

Sir Rose cleared his throat. "And convince King Ban to open the door without being killed."

"Sounds like a job for Petro," I suggested, but Merlin huffed out a breath.

"He hates Pixies. Plus, not knowing who Petro is, he will think it's part of Morgana's plan to get inside. No, we must figure out a way."

Phil set down his chicken leg. "Why don't we just smash our way through?"

Merlin turned to Phil, pouring more ale in his cup. "Some things we can't do. We need the walls of the castle and the extra swords from King Ban. Camelot is no normal castle. Behind its walls, we will be able to take a stand. If not, the castle may be destroyed. The Anger of the Grove is strong—more than I can handle."

I cut him off. "You seem to have taken a back seat for all the fights so far. You sure you're up for it in case we do get into the castle?"

Ale spewed from Sir Rose's nose. "Merlin has decimated entire armies. I have also heard of the Anger; we are on even ground inside the castle."

"Doesn't like Pixies," Petro huffed. "Let me tell you, he hasn't met one as charming as me." Petro scrunched his face in thought. "Hey, what about that cloak thingy Phil has?"

"Oh shite, I forgot about that," Phil exclaimed before taking down his freshly filled cup.

"Let me see it," Merlin requested. Phil dug into his infinity bag and pulled out the silky smooth cloak, handing it over.

Merlin grumbled under his breath, smelling the fabric before putting it on. "Yes, yes. This is something I can't believe you have." The old wizard completely disappeared. "Ah, the possibilities," he mumbled, knocking the chicken leg Tristen was reaching for.

"Hey!" the young man exclaimed.

"Right," Petro started. "Girls' locker rooms, free movies, sexy time."

"No," Merlin said. "I was thinking about sitting in on conversations meant for the wind. But if sexy time is your thing, then it could be used as such. No, this cloak is from the time before time. The time of the separation."

"From Terrum?" I asked as he pulled the hood back, nodding. It was odd to see his bodyless head floating around.

He smiled. "Yes. It was used by a very, very evil Fae to cross over undetected. You see, with this cloak, even magic can't see you."

"Score!" Phil barked while Tristen reached for the roasted

chicken again.

That was another thing. Merlin seemed to have freshly cooked food in his bag. In my head movie, I could see an army of maids cooking inside it.

"Yes indeed," Merlin said, taking it off. "If one of us can go to the castle under the power of the cloak, we may just pull this off."

He frowned.

I didn't like that frown. "What is it?" I asked, smiling at Gabby. She was listening. While she often didn't chime in, she was always listening. Her silence was absolutely not to be taken as weakness; she was lethal.

"Whoever makes the journey will be walking through the army of the undead. Not a simple task." Merlin sighed. "King Ban is another story. He may not take it lightly. But there may be a way; we just can't fully rely on magic until we're inside the castle."

"I'll do it," Tristen said.

We all turned to the young man.

"What?" He shrugged. "I'm young and good at sneaking around. I've been doing it most of my life. What is it you can do?"

Merlin sat back down. "I can talk to them through the fire; we will see when the time comes. We have to make it there first. The group we just encountered was small. Imagine an army a hundred times its size."

"Yeah," I said, "I've figured that. I'm going to call it a night." Standing up, I pulled out my sleeping bag.

***

The sensation of Gabby tapping my forehead with her finger was accompanied by the buzzing of Petro's wings in my ear. Yawning, I slowly shuffled my elbows under me, sitting up.

"What?" I asked, groggy from the night before.

"Time to go," Gabby insisted as Petro landed on my chest.

"Yeah, boss. Last night, you were all like, 'It's bedtime,' then just passed out. We stayed up talking. Tristen even showed us more of his magic."

Seeing everyone else was already by the horses on the other side of the trees, I hurried to get dressed. I agreed with Gabby. For some reason, I was oppressively tired. And as with most situations when I was super tired, I had vivid dreams.

While I didn't understand how it worked, my dreams had a way of guiding me. While sleeping, I saw darkness, and familiar faces. Tom and I sat at a table looking at each other, while Lilith danced in the background. The dream had morphed to me standing in a forest looking into the sky watching a plane go overhead.

"Hey, daydreamer," Gabby interrupted. "Put your pants on before you get on the horse."

Looking down, I realized I was standing up in my whitey tighties.

Don't judge me, they're comfortable.

Within ten minutes, we were all back on our horses, trotting off through the field we had fought in the day prior. Instead of the bodies of the fallen black nights, piles of ashes lay in clumps, topped off by the amazing mound of flowers the witch had turned into.

"How far?" Petro asked as Merlin glared into the distance. "We will be there by night."

"Depending on any issues, bruthers," Phil emphasized.

I noticed Sir Rose and Merlin exchange a glance when we reached what looked like the final hill. Merlin held his hand up, and we all stopped.

"Listen closely to my words. Everything you are about to see is not as it seems. We are going to take a shortcut through the field of ashes and bones."

Petro buzzed over to the old wizard. "The field of sashed and phone?"

He shook his head, starting to figure out that Petro didn't pay much attention to what others were saying. "It is a field in which a large battle took place. The battle of the Grays. Many lives were lost. After the battle, the bodies of the dead were left in the field."

"That doesn't sound good," Phil gulped.

"No, it isn't. Just stay focused and on the path. At no time are you to leave it," Merlin insisted. We all agreed.

There are things you see that don't always compute until you can reach out and touch them. Scenes of anarchy, death, and life. Amazing waterfalls and mountains taller than the clouds. Stars at night in a perfectly clear sky in the country, unmolested by light.

What lay before us was a scene only fitting for the worst of nightmares. Gloom permeated the entire field in front of us, two steep cliffs lining the macabre sight. Bodies as far as the eye could see were split by a narrow path of cleared ground.

Spears stuck onto the ground—clearly driven through the body under them—stood like pillars on a memorial, telling the last story of someone's life. In some areas, bodies were piled higher, showing just how ferocious the battle had been.

But worst of all was the stench. That was the confusing part. It was as if the battle had just occurred. Turning, I caught Petro already retching.

Merlin turned to us, once again bringing the small band of misfits to a stop. "This land is cursed. At night, one can hear the shuffling of the gravely injured buried under the already dead. I was in this battle, and the sorrow and misery did this. The mountains were so bothered by the scene, they didn't wasn't to see it come to a close and have to own the horror."

I shrugged, not fully understanding what he was saying. Phil spoke up. He was, after all, a graduate of the Guild, and these were the types of things they often studied: ancient human lore told through the eyes of the magical community versus the history I had grown up with. While in most settings Phil wasn't generally the type to be picked for trivia night, it wasn't because he wasn't smart; it was that he'd usually had several dozen drinks before.

"Aye," Phil said, clearing his throat. "The land can decide at extreme times to take the flop."

"The flop?" Tristen asked. Merlin and Sir Rose kept silent, knowing this was our conversation to work through.

I spoke up, knowing Phil's general expressions for things. "It can choose not to partake."

"That's right, bruther. The land doesn't want all the souls to haunt the ground. In this time-a-mo-thingy, they would leave their dead on the field of battle in some silly situations or whatnot."

"He is correct," Merlin finally interjected. "This land is sacred. When the battle was at its peak, a wave of earth crashed through the valley and stopped the souls of the dead from pouring into the land to haunt it."

Tristen shook his head, still not understanding.

"Young man," Sir Rose spoke, "it stopped the warriors' souls from leaving their dead bodies. The field is full of truly lost souls. If you stray from the path, that soul may take you as its own."

"Indeed," Merlin said, turning back to the path. "Imagine a soul that has been locked inside its dying body for over twenty years. They're all mad."

"Why not you?" I asked. Merlin pointed at a small rock jutting out from one of the cliffs.

"I was there," the old wizard said. "I saw it all happen, yet the fog of battle never reached.

"Sit this one out up there?" I asked, smirking at him.

"I had already ravaged their lead forces. I was on the ledge with my king to keep him alive, and he did." Merlin's face hardened. "No, I didn't sit this one out." Merlin lifted the arm of his robe. Under the sleek fabric, his entire arm, from a few inches above his wrist all the way up, was gnarled and burnt.

"I didn't mean anything by it. We just could have used some help back there," I replied as Merlin smiled.

"I'll teach you something yet. There are two lessons to learn here: First, why would you push your queen forward on a chessboard first? Your most powerful weapon." He paused. "Which may not be the case here." He was referring to my power. "Secondly, while all of you are clearly brave—"

Petro pulled the scarf down from his face, his nose still pinched. "You got that shit right! Now, I'm going back in the bag. It stinks out here." Just as fast as he was there, the Warrior of the Freeze was gone.

The brief moment of levity was needed as Merlin rolled his eyes. "As I was saying, at times, it is better to sit back and observe the battle while it forms and takes shape. Much can be gained in knowledge, as we found earlier. I'm no good when I'm dead."

Sir Rose moved forward, taking the lead. "We ride. Enough lessons for now," he grunted.

Gabby slid in line in front of me with a smooth wink as she passed. She looked great on that horse. Unfortunately, the view was spoiled by the backdrop.

No one spoke as we passed wretched faces frozen in an eternal scream. The smell oddly disappeared as we entered the small valley. After ten minutes of riding, a crossroads opened up, giving us room to gather around each other once Sir Rose stopped.

Merlin came down from his horse, squinting his eyes as he walked in a circle. With the clap of his hand, a smaller bubble came into existence.

"Time is short; something has happened here. We are not safe on the path. Max, when I give you the signal, you burn everything you can around you. It will be while we are leaving the valley. Do you understand?" Merlin was laser focused and razor sharp. I had yet to see him like this; it was almost scary seeing him like this. There was no world in which anyone would not follow his orders when he became this serious.

Merlin jumped on his horse as fast as he'd leapt off. Slamming his heels into the sides of his horse, he shoot forward while the rest of the group followed, with yours truly bringing up the rear.

The wind brushed my face as the thunder of hooves was absorbed by the dead bodies surrounding the path. What was truly bothering me was the sound of groans growing alongside the now visible shuffles of the dying. The battlefield was coming to life—or death, depending on one's point of view.

Petro had crawled up to my shoulder once more. Merlin had made it a point that he must not fly. "Boss!" he yelled. The thunder of the wind made him sound muffled. I could tell these horses were not normal, or maybe Merlin was doing something. They were moving faster than I thought possible.

"Yeah?" I asked, trying to stay focused. It was hard due to the sheer size of the battlefield now starting to overwhelm me: tens, if not hundreds of thousands of bodies writhing in pain.

"This whole place is waking up. I, uh, don't know, boss." Petro was genuinely concerned. Truth was, he could smell it in the air.

"We'll see, buddy. I'm not so sure myself."

"Oh snap. That means, according to the book I was reading, I need to confess!" He had recently read the Bible. After snickering at it because he knew some of the other stories surrounding J-man, he'd agreed to "try it out."

"Boss, I once used your toothbrush to clean my bedroom." He was screaming by this point, a spear flying overhead. "One time, I pooped in the glove box of Ed's car after you saved me and my bros from the freeze. One day—"

I cut him off. "Not now . . ." I paused. "That was you who pooped in Ed's car?"

"Yeah, I even pixed it to make it seem like a real animal did it."

"Sounds like you confessed enough. How far do you think we have to go?"

Petro stared forward, lifting his nose in the air as he shook off the stench. "Get ready, boss. Another minute or two."

A body lumbered into Gabby's horse's path in front of me. She swiped her sword down, trying to catch it, and it flew into the dark gray of the field. The truth of the matter was I was feeling Petro's concern.

A light flashed in front of me as the blue-silvery glow of Merlin's staff beamed for several seconds. Taking this as my queue to start literally raising hell, I pushed all my will into my arms and sent two streams of hellfire to either side of me. Pulling back the wash of hellfire, I summoned my whip, dragging it onto the bodies now lurching toward us. Glancing back, I confirmed this was efficiently setting swaths of whatever they were ablaze.

With my other hand, I slung several dripping balls of hellfire several feet away from the horses. After another couple of seconds, I switched sides. Again looking back, I saw an orange glow was starting to light up the foggy grounds.

My eyes shot open and I reared back on my horse, feeling as if something had happened. Speckles danced in front of my eyes until they finally came into focus, and I quickly realized I wasn't dead.

The horses all huffed with exertion, pushed to their limits. The once dark, foggy valley was starting to glow. I had done a decent job at starting the fire, even though the thought of what was burning didn't sit well with me.

"We don't have long. The army that survives the fire will be marching on Camelot. Morgana has taken over their souls and is commanding them. She knew we would come this way; it was a trap. She is trying to slow us down. Morgana knows we are coming," Merlin declared.

"Figured that," I replied, seeing the claw marks from the hands of the dead warriors on the side of Gabby's horse. She was leaning over, comforting her. "Lesson from the book of Max: Be unpredictable."

Merlin laughed again, turning his horse to the path leading out of the valley. "That was my next lesson!"

CHAPTER 25

Where Oh Where?
**The Atheneum
Present Day**

E d paced around the crucible room while Angel and Frank sat at the table with the box's main workstation. Jenny, walking in, handed Ed a cup of tea.

"It's been three weeks!" Ed exclaimed.

Jenny rubbed her hand on his back. "We knew this would take time." She walked to Angel and Frank. "Any changes?" she asked.

Angel shook her head. "No. I think the parameters are stable as well. If something changes in the story or history, we should see it." She turned.

"Unless we wouldn't know because it changed in the system previously," Ed replied.

"No." Frank stood up, an unnecessary gesture from a V. "That's the point of it being set up this way. We would know either way. Maybe next time we won't experiment with time."

"We really don't know. All we can track is if anything changes in the text." Angel stood as well, walking to the main screen. Trying to change the subject, she clicked her teeth. "No more murders since they all left, including Tristen. Have we heard from Aslynn or her brother?"

"No," Ed again huffed. He was a cable of tightly wound nerves and, as always, wore his emotions on his sleeve.

"Well"—Jenny smiled—"maybe we can occupy ourselves with that. I'll go see the Messenger."

"We can just use the box," Angel suggested. After all the time working together and forming a bond as friends, the group had worked with the Messenger to find a way to send messages through the box. While the Council also had this ability, it was done through magic. The team at the Atheneum used technology.

Jenny nodded. "True, I just thought it would be nice to take a break from this room," she stated, walking behind Frank. "Do you have the proper settings on?"

Just as Frank was about to work the keyboard, an alarm alerted them that the system had found something. The room froze. Frank clicked the alert, and several pages of old text populated the screen.

"It says," Frank started, "an alert of the word *hellfire* was found in a text from the general time and location."

"It says the text is from *The Battle of the Grays, a History of Camelot.* Hold on," Jenny said, leaning over his shoulder. "It's a book about battles that took place around the time of Camelot or that affected it."

"Right." Ed paused. "Doctor Freeman added some additional search parameters for stories that may pertain to the time."

"Open it," Jenny insisted.

Frank opened the file on the main monitor, which showed an old hand-drawn map of two cliffs overlooking a battlefield. Clicking the next page highlighted the word *hellfire* and an image of a burning valley of death.

"It says the Battle of the Grays left a field of souls unable to cross over. Three hundred years later, a group led by Merlin himself and several strangers from a strange land crossed the field and burned it with a flicker of hellfire," Frank read, turning to the next page. There, riding a horse, was a figure resembling Max and the armor they had taken with them.

"Son of a bitch," Angel breathed out. "This can't be real."

"Right, as long as the main story doesn't change, it means we have nothing to worry about. That book has probably had those pages in it since it was created. It's not like the book will chan —" Ed stopped in his tracks. Materializing out of nowhere was a footnote.

The field only half burned, still giving Morgana the additional army she needed to attack Camelot before the time of Excalibur. This was only one of many such attempts before falling to the loss of Lady Guinevere and the betrayal of Sir Lancelot, also known as King Ban's son, a young warrior said to have ridden on that very charge through the dead Battle of the Grays before joining the Round Table.

"This is seriously messed up," Frank grunted. "I'll grab the book from the stacks."

"Send that message first if you can," Angel insisted while Frank typed away.

The thing about the Fae was that they couldn't tell a flat-out lie. Leave out important facts? Sure. Tell a bald-faced lie? No. Understanding this fact, it was easy to ask a Fae something. Even Vs such as Frank and Angel knew all too well that when asking them something, it had to be specific and with a definitive answer.

As if they had been standing by the console, wherever Aslynn or her brother Jamison were, a message chimed back within seconds.

"Hmm," Frank again grunted.

"And?" Jenny asked as he pulled back from the monitor.

Frank's question had been simple yet thoughtful, forcing an answer. *"How is Tristen doing with you guys?"* They would have to tell them how he was if he was with them on the Plane.

The reply was likely Aslynn. *"We're sure he's fine."*

Everyone straightened up before Jenny spoke up. "What does that mean?"

Angel slammed her fist on the table, nearly breaking it. An indention of her hand remained as she lifted her fist. "They don't have him. He went with the others."

"How do you know that?" Ed asked.

She shook her head. "I like Aslynn and her brother, but they clearly don't have him," Angel said. "We do have a way to find out. They changed in the Postern, and we still have access to it. If he left with them, his clothes should be there."

Ed took off at a sprint, never questioning Angel's logic. Within seconds, the rest of the group followed, making their way to the Postern.

CHAPTER 26

Things About Quests

G reen trees contrasted with the gray sky as we entered the sprawling forest. After riding for another full day, we'd reached our destination. While Merlin mentioned it was a smaller forest, the term "smaller" had a different meaning in the past. While not as large as the one we'd passed through while leaving Merlin's castle, it was a monument to the lack of highways now cutting through the countryside.

Merlin stopped the caravan of misfits as we entered under the first grouping of trees. "We have a way to go, but we'll have to walk the horses from here."

"Why's that?" Phil protested, not wanting to walk.

"There are centaurs in these woods. They don't take kindly to us riding on horseback. I would prefer not to pick a fight today." Merlin paused. "Have you ever pissed off a centaur?"

"Can't say we have," I said as Petro nodded his head.

"Speak for yourself, we used to mess with them as kids. I farted in one's face one time, and it chased me for days. If they're in the woods, they for sure won't like seeing big bags of bones riding on horseback. It's a show of respect. They still know you ride them, though."

I shook my head. "Only you, buddy."

Phil meanwhile was chuckling as he whispered, "Farted in its face . . ."

"I can't deal with the lot of you sometimes," Merlin grumbled, turning toward the path.

"Just wait," Gabby said.

For the next hour, we walked through the forest. Plants I had never seen hugged old, wise trees. This was a living, breathing forest. Frogs hopped while birds chirped in a chorus fit for a fairy tale.

"How far are we from the castle?" I asked as Merlin looked up at the forest canopy.

"Two days on foot. We might be able to ride at some point.. The forest is long and narrow, and it ends within eyeshot of the castle; we should be safe on this path. As for the underground path to the castle, it is a half-day walk."

"Hey." Phil stopped. "I got to dillydally through that field for half a day?"

"What's wrong?" Sir Rose smiled. "Not man enough? I'm sure Tristen can make the journey."

"*Whaa?* Man enough? I'll—" Phil was flabbergasted. "I'll show you and all that." Phil fluttered his fingers at the knight's armor. "I'll tell Ed you were an overblown tea kettle. My arse, the kid is going. I'll handle the trip."

Sir Rose glanced at me, winking as Phil stomped forward. Even though several apples had fallen from the Rose tree, some of his traits had carried through the ages.

Phil kept grumbling under his breath as we walked. "Man enough. Total hogwash. I fought a chimera."

Gabby came to walk beside me as Petro went to ride on Tristen's shoulder, who was talking with Sir Rose. "Penny for your thoughts?"

We both watched Merlin several feet ahead of us. "It's Tristen; he seems so happy here. He's lit up like a Christmas tree and hasn't left Sir Rose's side since he got here."

"You noticed it too. You'd make a good father," Gabby

commented.

My heart dropped into my guts as I looked at her smile. Her lips were still red even though she hadn't put on any lipstick.

"Is there anything you want to tell me?" I asked, gulping.

"No, silly. I'm just saying. I see how you look at him and the other kids. They all love you. They look up to you. Hell, I'm just happy you asked me to tag along; I'll take the scraps."

She was giving me a hard time. In reality, she was the mayor of Salt City and a very important person in her own right. Smart and devastatingly gorgeous, Gabby was everything I felt I wasn't at times. She had her shit together.

"When else have we had the time?" I asked. She shrugged.

"Maybe I'm just jealous of all your other misadventures, but I must say . . ." she trailed off, thinking. "This one takes the cake." She pointed at Merlin. "He's stopping."

Merlin stood resolutely staring into the trees. Sir Rose walked to him, also looking into the thick forest. Meanwhile, Petro buzzed over to us, landing on my shoulder. "There's something ahead watching us. It's been in front of us for a few minutes."

"Any idea what it is?" I asked. He nodded.

"Smells like a Dwarf; one of the burly ones who never take baths. You know, like the ones who built that calf thingy for you, boss," Petro said, still staring into the deep-green foliage.

The thing about Dwarves, besides them being labeled incorrectly as little people in modern times, was that while they were in fact short, they were also massively strong and some of the best crafters on the face of the Earth.

It also went without saying that they were fierce warriors wielding unimaginable weapons. J. R. R. Tolkien had gotten that part right about them. Often loud and generally disgruntled, the Dwarves had sat the Balance out, preferring to keep to themselves.

The rest of the team walked forward, joining the two men.

"Trouble?" I asked as Merlin stayed still. Sir Rose didn't

have his hand resting on his sword, telling me there was no immediate danger.

The old wizard finally turned. "We are here, and if I'm right . . ." He held up his hand, and a flicker of fire launched from his hand, darting into the distance.

After a few seconds, a yelp disturbed the pristine quiet of the forest. Merlin smiled, clearly familiar with the yelp. The sound of something moving through the brush reached us, followed by an extremely grumpy voice.

"Might as well burn the forest down, wizard. Fire, really." The voice grew closer. Low and growling, this was obviously not the first time Merlin had slung a little bolt of fire at him.

"Gelf." Sir Rose smiled. "You know, you could have just let us know you were here."

With those words, a short, thick, armored Dwarf of the vale walked out of the low brush. "You could have just let me know you were coming," Gelf grumbled before pausing to take the rest of us in. "Hmph."

"*Hmph* is right; you stink like a moldy sock," Petro replied, buzzing off toward Gelf. I almost reached for him to stop him, but Gelf held out his hand, palm up.

"Ah, a Pixie warrior," Gelf announced, seeing Petro's armor. This was followed by Petro turning to show off his encased wings. The Dwarf poked him with his finger.

"Very nice, yes, very old. You must be of importance, Pixie."

"My name's Prince Petro. I'll spare you the details, big guy, but you can call me Petro."

"A prince. Well, we must feast with such a noble Pixie." Gelf lightly bowed his head as Petro flew back to my shoulder while Merlin walked forward and dropped a small sack of coins in Gelf's hand.

"What was that all about?" I asked Petro.

"That's right, we never talked about the Dwarves. They're our homies on the Plane. I mean, they kind of fall under the little folk category as well. We provide them with dust for making weapons and armor, and they treat us with respect. Total bosses. Don't ever piss one off if you think my gas is bad," Petro rattled off.

"I never knew," I replied as Phil leaned over.

"Oh yeah, bruther. I'd keep an eye on those two. Just think if Petro was that big with no wings and as round as a basketball."

You learned something new every day in the magical world. I was still fairly new to the show, on the grand scheme of things.

After ten minutes of walking, we came upon Gelf's camp, an old house that looked as if it were part of the forest itself. The cottage was covered in moss and stone, making it seem like the trees had grown around it.

"Come in, I'll fetch water for the horses," Gelf instructed, opening the door.

The inside of the cottage was just as eclectic as the outside. A fire burned in the main room with a pot hanging over it, the smell of stew lingering in the air. Several barrels of ale sat in the far corner, and two smaller rooms split off nearby, leading into the back of the space.

Standing up, my head was roughly an inch from the wooden ceiling, allowing for several loose hairs to touch it. Petro was already hovering over the stew when Gelf clomped back in, and Merlin had dropped into one of four cushioned chairs in the main living area. Sir Rose took off his sword, motioning us to do the same. "We're safe here."

Benches sat on either side of a knotted table carved from a massive tree, with plates and cups set out. He knew we were coming.

"The horses are good. Those are some fine animals," Gelf said, walking over to one of the large barrels of ale. "We have much to discuss. A storm is brewing."

"Indeed," Merlin replied as Gelf handed him a large cup of ale.

"But first," Gelf interjected, "who are these folks? They smell too clean."

"At least someone does," Petro joked while Gelf chuckled.

"Indeed," Gelf mirrored Merlin's response. I was certain that if I had been the one to say that, I would be in a fight.

"That is a story you will need to sit down for, Gelf." The old wizard motioned him to sit down as the rest of us made out way to the benches.

Phil and Tristen were already eyeing the stew. It smelled amazing, and even I found my mouth watering. It went without saying that such good crafters would also be good cooks.

For the next hour, Merlin told the entire story as he knew it. Gelf, by the end of it, had repacked his pipe of sweet tobacco several times and was literally staring at us.

"And that is that," Merlin concluded.

Gelf stood, walking over to us. The Dwarf sat at the end of the bench, getting eye level with us, then leaned forward, burning curiosity in his eyes while he stared directly at me.

"You, Max, is this all true?" Gelf inquired.

I nodded. "I'm afraid so." He was clearly trying to see if there was more to the story, which there of course was. Good thing for me, I had honed my skills in telling only what was needed from Ed in a way that came across as natural. While most magical types had a good bullshit meter, I had sat in a chair in front of the Council enough times to know.

Gelf grunted. "You're not telling us everything."

I had to admit, he was good at reading people, but I was also good at the game.

"There are some things that are yet to happen. We have to be careful. Yes," I proclaimed loudly, "there are some things we are keeping to ourselves, but I can assure you, it's for your own good. I'm familiar with your kind." I lifted my leather pants, exposing the rebuilt steampunk-like calf made by the Dwarves. Merlin looked shocked to see the odd contraption that made up my lower leg. Mixed with flesh and fine gears and metal, it was in many ways a work of art in itself.

Satisfied with my answer, Gelf walked to the small cooking area, grabbing a ladle. "Well, I see your way of thinking. Plus, no Dwarf would do work like that on a nob."

Phil snickered. "I wouldn't say he's not a nob there, bruther."

Serving the first bowl of stew, Gelf set it in front of Phil. "Aye," Gelf replied, looking at Phil. "I see the fire in his eyes." He pointed at me. "The heart for your friends in you." He pointed at Phil. "The strength of a warrior in Petro, and the warmth of the bloodsuck—" He interrupted himself. "The warmth in the lady. Sorry, miss. Habit. I see the power and weight of responsibility you keep."

He shifted to Tristen. "As for you, young man. I see valor, and . . ." Gelf cocked his head. "Yes, and power." He had clearly seen something.

Tristen was the next to be served. "A young man with much ambition. You will choose your fate, young one. We all do."

"Alright." Merlin stood up, heading to the table. "Now that we have that out of the way, let's make merry for the night, for tomorrow, we go to the forest's edge and see what perils await us."

CHAPTER 27

Dream a Little Dream
Max
Dreaming That Night

Ocean waves crashed on dark, stony cliffs under the cover of night. In the sky, stars twinkled as if someone were turning them off and on at random, making the entire gray, rocky beach leading up to the cliffs look as if it was under a strobe light.

Thunder growled in the distance like a freight train, and muffled voices sounded in the horizon. I stood on the edge of the cliffs, looking out into the endless black of the night ocean. Turning, I could see a battle taking place over rolling hills. Blurred figures clashed as dots of fire peppered the countryside. Between me and the struggle, there was nothing but calm land.

The longer I stared in my dream, the more two figures started to appear out of the gloom of night. My feet felt light as I began to float toward them, not of my own free will. Something was pulling me to them.

Within seconds, familiar stances and features made it apparent that I knew the two figures I was about to come face-to-face with. Unlike most of my dreams, this one felt real. I had experienced this only on a handful of occasions, and each time, it was a powerful force sending a powerful message.

Bo had explained that this was the mix of demon and Tom in my blood. Tom, on the other hand, had approached it with caution, telling me the ability to meet with others in dreams was a trait of a necromancer, something I'd had no success with. Yes . . . I had tried my hand at Tom's craft with no luck.

The familiar face of Metatron, the all-seeing and all-knowing angel, stood stoically beside Penance, the Overseer. Unlike the archangel's usual gleaming armor with eyes looking in all directions, he was in a normal set of light armor. Penance, as always, was in a large black cloak.

"Max," Metatron started. His voice wasn't crushing, as it was on some occasions, but more human. All knowing, but more human. "What do you see?"

I felt his words as Penance took off his hood. "Yes, what do you see?" he echoed.

Not feeling this was the time for a reunion, I rolled my eyes enough to make do. "A battle. I thought you knew everything?"

"I see all. Past, present, and future. The here and the now; what may and may not be. With you here, my vision splinters. What do you see?"

I squinted my eyes in this dream realm as two massive wings came out of the dark sky through the thundering clouds sweeping over the battlefield. They were asking me to look with everything I had. This meant something.

"A dragon in the sky over the battle. It's hunting something," I replied as Penance nodded.

Metatron wasn't satisfied with my answer. "What do you see?"

This time, I focused on its wings as it swooped down over the battle. The flame of the battle lit up its underbelly. Breasts and the features of a woman came into focus as slender-clawed hands scooped up piles of warriors, taking them into the sky, only to drop them.

"Part woman, part dragon; killing," I answered as the dragon unleashed a ball of flame onto the battlefield.

"Not a dragon—a demon," Metatron breathed out. "One familiar to you." When Metatron spoke, he often did so in absolutes.

I again focused on the swooping wings. "I've never seen anything like that in my life."

Penance turned this time. "That you know of. Demons take on many forms. Bo, as you know, can be many things. Of more concern, you have yet to break the stream of time on your journey. You must not burden yourself with things such as these." He waved his hand over the battle.

"Lady Morgana and something called the Anger are going to take over Camelot. I don't remember seeing anything about this?" I asked. Penance and Metatron shot each other a glance.

"The Anger." Metatron pointed at the winged creature swooping down for more warriors. "She has many names."

"She?" I asked as Penance again took over the conversation.

"To stop death is not to kill it. This is not your fight, just your station here and now. We watched this happen, but as Metatron said, there is a fork in his vision."

"I get we are here to do one thing, but in turn, have done many others," I said.

Metatron nodded. "As it was written."

"What does all this mean?" I asked just as they turned to dust in my dream.

A screech of the creature in the distance pulled me back from the horror unfolding in front of me, and the vision slowly faded away.

CHAPTER 28

The Fields of Glory

I jerked awake as the cool morning air touched my lungs. Gabby sat beside me, still in her clothes, rubbing my forehead; she had clearly been doing this the entire time I'd been asleep. Vs needed very little sleep and usually did so when they were fully comfortable. Angel had once told me she only slept once a week, but I was sure that had changed since she and Frank had been together.

"You were talking in your sleep. Petro even came in to check on you."

I looked around the small room, seeing piles of garments and random pieces of armor. Sweat covered my body as I pulled myself up. "What time is it?" I asked.

"Midmorning. Everyone else is outside. Merlin insisted we let you sleep; he came in and did that eye-squinting thing, then left. He's a funny old wizard, but strong. Stronger than we think."

"Listen," I started, "I had one of those dreams I told you about. It was a warning."

I reached up, and Gabby pulled me to my feet. "Warning? Your whole life is a warning."

"True." I smiled. "There was a battle. A fire burned the field as a demon came from the sky. It was the Anger; it's a *she*."

"She? You're saying the Anger they keep talking about is a

woman? Makes sense." Again, her humor cut through. There was a reason we got along so well.

"There was more to it. We aren't supposed to get involved in this fight. I know we are, but we both know that there is no history of this siege on Camelot. Something is going to happen; I don't know what, but we must be ready."

"A she, you say?" Merlin's voice boomed from the doorway. "Interesting. I heard the rumor, but your dream might just confirm this."

"A demon," I followed as Petro darted into the room.

"Your horse is ready, boss. I think she was worried. Anywho, we're ready to roll out!' Petro exclaimed, zipping back outside.

After explaining what I had seen in my dream, a look of concern took hold of Merlin. He knew something he wasn't yet letting us know.

Gelf, and Phil nodded as I walked outside, only to see Sir Rose and Tristen practicing sword stances. "So, bruther, you good?" Phil asked, knowing I had had one of my dreams.

"Yeah. We need to get moving and focus on why we came," I replied while the rest of the group mounted their horses.

"How goobered up was it?" Phil asked, still wanting to know more about my dream.

"I saw a massive demon with the body of a female and wings of a dragon. Plus, old Penance and Metatron were there. It was a warning not to get too involved here."

"You saw boobies in your dream?" Phil asked, cocking his head.

"Boobies?" Petro echoed, landing on my shoulder. I had their undivided attention.

"I literally talked to Metatron and Penance, and that's all you guys care about?" I asked as they replied in unison. "Yup."

Gabby turned. "Good thing you two don't know about Vampire skin clubs." Petro buzzed over to Phil, and the two started a heated conversation about the topic.

"Is that a real thing?" I asked as we trotted to catch up with Merlin and the others, who had already started toward the trail.

"Totally made up. Why would one of my kind need something like that? I just like to watch them squirm."

"Pure evil," I whispered as she shrugged.

"I've been called worse. Let the dream set for a while, and we can talk about it again. You said that helps."

Nodding, we all fell in line as the trail narrowed under the protective shade of the forest. Minutes turned to hours, and light started shining through the trees in front of us; we had made it to the edge of the forest.

Phil and Petro had on several occasions rode up to ask Gabby more questions about these skin clubs, only to have her fuel their fire. They'd asked everything from "Are Pixies allowed in?" to my favorite from Phil: "Do they serve vitals when doing whatever it is they do in there?"

"We walk from here," Gelf instructed the group, and we dismounted our horses. Tristen, now sporting his sword on his side, still struggled with maneuvering the weapon, and when he jumped down, the sword stuck to the ground, almost making him fall.

Sir Rose's steady hand grabbed the young man's shoulder and lifted Tristen to his feet. "Always pull your sword back when dismounting. It makes it faster to draw and keeps you from doing that." He pointed at the ground.

Gelf motioned for us to follow as he lowered his posture. It was time to be quiet. The closer we got to the edge of the forest, the lower we got, until we were all on our knees looking over the rolling hills leading up to a shockingly massive castle.

Even after all the movies and drawings in books, nothing could have truly portrayed the sheer size of Camelot. I saw even Tristen, who was familiar with this part of the country, mouth WTF.

Tall spires jutted into the sky as a massive wall hugged the grounds of the castle as if it were protecting its newborn child. Birds circled the towers, and an even larger wall surrounded the inner section of the castle.

Grand, regal, and like something from Titania's castle on the Plane, I had questions about how such a massive structure could not stand the test of time. Pushing my will into thoughts, I sent out a simple message: *"Don't mention this not being here in the future."*

Simple nods let me know my message had been received. The less the others knew, the better.

Gelf pointed at the dark clouds surrounding the castle, the black line slicing the already gray sky in half. "Morgana's army of the undead is under that soup."

I looked up at the clouds. "And what is that in the sky?" I asked. Gelf shrugged.

"Clouds for now. As long as the Anger is here, the countryside is fouled with this thick muck," Gelf noted, turning to Phil. "You will need to make the journey across the fields. There's a small ridge that leads to the water pipes leading into the castle. There, you will find a secret entrance."

"How will I know where to stick my head in?" Phil asked.

Merlin smiled this time.

"You will take this amulet with you. Once you are where the water meets the pipes, the entrance is marked with several flat lines that look like this." Merlin drew a symbol in the dirt in front of us. "Hold up the amulet, and the way will open. From there . . ." He hesitated. "From there, you will need to make your way to the inner keep and King Ban. Before you ask, I'll figure a way to let him know you are coming. Maybe. Perhaps."

"Maybe?" Phil scoffed. "Perhaps? It's my arse on the line."

"Worst case, show him the amulet; it will at least get him to listen. I know you are strong; just be ready. But no matter what you do, don't take on the castle guards and make sure you close the passage. He will know the door you need to open if everything works out."

"This sounds a little loose," I said.

Merlin shrugged. "As all plans. We will be waiting in the tunnel. Knowing Morgana, she will have something waiting for us."

"They wouldn't have gone through the entrance we will use," Gelf said.

Merlin nodded. "It doesn't mean she didn't dig into the earth or gate someone there," he replied.

"Why can't we just gate in?" Tristen asked, leaning back on the damp soil.

"Two reasons, as mentioned before. She will know if we gate, and the castle is heavily warded. I'm sure they have those in your time." Merlin frowned.

Nodding, I pointed toward what appeared to be a stream of fog leading to the castle. "Is that where her army is traveling?"

Sir Rose nodded. "Yes. We will stay in the fog; I've seen this before."

A thought formed in the old head movie. The more I looked, the more the rolling hills resembled my dream. A fight would happen here regardless.

"What if this doesn't work?" I asked, but Merlin again shrugged.

"Then we fight. Or die. Either way, you are getting into that castle. I'd prefer not to die; there will be plenty of time for that later. Plus, you already stated I live much longer than Excalibur being taken by Arthur," the old wizard noted.

"Yeah, probably shouldn't have told you that, but it's true," I said as Sir Rose turned. We hadn't mentioned anything about his future, and truth be told, we had no clue. For all we knew, he survived to see Camelot thrive.

"Petro," I called him. He left Gelf's side.

"Yeah, boss?"

"How long would it take you to fly to the castle?" I asked as he held up his fingers like he was counting.

"Thirty or forty minutes, give or take. Depends on how windy it gets."

I tapped his armor-covered wings. "I'm fairly certain that armor will protect you from the wind."

"Oh, yeah, I never thought about that. You want to blow in the air and see?"

Sometimes, Petro wasn't cooking with fire, and this was one of those times. He was nervous.

Phil glanced up. "If you say I'm the only one full of that much hot air, I'm going to get Trish to close your bar tab."

"Is that a thing?" I asked while Gabby, Phil, and Petro nodded. "Well, let's not be hasty." The levity was needed, though Merlin and Sir Rose looked confused. "Petro, I want you to be ready to fly to the castle if anything happens in the tunnels. You know. Plan B."

He saluted.

"When do we go?" I asked as Gelf finally stood. In reality, he'd never needed to duck down.

"Now. It will take several hours. Plus, Phil will be moving like a cow in the mud. Here." Gelf pulled out a rolled-up map and laid it out. "You will need to follow this ridge to the water," he reiterated the route. "You will know when you get to the water outflow."

"How?" Phil quickly asked, picking up the map.

"You'll smell it before you see it. But never fear, warrior. The secret entrance does not go through the sewers," Gelf promised, only to have Merlin glare at him. "Okay, maybe a bit, but it's not that mucky."

CHAPTER 29

The Path to Nowhere

The entrance to the hidden underground passage to the castle was a work of camouflaged art, a large tree with a massive set of moss-covered stones sitting beside it. It looked the same as every other clump of trees.

Six boulders sat together, hiding the entrance to the tunnel. The first step in accessing the opening involved Merlin and Gelf shutting off the ward, which entailed chanting a specific phrase over and over.

Petro got so tired of hearing it that he decided to take a nap in my infinity bag. Next, the pair located two small holes on the opposite side of the boulders, and each pulled out a gleaming silver spike, unlocking some mysterious mechanism.

The last step, which seemed completely odd, was them both kissing the boulders at the same time. After Phil started snickering, Sir Rose explained it was more like kissing one's mother on the cheek and not so much telling the rock you loved it. They were showing their respect for the earth itself.

Phil, of course, had something to say. "If Mother Nature could gander at Gelf kissing her, she would open that hole to keep you from scaring the rest of the lady folk."

Merlin motioned everyone to stand back as the six boulders slowly started moving like a blooming flower opening, exposing a set of stone stairs leading down. Tapping my bag, Petro flew out.

"There spiders down there?" Petro asked.

Gelf nodded. "Aye. Big ones, with nasty hairy legs and teeth," Gelf said, picking up a torch. "What we need to be worrying about is Morgana's undead army. It is said they can climb through the earth itself. Plus, there may be a few ghouls. No idea what was locked down there last time the passage was used."

I focused on Phil. "You good to go, man?"

Phil held the cloak in his hand. "I could sure use a nip of liquid courage. Just a long walk through the countryside."

Petro flew over to his partner in crime. "I read that dating profile you put together once. You said you hated long walks on the beach. I think you then listed off every other place that involved long walks."

"I-I," Phil stammered. "It was for scientific purposes. I . . ." Phil blushed as Gabby beamed a smile at him before he play-swatted at Petro. "You weren't supposed to say anything about that, bruther. We even did the pinky swear."

Sir Rose stared down the dark stairs before turning back. "What is a dating profile?"

Gabby took this one. "It's better if you don't know. It would ruin the vibe way too early in history. And before you ask, in the future, the pinky swear is a powerful bounding spell."

Merlin looked at his hands and grumbled, "Pinky Swear . . ."

By this point, I was fairly certain Merlin would invent an actual bonding spell, and once again, we would be the reason it was invented, even if it wasn't truly magic to regulars.

After saying our goodbyes, Phil vanished into nothingness, pulling the cloak over his head. After everyone continued to just stare down the stairs, Gabby walked forward into the dark abyss. Vs, after all, had perfect night vision.

Large enough to drive a truck through, and as ominous as an underground medieval passage could be, the journey ahead screamed danger. Merlin's staff glowed as if made of pure light. Bright enough to illuminate the passage, it also had the ability to not project past our immediate area. If needed, I could always sling a little hellfire around.

Gelf lit his torch, walking in front of the group beside Merlin. Tristen, as he had for most of the journey, stayed close to Sir Rose, while Gabby and I followed behind. Petro was, of course, hitching a ride on my shoulder.

Random crates and empty carts sat at random intervals, showing varying levels of age. In one cart, several barrels of ale sat untouched. Phil would have insisted on a pit stop.

Merlin's voice finally broke the silence after several minutes of walking. "Tom used to come down here. I'm not sure what he did, but he was always coming down here."

Gelf stopped. "That's right. He had a room off the passageway down here that he made. I never saw it, but he talked about it a few times after a few ales."

"It might be a good thing to find this room," I said while the others nodded. "Any idea how to find it?"

"We have a Pixie; just sniff for it," Merlin suggested, but Petro shrugged.

"It smells like dirt and poop down here, but I'll do my best," Petro promised with a salute.

"Finder of the room," I drawled out. "You find the room, and it's totally getting added to the list." This, of course, was the list of Petro's titles that, by this point, was a good twenty items long. I usually cut him off after he got to the "Slayer of the Eye"; after that, it could get fairly adult oriented.

"Piece of cake, boss. Leave it to the professionals." Petro took flight, going to the front of the group.

As with any medieval tunnel built underground, a shriek echoed from the far distance. Gabby's ears pinned back as she listened.

"Only one," Gabby spoke up.

"One what, my lady?" Gelf asked.

"One something," she replied with a smile.

Merlin glanced at Gelf. "We knew there would be obstacles. Morgana knows of this passageway."

I stepped forward. "I'll take point; put out the torch. Worst case, I light up the passage."

Gelf scratched his red beard. "Hellfire. Hah," he scoffed. "Can't wait to see it." He was being sarcastic, even after hearing the story. Doing what I did best, I let hellfire dance through my eyes before it concentrated around my hand.

"Well, tickle my berries. I thought you were all gassing me on. Let's go," Gelf concluded, now looking unimpressed. He was a hard sell.

I took a step forward while Merlin pushed more energy into his staff. Petro joined me, still sniffing the air every few minutes. It was at times like these that I thought about all the other bad situations we had been through. I was strong—not just strong but fast, and able to take on most of any creature I had come toe to toe with.

The gauntlet, as I'd experienced earlier, was able to deflect one good shot, pushing the energy of the attack back at its originator, but I realized it needed time to reset itself. I'd felt drained after the run-in with the black nights. I would save this for when it was needed. My main concern at this point was how bad of an idea it would be to sling hellfire in the enclosed space.

Another—now closer—shriek echoed down the passageway. Whatever was in the tunnel with us was closing in on us. Even more off-putting was the water now dripping from the roof. Every drop echoed off the damp floor, creating a chorus of plunking taps.

"Are you going to say it, boss?" Petro asked, sniffing extra hard after asking.

"Oh yeah, I said it to myself a few minutes ago. I got a bad feeling about this." I paused, seeing Petro starting to home in on something. "Got something?"

"Yeah." Petro continued to sniff. "Not whatever is howling at us. Over there." He pointed to a flat spot in the tunnel wall carved out of stone and mud.

"We got something," I mumbled behind me. By this point, we were whispering at best when talking.

Merlin stepped forward while Petro dusted the area, continuing to sniff. The old wizard placed his hand on the wall. "I think you found it." He nodded, pushing both hands into and through the mud and stone.

A light sucking sound pulled Merlin into the wall, and he disappeared.

"I'm not doing that," Petro huffed just as the ground began to rumble, followed by a shriek fit for hell itself.

CHAPTER 30

The Field of Dreams
Phil

Mud clung to Phil's boots as he trudged along the foggy path laid out by Gelf. To his right, massive swaths of the undead stood like mindless shoppers waiting in line to check out, staring at the ground. To his left, a small ridge lined the side of the used path covered in odd-looking carts and nightmare-inducing animals also in various stages of decay.

While the first thirty minutes of the journey had been relatively pleasant, it'd quickly devolved into organized chaos. Even more unnerving was that none of the army he was slowly walking among had moved. It was as if they were statues waiting to be brought back to life.

The one plus was the cloak's ability to hide his footsteps, and after looking at the road he had just walked on, it also made any trace of his movement disappear into nothing. Even though his nerves were tickling his thoughts, Phil was moving along at a good clip, focused on the mission.

"What the bloody hell?" Phil whispered to himself as a large tent, looking as if it housed a carnival, slowly appeared in front of him.

For a brief moment, he considered passing the obnoxiously

red tent, but then he smelled food. Even more compelling was what appeared to be a living human in opulent armor walking inside. This was a command tent, and in Phil's mind, a quick pit stop for intel was just what the doctor ordered. He would be in and out in five minutes.

The closer Phil came to the entrance, the more he started feeling a knot in his stomach. It was at times such as these that he wished at least Petro had come with him. Phil quickly realized that Merlin had suggested it be a one-person trip in case something went wrong, and Sir Rose had known this when prodding Phil about sending Tristen.

Standing to the side of the tent flaps, Phil timed his entrance to follow two suited figures about to walk in. With a quick kick of his heels, Phil entered the tent. What he wasn't expecting was the massive model of the castle and the surrounding fields sitting in the middle of the space.

The three figures he'd followed were all standing next to the table, talking about something important. Wearing black armor, each had a sword hanging from both hips; they were clearly not only leaders but also fighters. Each of the men had a cape covering their backs in different colors. To Phil, this most likely identified the units they were in charge of.

Scanning the sides of the tent, lavish piles of food sat on tables, with wine and ale sitting in large barrels. This tent was not only their command center—it was also a space for entertaining. Upon closer inspection, Phil noticed most of the food was rotting.

He backed up to the entrance, just off to the side, so he could make a quick exit; he had no desire to get any closer. Just as Phil was thinking of leaving as soon as the entrance opened again, a flap on the far end fluttered, immediately shutting up the three men.

Holding his breath as if he would never breathe again, he finally saw her. All three of the men took a knee with the clatter of their armor, then one of the leaders with long black hair slicked back on his head stood first.

"Lady Morgana, the armies are set."

Morgana walked closer, motioning the others to stand. "I see. And what of this band of travelers with Merlin? I received word of them taking out a squad of our finest black knights. Do you bring word of this?"

Unlike most cowering commanders who did not want to bring bad news, the knight didn't flinch. "Yes."

"Proceed." Morgana waved her hand. She was average height, thin, and full of intensity, like a wound-up cobra about to strike. She wore a blood-red set of robes that were both formfitting yet looked to be part of some type of armor. A rapier hung from her hip, with a wand sitting in the same scabbard. To Phil, she was beautiful in a dangerous way, like a predator using her looks to lure in prey.

"Lady Morgana, we received word from our scouts at the Battle of the Grays that Merlin is traveling with five others and a Pixie. Sir Rose is with him, but the others are unknown." The other men remained silent.

"Unknown. There are not many who are unknown in these lands. What else did the scout report?" Morgana pressed, the intensity in her voice escalating.

"They were on the back and were likely the ones who attacked the squad."

Morgana let out a cackling laugh, warning of violence. The three men again didn't show any signs of fear. They were warriors. "Likely?" she asked, walking closer.

"My lady, there is also news of hellfire being used in the valley." That got her attention.

"Hellfire," Morgana drawled out, walking behind the men. Faster than the blink of an eye, she pulled out her wand, clanking on one of the other two knights' armor.

The brown-haired knight immediately fell to his knees while the other two remained unmoving. Walking back in front of them, she knelt down and got face-to-face with the man she had just tapped with her wand, lifting his chin with her sharp finger. "That was one of your scouts, Paragon, Lord of the Valley of the Damned. When I say was, I mean *was*. I had him flayed and fed to the men, if you can call them that."

The man didn't speak, even when the sound of armor being crumpled like a beer can started clunking. Phil stood in shock as the knight's chest armor completely collapsed, caving in the man's chest to nothing more than a few tight inches. Blood pooled at his feet as she let his chin drop. Paragon fell forward, dying instantly.

Standing up, Morgana put her wand away. "He will be part of your unit, Lord Valin." This was the lead knight's name. Phil was taking note of everything by this point, not paying attention to time. He was also getting concerned that the woman in front of him was powerful enough to sense him if she started paying closer attention to her surroundings.

"Yes, my lady." Valin bowed.

"You will also find where this group is and kill them. You know the dangers of Merlin. They are surely heading our way; they must not stop what is coming. And remember, my knight"—she walked around Valin—"the Anger is not as forgiving as I."

She quickly shifted focus, looking over the massive table with Camelot sitting in the center. "I took the liberty of leaving them a few surprises in case they are stupid enough to take the tunnels or go by water." This piqued Phil's interest. "A few mermaids ought to do the job." Lethal and much more dangerous than the romantic tales of them, Phil knew what this meant.

He could handle them as long as he kept the cloak on and didn't use magic around the water; he had dealt with them before. The thought faded as Morgana continued.

"The Anger will be here in a day's time at most. Once she arrives, we'll take the front gates. Lord Tate." She shifted to the other knight. While shorter, what he didn't have in height, he made up for in thickness. Slabs of muscle on slabs of muscle bulged from the man. "You will take on Paragon's forces. I will send a replacement."

With the conversation over, the two knights bowed. Phil, not wanting to spend another second in the tent, followed as the two men left, dragging the body of their counterpart. Phil had lost his appetite for the food.

Once the knights were out of eyeshot, Phil redoubled his efforts, taking off at a sprint.

CHAPTER 31

Tom's Time Capsule

T he last of the shrieks from the creature in the passage faded once I finally walked through the wall into another chamber. It was clear we would soon have a fight on our hands.

Unlike most things that took me by surprise, this place was on another level of confusion. The large room we stood in was full of shelves and tables. Sitting like shrines, various items from a future time sat like trophies.

On the first table, an Etch A Sketch sat next to a Game Boy and several other games. To the right, various weapons and guns sat on a rack next to a TV and VHS player. A bike and what appeared to be a motorcycle leaned against the far wall, while a hallway opened on the far end of the room to another section of what could only be described as Tom's literal man cave.

Sir Rose and Merlin both looked confused as Gabby stepped forward. "These are from our time, or thereabouts."

Tristen picked up the Game Boy. "I've seen these on the internet. I always wanted one."

"Internet?" Merlin asked.

I stepped forward. "It is something we use to communicate with and do things in the future. I'm sure you've used an Atticus board; it's something like that, but way cooler. Let's see what's in the back." I started walking as Merlin nodded, holding up a Simon Says game.

Gabby pointed to several guns. "You think we should grab some of these?"

"No, I'm not going to be the reason Morgana gets a flame thrower." I pointed at the literal flame thrower from World War II.

Merlin continued to scan the items as we walked through the room "Tom used to talk of these things, but he never showed me. I know of the TV; such magic in the future is a thing of wonder."

Sir Rose looked a little more uneasy with the current state of affairs. I could see in his face how insignificant all these things made him feel. We were now the gods in a foreign land.

Walking into the next room, it was clear Tom had been taking more than a few toys. Pieces of priceless art and stacks of gold bars led to an honest-to-God La-Z-Boy recliner facing another TV. Besides that, a small fridge sat with a cable running to a glowing yellow ball; he had used some type of magic to supply power to everything. It was then that I noticed actual electric lights illuminating the space.

"This place is awesome," Tristen said, opening the small fridge to find several beers.

"Yeah," I huffed. "Gramps was always up to something. I wonder if this place is still here in the future."

Gabby shot me a glance; she was right. After seeing the sheer magnitude of Camelot, I was starting to reconsider what actually happened here.

Merlin, unfazed by the riches, was feeling the wall.

"What is it?" I asked as he continued to run his hands over everything.

"Knowing Tom, he most likely had another way out of here, or a shortcut to the end of the tunnel. It may save us some time and effort."

"Effort not to die," Sir Rose followed, picking up a picture.

"Who are these people?"

He handed me a photo in a cheap frame. I had seen this picture before; it was Ed, Vendal, and Tom all holding up mugs of beer. The other version had a few others in it, but this one looked more intimate—friends making a final cheer before moving on to their next adventure. Even in this picture, Tom was clearly older than the others.

"It's Tom and some of his friends. There is a war in the future, a cruel war. Millions of people die," I said.

Sir Rose looked up. "Millions?"

Petro, having been distracted by a stack of romance novels, threw in his opinion. "Oh yeah. They like fighting, and when they do, they don't mess around. They also like slushies and pizza. Oh, and don't get me started on techno music."

"We get it, buddy. Listen, there are a lot more people in the future, and the world is a big place. Let's just say time is the one thing you can't outrun," I said reflectively.

"Words you should abide by, Max," Merlin added, pressing into a part of the wall, only to have it give way, crumbling to ashes. "Ah. Here we go. Anyone else want to avoid whatever it is in that tunnel?"

"I'm in," Tristen spoke first.

Gabby was already walking toward the small passageway, picking up a dusty flashlight. I cocked my head as she shrugged. "What? I don't have a built-in flashlight." She smiled, pointing at the gold. "That's a fortune."

"It is indeed." I pointed at the paintings. "And that's the lost treasure from World War II. Guess they got that movie wrong." While it would be interesting, not to mention lucrative, to look for this place in the future, it oddly felt like a tomb to things that needed to stay buried.

Tristen cleared his throat. "What if she knows about this place and it's a setup?"

"Nah, this place smells old; no one's been in there in a long time," Petro affirmed. Seeing Tristen's face drop, Petro shifted. "Way to think ahead. I was worried about the same thing till I got a whiff of it. Elbows and assholes, let's get moving."

"Why is he so chipper?" Gabby asked, referring to Petro.

I picked up a necklace full of gems, sliding it into my pocket with a sly grin. "He dropped a few romance novels in my bag. Gramps had some doozies. Plus, he wants to get aboveground as soon as we can; he doesn't like it underground. When we found the Fountain of Youth, he didn't act like it bothered him, but later on, he made sure we knew his opinion on not seeing the sky."

Taking one last glance at the room of spoils, we slowly entered the narrow hall. Christmas lights illuminated the way, different types and styles lighting the path forward. Colored lights flickered, while solid white bulbs broke the strobing effect. Within four hours, including a break for lunch in an area full of more weapons, we finally made it to the door leading into Camelot.

Large enough for a train to pass through and part of the stone itself, the door was more than just a way to another place; it was built into the foundation of the castle itself. No weapon or ogre could get through the door. Even hellfire would have trouble making its way through.

We all stood with our heads leaned back, taking in the sight of solid silver and cold iron adorning the gate. Several skeletons sat against the side walls—people who had tried to get into the castle undetected and failed. There was no sign of struggle, just simple death from starvation.

Sir Rose walked to one of the bodies, looking at their armor. "French."

"They smell French," Petro added, landing on my shoulder. "They wee-weed their last wee-wee."

"How do you know they smell French?" I asked as Petro pointed to the small crate of wine with a French flag on it.

"The wine; I can smell it from here. The corks are rotting. I don't see what the big deal is with French wine—it sucks. Now, Mad Dog . . . that's the stuff," Petro ruminated.

Gabby let out an echoing snort. "You know, you can start a car with that stuff."

"Yup." Petro smiled. "It will get you schnockered *and* run the car. See? Perfect."

Shaking my head, I felt a prickling sensation on the back of my neck. Turning to the passageway we had avoided, the sound of thundering hooves started booming from the dark tunnel.

"Gods and graves," I huffed as everyone started taking their positions with their backs to the massive doors.

"Hey, I thought we hit the cheat code!" Petro complained. Swords were drawn as my hellfire whip snapped into existence. It was time to get the long-expected fight over.

Right at the edge of the darkness, the thunder stopped, dust shaking from the ceiling and wafting down. Merlin stepped forward. Pulling off a scene that would make Gandalf jealous, Merlin slammed his staff into the ground, illuminating the entire passageway.

There, standing like a monument to all that was dangerous in the world, was a massive battle cat. Its foot-long claws dug into the ground, while huge teeth protruded from its raised gums. Eyes the size of basketballs gleamed an angry yellow, and a scar traced the feline's face from ear to nose.

I had witnessed such a creature only once, and Oscar was hell on earth when in this form.

In front of us stood an old battle-worn shifter.

"You know them?" I asked Merlin, who shook his head without turning.

"No," was all the old wizard said.

Stepping forward, I let my hellfire dissolve into nothing. Holding my hand up in front of me, I passed Merlin. "We mean you no harm. Why are you down here?" I asked. The massive feline didn't move.

Just as I thought the cat was going to pounce, the massive beast leaned forward, smelling me. He also gave Merlin a passing sniff before raising his head.

His voice rumbled as he spoke. "You were in my home and have brought death with you."

Not knowing where this was going, I decided the best course of action was actually telling the truth. Plus, I figured he meant Tom's old hideout, meaning they knew each other.

"My name is Max, and I'm Tom's grandson," I proclaimed. I could hear Sir Rose gripping his sword. Fanning my hand to the ground, I motioned for the others to stand down.

"Yes. The truth, I see. I could smell him on you, and especially that one," the massive cat growled. "Merlin, Tom's father."

I turned to Merlin. "You sure you don't know each other?"

"No," Merlin stated flatly, backing up.

I recentered myself, figuring if he wanted to eat us, he would have started already. Petro flew to my shoulder, leaning into my ear. "He smells familiar."

"Yeah, buddy, I'm starting to do some math." I shifted back to the massive creature. "How do you know Tom?"

If a cat could roll its eyes, this one managed to do it. "Several years ago, Tom found me floating off the coast. I was coming from France." Sir Rose let out an unapproving scoff. The cat turned, quickly shutting him down. He clearly was not a fan of the French. "I came through France from the land of the pharaohs."

"Egypt?" I asked.

"Yes, as you call it. He saved me and brought me here, along with my son. We were looking for an object of great power, sent by one of the sun gods."

I interjected, figuring the math I had done in the old head movie was right. "Oscar?"

The cat's eyes widened, and his posture relaxed. "Anscharus

Oscar, is my son. When Tom disappeared, my son was with him. What do you know of this, and how do you know of my son?"

I knew what this meant. One late night, Oscar had explained his original name was Anscharus, meaning God's spear. "I know much of your son. God's spear."

Petro decided to cut in. "Yeah, he sits around and eats all our snacks. When he's around, that is. And one time, I caught him licking his butt on Max's couch."

As I had witnessed on many occasions, the massive, hulking battle cat started morphing into the size of a regular human.

Sir Rose was stunned; there clearly weren't many shifters in medieval England.

Putting on a small pair of cloth shorts, the cat walked within reach of me. "I have been in this underground lair since we arrived in this place."

"Clearly, Tom liked keeping secrets," Merlin said, shaking his head.

"Liked?" the cat asked.

"He left many, many moons ago."

"My name is Lashar, but Tom called me Lash. What news of my son can you offer?"

This was once again the time to lay it all out. "Tom, as you said, left with your son. It's not so much where but more of when. From what I gather, he left here with Oscar and became stuck. It's complicated, but here we are. What I can tell you is that he is very much alive and well. He comes and goes, but we've been through a lot together."

Lash continued to relax his posture. Even in his half-human, half-cat form, he was still covered in layers of battle-tested muscle. While elated to hear news of his son, something shifted.

"And what about Tom?" Lash asked. It was evident he cared for Gramps. He had, after all, saved him and his son.

My eyes gave it away. "We don't know. Again, it's complicated."

"Very well," Lash growled.

"Why have you stayed down here?" Gabby asked, stepping forward. Lash bowed; he had manners.

"My lady," he purred, taking her hand in his paw. Gabby pulled her hand back, smiling as only a predator could. Lash, seeing this, breathed in the air around us.

"Yes," Lash said as Gabby genuinely smiled. "I have everything I need here. Plus, Tom was going to look for the item I was sent here to get. In this land, it's not safe to be seen, though I have wandered out at night on occasion."

"So you just stay down here?" I asked.

Lash pointed down the dark corridor. "And take care of the pests. I handled several ghouls that arrived several hours before you showed up. They appeared out of the ceiling, crawling through the earth."

"Morgana sent them. Did Tom ever mention her?" Merlin asked as Tristen and Sir Rose stepped closer.

Lash hissed. "Yes. My son vowed to help Tom stop her, but here we are, and they are not. What of you?"

"We're going to the castle. Morgana has it surrounded, and Arthur and his main army are away," I explained. Lash stared into my eyes.

"Half truths. I see much in you, Max," Lash proclaimed as I nodded.

"So I've heard. I have to ask, what item were you looking for?"

"A very important artifact was taken from my queen: the sun stone."

"Hah," Merlin scoffed. "One of the four Pillars. A fool's errand."

Petro and I smiled. "Yeah, well, we sort of had to find one on the Plane after it was stolen."

"Let me guess," Tristen spoke up, "it's complicated."

Petro took flight. "You got that bag of biscuits rights. Remember that story about us being in the Crystal King's castle?

Well . . ."

Tristen knew that had been his jail for hundreds, if not thousands, of years, though we hadn't told him the full story. There would be time for that later.

"You know where they are?" Lash asked, but I shook my head.

"One is lost, but the others? I think we can find them if it comes down to it," I said, refocusing my thoughts. "Hey, why don't you come with us?"

The others turned to me, but Merlin bobbled his head at the suggestion. "Yes," Merlin agreed. "You should join us."

"You mean to fight with you." Lash had Merlin figured out. Oscar was the same. Shifters had a way of doing that. Al, the alligator shifter, was the same way.

"That's precisely what he meant," I added as Lash stilled with a serious face.

We all stayed quiet as Lash burst out in a full-on belly laugh. I found myself joining in as he slapped my shoulder. Luckily for Petro, he was on the other side.

"It's about time I stretch my legs. Plus, I'm sure more ghouls will drop into the tunnel soon enough. I would rather not be backed into a corner. I say yes—on one condition."

"What's that, big guy?" Petro asked.

"You tell me of Tom and Oscar's adventures."

I looked back at the door. "Well, it looks like we will have plenty of time while we wait."

CHAPTER 32

The Moat
Phil

Mud turned to stone and the fog thickened the closer Phil got to the castle; Morgana didn't want anyone inside to see what was at its gates.

Surprisingly, Phil had actually followed Gelf's instructions, laser focused on getting his friends out of the tunnel, through the gate, and into the castle. Seeing Morgana and her generals had lit a fire under his ass and put him into a gear he didn't know he had.

Breathing heavily and scanning the edges of the dizzyingly large moat, Phil knew finding the water outflow drains wasn't going to be easy. He could see his breath as he turned his head, listening for the sound of moving water.

At least three hundred feet wide and roughly one hundred feet down to the water, the only way apparent was a narrow stone staircase hugging the cliff wall, zigzagging its way down to the water. Considering there were mermaids in the moat, swimming across was likely not an option.

A thought crossed Phil's mind. What if the drains were on the land side of the cliff walls and stretched underwater? It made sense. Instead of leading directly into the castle walls, if the drain was on the land side, it could be collapsed in case of intruders. He recalled taking a class on castle defenses while at the Guild. Rule number one was no paths into the castle from the walls themselves. Gelf should have given him this little piece of information. Either way, he would find the entrance.

The shriek of a creature overhead forced Phil's legs into motion. With no rails on either side, one slip would see him fall into the massive chasm. Even more worrying was the likelihood of something other than the mermaids being around the moat.

Focusing on the path and only the path, Phil continued to move down the long, narrow walkway, grumbling various curse words while doing so. The size of the army he had just passed through was starting to come into focus. Even worse was the massive size of the castle.

Pausing for a brief second, Phil looked up, unable to see the top of the outer protective wall. By his estimate, it had to be twenty stories tall. The army would have to come in through the front gate or from the sky, something that was starting to concern Phil after hearing the shrieks above.

Finally reaching the bottom of the stairs, a five-foot-wide path skirted the outside of the moat, giving Phil a chance to steady himself. Looking into the gray water, Phil swore he saw something rippling by underneath.

"Damn mermaids," Phil grumbled. "Not today."

Walking, Phil quickly realized just how far he had pushed his body. His legs ached, having just jogged at least three miles through an army of the undead. Another mile passed as Phil continued to realize just how massive the castle was. Just when he started thinking about taking a break, Phil heard the rush of running water. Now getting his second wind, he lurched forward to find two small water drains.

"This is some bollocks. There's no way they expect me to fit through one of those." Bars spanned the small dog-size opening as Phil homed in on the vertical lines etched into the walls between them.

Without hesitation, Phil pulled out the amulet, pressing it against the symbols. The stone wall started deconstructing inward to reveal a passable opening. "That's more like it," Phil mumbled to himself, only to hear the splash of a fin in the water behind him.

Not wanting to face the mermaids, he lunged forward, getting inside before turning. A mermaid had risen from the water, her face the mix of a nightmare and an angelic dream at the same time. Before she could open her mouth and let out the haunting song that could draw the strongest of men, Phil pulled the lever beside him, quickly closing the entrance.

Pulling back his hood, Phil dropped to the floor, finally letting himself relax. She could see him, or had at least heard the passage open. Pulling out a small ball, Phil blew into it, and light emitted from the small charm. While not overly bright, it was enough to lead his way.

Around Phil's feet, several rats scurried off into various holes in the walls, but that was all slung to the back of Phil's thoughts once the smell hit him. He was indeed in the sewers.

It wasn't the several-story-tall, rickety wooden ladder he had to climb down that was nagging at him; it was the narrow tunnel which forced him to turn sideways to walk down. Claustrophobia was one thing that Phil had never really considered until today.

Phil was starting to believe that if he continued to push forward, he would get stuck. With the sound of rushing water all around him, using brute strength would not be an option. Just as the narrow passage forced Phil to suck in every bit of gut he had, the tunnel opened into another room with a ladder leading up into the city. After roughly an hour, Phil finally pushed a wooden hatch opening into a room surrounded by metal bars.

"Fine hello this is," Phil breathed out, walking up to the metal bars, shaking them.

"What was that?" a gruff voice boomed from behind him on

the other side of the bars.

Turning, Phil saw a knight dressed in sleek armor, a helmet with a nose guard giving way to a slender face. Phil stilled as another two guards entered the room.

"You hear something?"

Phil was hoping the answer was no.

It wasn't.

"Yes, something opened the hatch. We must warn the wall guards."

Phil ran his fingers on the bars, quickly realizing they were made from a mix of cold iron and silver. He wouldn't be pushing his way through them.

Taking a steady breath, Phil pulled back his hood, materializing into reality. "Oy, I'm not here looking for a fight. Merlin sent me."

The guards stilled at the mention of Merlin as an even bigger guard walked in, adorned in gold armor. "Everyone back. Now." His voice was one of authority not to be questioned.

"You. What's your name?" the commander asked.

"Phil. Bruther, I got to get to King Ban. Merlin and the others are waiting by the tunnel entrance under the castle. The Anger thingy is coming."

"You talk in weird tongues. My name is Valute. Who are the others you speak of?"

"Sir Rose and a stinky small fella named Gelf. Plus, my companions," Phil replied.

Valute paused. "How did they get to the tunnel?" he asked, cocking his head.

"A big tree and some rocks. I left once they did their magic stuff, opened it, and left."

Valute cocked his head to the other side. "And just how did you get here?"

"I wore this cloak and walked here from the forest. Oh, and I snuck into Morgan . . ."

"Stop!" Valute screamed. Phil took a step back. "Don't say her name. Only those in the main keep can do so without being found."

Knowing this type of magic, Phil nodded. "I was in the creepy lady's tent. They're coming in two days tops, maybe sooner. I need to get to King Ban." Phil pulled out the amulet as Valute squinted.

"Take off the cloak and hold up your arms," Valute instructed. "Dano," he barked, "bring the Caller. You stay put."

Phil took his cloak off, shoving the small garment into his pocket; this would stay with him. A few minutes later, a woman older than the sands of time scurried into the room. Hunched over and looking as if she had followed Phil up from the sewers, her rotted teeth and foggy eyes made her resemble a walking corpse.

"You," she breathed out, raising a gnarled finger. "Come closer."

Phil did as he was told, walking to the bars in front of the woman, his tattoos finally showing in the light. Before Phil could react, she grabbed his forearm, immediately shooting her head to the ceiling. If Phil wanted to react, he couldn't, as his body froze. She was a powerful mage.

The old woman started rambling. "Stronger than stone, braver than night. Not from this place. Unmatched through time, brings hell with him."

Once she let go, Phil could feel his life pouring back into him. Whatever the woman had done, it was over. Turning to Valute, she nodded before shuffling back out of the room.

Valute, without any other words, pulled out a key and opened a section of the cage. The other two guards tensed as Phil smiled.

"You are to come with us. You will hand us that bag, and"— he threw a pair of silver cuffs on the floor—"put those on. Any deviation will prevent you from leaving this building."

"Not to be threatening or anything, but we got to get a move on." Phil smiled, throwing his bag on the floor while cuffing himself. Valute looked impressed at the speed at which Phil moved. Satisfied with his lack of pushback, the other guards entered the cage, grabbing Phil by both arms.

"You know, I can dance either way, bruthers. Stay away from the goods, and we'll be just fine. Oh, and if you have a nip of drink, it would be mighty appreciated."

The two guards didn't talk as they walked out of the room. Valute closed the gate and turned to the door, leaving the room. The old lady stood next to him as he looked down.

"Seal the room in perpetuity," Valute ordered. She nodded.

CHAPTER 33

The King of Many Kings
Phil

The journey through to the castle took an hour on foot. Knights in small groups sat guarding large intersections of the outer city. With only a small army and such a vast area to cover, King Ban had spread his forces thin outside the inner walls. What caught Phil off guard was just how massive the inner protective walls truly were compared to the outer perimeter.

Once the massive gates to the inner walls were opened, a carriage awaited to take them to the inner core of the castle.

More guards joined Phil's parade while prowling eyes stared at the cuffed man being escorted to their king. Again, Phil noted the lack of large groups of soldiers. But even though they were spread thin, the resolve on their faces was unquestionable.

Within another thirty minutes, Phil had walked up several staircases and even more gates before finally reaching what could only be called the top of the main spire overlooking the fields around the castle. This was a location a king would use to oversee his armies and lands.

King Ban sat stoically on a granite throne. He held a scepter with his hand and had a crown sitting neatly atop his head. His armor was red with streaks of gold, all leading into sleek leather sleeves. A short gray beard salted his face, knowledge flowing through his eyes. Phil liked the guy on sight alone. He was strong, wise, and showed genuine care for his knights.

Smiling at Valute, King Ban nodded. "Thank you, Sir Valute. I heard of you closing the moat passage; you are very wise. I would ask you to stay." He stood.

"Yes, my lord." Valute saluted with his sword, handing Ban the amulet before walking up to Phil. Leaning in close, he whispered, "Show the king due respect, and he will do the same. You don't . . ." Valute glanced down at his sword.

Phil nodded, knowing there was more at stake here than his pride. King Ban waved his hand, and Phil's cuffs dropped to the ground. Valute's eyebrows rose as he stood back.

"I haven't seen this amulet in many moons. What is your name, young man?"

Phil, figuring he would use his manners for once, nodded in respect. "King Ban, my name is Phil. Merlin sent me through that field over yonder to let them in through a tunnel under the castle."

"Sir Phil," Ban started.

"No *sir* here, Your Highness. Just Phil."

"Humble. Looking at you, I would say you could take on my finest knight. Very well. What other news do you bring?"

"That army is going to attack in no more than two days. Something called the Anger is coming," Phil explained, not realizing the profound effects that name had. It was clearly a known story.

Voices whispered in the background, repeating the name. King Ban rubbed his beard. "Troubling. Yes, very troubling. If what you say is true, what do you bring other than Merlin?"

Phil chewed on the question. "Backup."

"Backup?" Ban asked, not knowing the phrase.

"A whole bunch of ass whooping." Phil, realizing he was

not being respectful, corrected himself. "Sir, my lord. King," he stammered.

King Ban beamed a thousand-watt smile as he laughed. "Hah hah. You are from the gods. A rogue warrior, and Merlin brings an army of his choosing. This will be one for history."

Phil, knowing he had never heard of the battle about to take place, simply nodded. Liking the label of being a rogue warrior, Phil smiled back. "My lord, can we let them in?"

"In a moment." Ban held up the amulet, breathing into it. While Phil could tell he wasn't a full-on Mage, he could feel the pull of energy coming from him, similar to that of a sensitive.

Merlin's face appeared in a bloom of dust as King Ban stepped back. The old wizard's disembodied voice floated around the open space. "We come from below the castle. Excuse our emissary; he is different in his ways. Make haste."

The area stilled as King Ban snapped into a ferocious state of alert. "To the tunnel gates. Valute, let the men know to prepare the air spears. Ready our forces and meet us at the round table with Sir Rain."

Valute took off at a sprint while the two guards who had escorted Phil handed him his bag. King Ban turned to the entrance doors and began walking at a brisk pace.

"What's next?" Phil asked the guards, who shook their heads.

"We follow him," the younger of the two said.

"What are your names?" Phil continued as they both rolled their eyes.

"Name's Pettie, and that's Scoff. We're brothers," Pettie replied, his armor clanking while trying to catch up with Ban.

In the main entrance hall, the old woman who had read Phil stood, whispering in King Ban's ear. There was a message being given, and Phil could feel Ban's eyes flash back at him before the king nodded, taking off once more. It was shocking how she had gotten there so fast.

To Phil, this was one of those scoots-per-minute types of old witches. She smiled at Phil as he walked by, no longer wanting to be around the woman.

No words were spoken as the ground dove into the heart of the castle. Floor after floor and stairwell after stairwell, they passed by opulent rooms. If the outside of the castle was impressive, the inside was even more so.

Arriving at a large room with massive columns strong enough to support the castle and covered in ornate artwork, King Ban walked forward before turning to Phil.

"On your honor, no harm will come of me opening the gates?" King Ban asked. Phil was almost certain the old witch had told him he was hiding something.

"None," Phil replied as Pettie and Scoff shuffled nervously, drawing their swords.

As if the door were made of paper, King Ban walked to a small handle on the bottom of the doors and pulled them open.

CHAPTER 34

Off to the Races

The sound of the massive doors opening took me off guard. Why, you ask? Good question. As of one minute ago, a large section of the tunnel had caved in, and several somethings were heading directly toward us.

Glancing back, whom I suspected to be King Ban stood with a stern look on his face. He was taking in our group before finally locking in on Merlin and Sir Rose.

"Oh shite," Phil huffed, stepping forward.

"Merlin. Explain?" King Ban asked as several howls echoed into the large room.

"No time," Merlin replied, turning as Sir Rose stepped beside me, ready for a fight. Petro was hovering in front, sniffing the air. "Whatever it is, it's rotten, boss!"

"Get behind the doors!" King Ban ordered.

By the time the words left his mouth, Lash had already shifted back to battle-cat form, getting a second look from Ban. I let my hellfire whip come to life as the first creature came into view.

Gnashing teeth and glowing yellow eyes erupted from the dark chasm. Phil and two unfamiliar knights were standing by the doors as Tristen let loose a stream of blazing power down the tunnel. The young man wasn't waiting.

Taking our cue, I let a ball of hellfire loose as the first demon pig reached the group. Sir Rose was already in motion, slicing his blade down at another creature. At the same time, Gabby was already going to town on the flaming demon pig, which had yet to drop over.

"Step back as we fight," Sir Rose commanded, his tone final. He was taking the lead on our retreat into the castle. "We need to close these doors."

I swung my hellfire whip, slicing through two more of the demon pigs. Between the squealing roar and the smell, I wasn't going to argue. Centering myself, I came up with a plan.

"Everyone, get back; I'm going to light this place up!"

Petro darted by after activating his lawn-dart-of-death mode. I was fairly certain he had taken a few eyes before doing so; his new armor gave him more confidence. It had almost been a tradition for him to break a wing when fighting, and he had learned his lesson.

Snapping my whip one more time, a wave rippled in the darkness. There was a literal wall of demon pigs coming. Pulling my will in, I slapped my hands together, pulling together my new favorite move: the hellfire boom. I, of course, named this after my favorite move on *Street Fighter II*, the sonic boom.

A pillar of hellfire erupted between my hands, which I fanned out in a wide arch in a literal wave of hellfire. Red flame enveloped the tunnel, followed by the shriek of something dying that was already dead. I would remember this sound.

Finally turning to run, King Ban and his knights slammed the doors shut once we were inside. Silence took hold as I stood up. Our group, now including Phil, all stood by the massive doors while King Ban and his knights stared at us.

"My lord, we are here," Merlin spoke, breaking the ice.

"I see," King Ban replied, then the two exchanged pleasantries.

Petro, having gone under my cape, flew out, landing on my

shoulder. King Ban shook his head. As we had been told, he wasn't fond of Pixies.

Petro leaned over. "Don't worry, boss. I got this."

"No, don't! Shit," I grumbled as Petro took off toward Ban.

Valute, now front and center, stepped forward, but King Ban motioned him to stop as Petro hovered a body length away.

Petro, knowing the hierarchy of royalty, didn't speak but rather bowed.

King Ban nodded. "Pixies are not allowed inside the castle walls. That being said, you showed great bravery just now. What say you, Pixie?" His eyes flickered to Tristen and me before he refocused on Petro.

"My liege, my name is Prince Petro, Warrior of the Freeze, Slayer of the Eye, Taker of the Ladies—well, Lady Casey—Saver of the Max and Phil and Ed and Jenny and world. Eater of the Golden Food, Savior of the Plane Pixies, Finder of the Fountain, Destroyer of the Thule Society, Savior of the Saved, Nightmare of the Hellions, Judger of the Soul Dealers, Champion of the Hell Wars, where I saved Max again. Mourner of the Ford Escort. Inventor of the Piña Colada—you get the point," he concluded, only choosing his favorite titles, along with some recent additions. He was wising up to reading the crowd.

King Ban chewed on the rattlingly long list before he focused on Petro's armor. "That is fine armor you have; armor fit for a prince—a prince of such noble cause. Prince Petro, you are welcome in Camelot under my invitation. Do you swear to uphold the rules of hospitality and not sneak around?"

"Yes, my lord." Petro bowed again.

"Do you swear to honor and protect my men and women in battle?"

In typical Petro style, he could only keep it up for so long. "What kind of question is that? We're bros now." He paused, correcting himself. "Yes, my lord."

"Bros?" King Ban raised an eyebrow while Sir Rose, of all

people, cut in.

"Friends."

Gelf chuckled. "A Pixie in Camelot. Hell has frozen over."

King Ban knew how Pixies operated and how to talk with them. I was starting to think he'd had a bad run-in with a rogue group of Pixies. That or the ones back then were all dicks. I was betting on the latter.

"And you, the rest of you. Your emissary has stated you are here to help," King Ban continued.

Merlin was about to interject when I stepped forward. "King Ban. We are here to help, but I must state we cannot become too involved in the affairs of the castle. Merlin can relay what we have already done to support the cause of King Arthur and the Knights of the Round Table."

"You speak the truth. I respect that in a man." King Ban cocked his head. "But you are no man. No. *Man*, I know. You are everything and everywhere; I can see it in your eyes. You wield hellfire," he noted. "You and your people are welcome. I must state that you are already involved; it may not be by choice. The darkness is coming."

King Ban shifted his focus onto Lash. "Shifter. You look as if you've seen a lifetime of battle. What say you?" He could tell he wasn't part of our core group, but he was Oscar's father, and by default, part of our group.

Lash growled. "I bow to no king other than my queen. I am not of this land; I will provide my fang and claw, but not my loyalty."

King Ban's face hardened. The room stilled. Valute reached for his blade just as King Ban let out a howl of laughter.

"A wandering warrior. We will see; I have faith in you, warrior. You are welcome in Camelot."

Lash bowed. I had to give it to him—he had principles and was sticking to them regardless of the situation.

"Alright, alright," Merlin interrupted. "Now that all that is out of the way, we must make haste. Phil," he turned, "I feel you have a tale to tell?"

"Aye, bruther. It's a mouthful, and I could use a drink," he replied, turning to Valute, who rolled his eyes.

"He's been asking for a drink since he arrived." Valute shook his head.

"Oh shit," Petro said, landing back on my shoulder. "If he hasn't fought all of you yet and he's still talking, then it must be bad if he's been that patient."

"I got a bad feeling about this," I added as Phil blew a raspberry.

"I'll fill you all in on the way to wherever we're going. This place is bigger than Aunt Martha's butt."

After twenty minutes of climbing mind-numbingly annoying steps, my jaw dropped, as did everyone else's. There, in the center of the massive room, was the round table.

Massive stone chairs with various symbols etched into them surrounded familiar sections of ornate table. A handful of swords sat in front of a handful of chairs. According to the stories, these were seats that had yet to be filled. The rest of the swords were with the knights riding with King Arthur on his current quest.

"Don't let your eyes wander here," Merlin said, knowing we also had other work to do.

"Well, Merlin," King Ban started. We all stood in the room, facing the table. "You are here, and we are about to be attacked. Tell us of this Anger Sir Phil has been speaking of."

As if we were in a chorus all singing at the same time, we all spit out, "He's no *sir*."

Phil shrugged while several servants rushed into the room carrying food and drink, setting them on a long table at the far end of the room. I glanced at Tristen, noticing him staring starstruck at the king. He looked as if he were staring at his favorite rock star.

"Yes, we must prepare. It is of the utmost importance to protect this." Merlin pointed at the table. "The Anger is here to take, not to give."

"You speak as if that is all they are here for," Ban said, concern sweeping across his face like a broom.

Merlin set his face like a statue. "Because it is. Listen closely. All we have to do is hold the castle until Arthur arrives. That army of foulness will be no match for the Knights of the Round Table. The Anger, on the other hand, will be another challenge. A demon from hell itself, set forth here by Lady Morgana, it is said to have taken out entire armies and to be death incarnate."

"We will be ready to hold the castle walls. No filthy demon can take down these halls!" Ban proclaimed as the rest of his knights cheered. "Hoorah!"

"We shall see," Merlin killed the mood.

King Ban ushered us to the table after Phil and Petro, who were already heading that way. I was starting to think that the battle about to take place would probably end in a victory for the good king and his knights. While Morgana had a part to play in it, she would also clearly make it through the battle about to take place.

The magnitude of the situation was starting to set in. Even Gabby stood by pensively. I noticed how no one had mentioned she was a V. Everyone was on edge, and as Phil had stated, these fellows were on the thin, which meant there were not enough soldiers to guard the castle.

I watched as King Ban and Merlin continued to talk. In some ways, they looked to be politely arguing. Merlin was on even footing with the king. While not as senior as King Arthur, Ban was the second in line since Arthur had yet to have any sons. The math was getting foggy the more I thought it through.

It was at times such as these that Bo would come in handy. A little bravado and some blood spilling were on the menu soon, and I figured whoever the Anger was, Bo would likely take dibs on their liver or lungs. I missed the fabulous demon.

Could we truly bring balance to the fight? Were we the reason the castle didn't fall? Were we meant to be in the fight? All these were the questions I figured were going through Gabby's mind as we looked at each other. I loved her. In many ways, she was my escape. A beacon of light in the otherwise hectic life that I now find myself in.

Did I miss Kim? Yes. Did I care for her and love her? Yes. Did I hate the fact that she hadn't embraced the life I now led? In many ways, no. We were star-crossed lovers with no path forward. Time was a fickle bitch that I'd never truly appreciated until it slowed down.

Once I came to terms with the fact that I would live hundreds, if not thousands of years, I realized how much precious time I had wasted in my youth. Drinking and chasing women, the latest fashion trend, the perfect hair, the right kind of car to draw attention. All of it. All of it was bullshit. Bullshit that I took for granted. It was no wonder Vs and older Mages were so oblivious to the mundane things in life. Davros was a prime example.

After a few short seconds, he was often done with even dire conversations. Time was an abstract to him, a toy to be played with. He saw the rise and fall of everything. Tom, on the other hand, played with time—something everyone was warning me to stop doing.

Snapping out of my thoughts, I was greeted by a mug of ale from Lash. "Thanks."

"No need," Lash replied. "While they are talking, I want to ask about Oscar. I know you and Tom are, well, close, which means Oscar has imprinted on you if Tom is gone."

"Imprinted?" I almost spit out my ale.

"Loyal. How is he?"

"Last I saw him, good. He hangs around an acquaintance of ours a good bit. He's brave and, well, he's probably the same

Oscar you remember. Funny and smug." I smiled, and Lash actually let his lips curl.

"That he is. Those two were insufferable. We were planning on leaving the tunnels before they left and, well, never came back. Hearing this warms me. You are a brother." Lash, in a move so fast I couldn't register it, slashed my hand with one of his claws. Blood slowly seeped to the surface while he fully smiled.

"We are brothers now," he concluded, emptying his mug in one pull.

"Cats," I huffed. "What's your plan after this?"

He wiped his lips off on his furry forearm. "Continue my journey. Your journey ends here; I can see it. You are not here to fight. I don't know what it is, but I can smell it on you, see it in your eyes. If I were to guess, it is something the others in this room would not approve."

He was as wise as he was old. Shifters had a way of being like that.

"Maybe. I know what I know. I also know what will be." I chuckled while Lash looked at me as if I were crazy.

"What is it?" he asked, pinning his ears back.

I set my mug down. It was time to focus. "What I said sounds like something Metatron would say."

As casual as a priest in church, Lash nodded. "Indeed, it is."

The conversation was cut short when the old witch Phil had described walked in. His explanation of her was accurate. According to Phil, if you were a princess around a bunch of Dwarves, you shouldn't eat any apples she offered up.

Cutting through the various conversations in the room, the witch spoke up. "The Lady of Shadows wishes for an audience."

The room stilled. Petro buzzed off the table. "The who? What's it?"

"Morgana," Merlin spit out. Turning to the old witch with warm eyes, Merlin bent down. He respected her. "When?"

"How about where?" I interjected, but the old witch ignored

me.

Merlin turned to me. "She will want to meet in the dream realm."

"The Everwhere?"

He nodded. "We will be on even footing. You, Max, and Ban will be joining me."
He paused. "And the youngling." He was referring to Tristen.

The old witch cleared her throat. "Yes, the demonborn."

I glanced at Phil, who shook his head.

"Lady of the Spire." This was the old witch's title. "When?" Merlin asked, focusing.

"Now . . ." the old witch breathed out.

CHAPTER 35

The Everwhere

Purple skies rippled as if we were standing on an alien planet. Stars twinkled, only to be swallowed by other stars, all following the same cycle. The familiar sticky cold of the Everwhere seeped through my light armor as Tristen gazed around in amazement.

Much like the Postern, Camelot had a room full of gates. In my opinion, this very well could have been the start of the Postern. The one gleaming abnormality of the Everwhere in the past was the lack of Camelot.

The Everwhere I had grown accustomed to was a nightmarish mirror of the real world. Here, for some reason, instead of the castle, a set of ruins similar to Stonehenge stood like monuments to an even further past.

Merlin, seeing my face, scanned the surrounding area. "She's not here yet. And before you ask, Camelot was built on top of these ruins. They are strong and old—so strong the castle can't overtake this version."

"It looks like Stonehenge," I said.

"Stone-what?" Merlin asked, motioning for Sir Rose and Tristen to stand next to him.

"In my time, there is a place just like this in the general area."

"Ah, that place. It is a portal to the hellion legions. Do you know of this?" Merlin asked.

I nodded. "Yeah, we sort of figured that out. In my time, there are—well, were people called Soul Dealers. We sort of blew the place up."

Tristen cleared his throat, having stopped gawking. "I heard about that. Inspector Holder told me all about it on our way over. I thought he was joking."

"No joke," I replied. I'd lost a good friend in that fight. I turned to Merlin. "Tom was there, and we fought off unimaginable odds side by side. You would have been proud."

"I bet I would be." Merlin froze, sniffing the air. "She comes. Everyone, by the gate."

A reddish glowing fog spread over the countryside as the sound of a thousand howling souls echoed. In front of the brewing storm was a lone woman who floated effortlessly, finally landing on the ground in front of us.

Dressed in a solid black cloak, the woman's pale, stunning features were offset by the danger present in them. While her backup wasn't visible, I was certain there was an army of the souls of the undead behind her.

"Merlin," she purred, sounding like a former lover. I knew Tom had been born of Old Gods' blood, so this probably wasn't his mother. She took a longing breath. "And?"

Merlin didn't skip a beat. "These people are of no consequence to you."

"Are you sure of that?" She turned her focus to Tristen and me.

Not having the patience for any of this and knowing she had a long run ahead of her, I stepped forward. "We're not from here." Merlin clapped his hands. While he didn't approve, he knew I was his blood and, with that, a pain in the ass. He was, of course, right. "I'm not here to get involved in whatever all this is, but I'm afraid if you attack the castle, I will."

Morgana took in my words like a knowing mother. "Is that

so? And why should I be concerned? I'm here to talk about the terms of the castle's surrender."

"Camelot will never be yours," Merlin spit out. The disdain in his voice dripped like snake venom in its victim.

"So you say," Morgana smoothly replied. I knew the truth. Eventually, she would lead it to its downfall.

"You have a mouth on you," I spoke up. "This is your last chance." Tristen took a step forward, and she locked her gaze on him.

"Brave, this one. Ambitious and full of life. It would be a sad day for him to die at such a young age," she purred.

I was done with this show. I let hellfire dance through my eyes as a ball engulfed my hand. "Yeah, lady, I'm about out of patience. Let me just tell you, we aren't the only ones here. I've got an army of folks just like the two of us in that castle ready to jack you and your goons' shit up, so I'd appreciate it if you could save it for another day."

She clearly didn't understand half of what I'd just said.

"Tristen," I followed. "Let's see a little light in all this darkness."

Like myself, I was certain he knew how to show off his powers. On cue, Tristen held up his hands, and a familiar silver glow lit up the entire area. In many ways, I wanted to tell them all just who his parents were. They would know.

Her face froze as she took the both of us in, while Merlin looked at us with caution in his eyes. Morgana, on the other hand, was heavily contemplating just who we were. She knew I was letting hellfire dance around my hands, while Tristen was using celestial magic. She was weighing the scales.

The math was simple. I was a demon of sorts, and Tristen was a celestial.

"Merlin?" she asked with a slight air of confusion.

"It would not be wise to attack the castle," Merlin said flatly.

"And wait for Arthur to return? No." Her mood shifted. "The

Anger is coming, and I'm not sure even these"—she waved us off —"abominations will be enough."

"I wouldn't count on that," I replied. "Merlin, we need to leave; I've heard enough. If it's a fight they want, it's a fight they'll get." I was also thinking about the main reason we were there. To get the missing section of the table.

"Very well," she scoffed. "You may want to get back then. I have a feeling things are already in motion. I would say may God have mercy on your souls, but you won't have any when the Anger is done with you all."

Merlin activated the gate. "We must leave, now."

"Oh, and Sir Rose," Morgana added as we backed into the gate between two large stones. "I do miss you."

We leaned back, disappearing into the void of the gate.

CHAPTER 37

A Dandy Day to Die
The Castle Gates
Phil

Massive gates stood open as the army of the undead pressed over the main bridge to Camelot. Wide as a small village and long as a runway, the mass of bodies heading to the castle entrance was staggering against the smaller army. Leonidas and his three hundred Spartans would have been proud at the display of bravery.

Phil gasped when Merlin winked into existence beside him. The show in the skies had yet to start, but on the ground, the battle had already begun. Valute was instructing a group of his men to set up more blockades on the drawbridge.

"What the nutter butter, bruther?" Phil huffed. Merlin handed him the coin.

"I see you're all about to get busy. This coin is your connection to your friends; when the time to leave is here, it will pull you to them," Merlin explained, getting straight to the point.

Lash and Gelf turned to Merlin, seeing that Phil's time in the fight would likely be short-lived.

Valute, done doling out instructions, grabbed Merlin's arm. "Thank the Gods. Merlin, can you help here?"

Merlin looked past Phil, taking in the situation. "Perhaps. Perhaps not."

Valute shook his head. "Please," he added.

Merlin finally nodded. "Yes. How many souls do you have? And how many archers are above the gates?" he asked. He was referring to the hundreds of slits facing the bridge surrounding the gate entrance. Stepping forward, he reached the blockade Valute's men were setting up. Turning, Merlin looked at the gigantic gears used to operate the bridge and gate.

"Four hundred total. One hundred of those on the battlements," Valute spit out, now looking at the oncoming onslaught. "They're coming!"

With any battle, there was always an opening move made by the aggressor. Several rotted bears charging forward were Morgana's army's opening play. Merlin, unfazed, slammed his staff down and started chanting.

"What's this all about?" Phil asked, taking a pull from a leather flask and handing it to Valute. He had taken it from the table where the meal had been laid out, and it was undoubtedly full of ale.

Valute shook his head, taking the flask. "Hopefully, the old wizard is fighting."

As the knight took a sip, Phil let his hammer twirl in his hand. "Aye. He has a habit of picking flowers when things get sticky."

Not knowing what this meant, Valute turned to prepare his men. Merlin continued to mumble under his breath, frozen like a block of ice. The noise stopped, and time stilled on the drawbridge. After a few seconds, his lips started moving in slow motion, but the bears looked as if they had been frozen in time.

"Archers! Light arrows and fire at will!" Valute yelled, and thousands of firefly's zipped overhead, punching into the bears. Fur burned as Merlin started moving again. This time, he held his staff overhead.

"*EXPLODERE!*" Merlin commanded, and the surgically placed arrows sticking out of the bears exploded in a flash of fire.

Gore splattering the bridge, all the battle bears lay dead, the largest pieces left of the creatures their mangled skulls, flesh clinging to the exposed bone. Even Valute's men had a hard time computing what they had just witnessed.

Merlin turned as if he were looking for the bathroom. "That should do for a few minutes while Morgana reconsiders crossing that bridge." He turned to Valute. "What happened to the drawbridge and the gates?"

"Morgana's magic, I suppose. They are working on the gears; something has them stuck."

Merlin turned to Phil. "Something you may be able to put a little gusto into?"

"Well, I suppose. I'm not much of a fixer; more of a breaker type," Phil replied.

Merlin pulled Phil to him, whispering in his ear, "You need not be here; you can just unlock the gears." As the words left his mouth, the sky erupted in the reddish glow of hellfire. "Hmph," Merlin breathed out. "The game is afoot. Phil, your reason for being here is complete." He knew Max and the others had already taken the needed piece of the round table. "What you do now is of your own accord. Now, go loosen the gate and drawbridge."

Gelf stepped forward, nudging a hyperfocused Lash. "I mean, between the lot of us, we may be able to get those gears moving. My father worked on those."

Lash, slowly morphing back to his normal self, nodded.

Phil turned to Valute. "Bruther, you good?"

"If you can get the bridge to rise while these foul vermin are on it and close the gates . . . yes."

For some reason, Phil knew this would be the last time he would ever see the noble warrior standing in front of him. He reached out to Valute, who took his hand.

Merlin nodded. "Take care of Max."

"We got this shite. Hold them at bay." Phil focused on Merlin. "I'll look after Max. I always have and always will. Oh, and remember: pancakes."

Taken off by the statement, Merlin cracked a smile. "I know you will. And no worries, I will make them for King Arthur himself."

Phil took one last look at the group around him. "Camelot will stand. You will see." Phil saluted as Valute motioned for one of his men to escort them to the control room. While the castle would stand, a significant number of roofs would need to be replaced.

As Phil, Lash, and Gelf entered the protective walls, they all took in the bats covered in hellfire dropping onto the roofs of the surrounding buildings. It was as if they were in Pompeii, the city getting buried under ash and flame.

CHAPTER 36

Crash

"**B**OSS!" Petro exclaimed as the sounds of organized chaos took hold. The last of the knights clattered out of the room we had gated through. Petro and Gabby had been right by the gate waiting for us to come back.

"Yeah, we figured things just kicked off here; Morgana wasn't too shy about it. Where's Phil and the others?" I asked as Petro sniffed me to make sure I was okay.

Gabby stepped forward. "Lash, Gelf, and Phil went with Valute to the front gates. King Ban is on the roof. There are apparently these big bat things flying everywhere, keeping his archers off the walls. It was like they knew this would happen."

"They probably did," Merlin grumbled. "I should have known. We need to get those things out of the sky. They're skelabats; they don't like fire." He turned to me. "Max, I'm needed at the front gates. The rest of you go to the overwatch tower and handle the skelabats."

"Petro, you good with Phil being down at the gates?" I asked, wanting to get everyone's opinion.

"I don't know, boss. I don't like splitting up, but Phil was insistent. Lash and Gelf were like, 'Come on, big guy.'"

Merlin pulled out four small coins, handing us one each. His shoulders slumped. "If you are in need to pull everyone together, these coins will do so. I will ensure Phil gets one. All you have to do is push your will into it, and they will all come to this coin."

He pointed at the golden coin he was still holding before handing it to me. Knowing this was similar to a gate rope, I nodded. This would have to do. I also started sizing up where we were in the castle in reference to the round table. We would pass by it on our way up.

"Alright. How will we know when he gets it?" I asked, referring to Phil.

"It will change colors; it will no longer be dull but rather shiny," Merlin stated as Sir Rose cocked his head.

"Where am I needed?" he asked.

"Go with them; ensure they are safe. There will be others on the overwatch," Merlin said with finality. Something in his tone was troubling. It was like he knew something but didn't want to get into it.

With those words, Merlin disappeared in a puff of smoke and ozone; he had transported himself to the front gates. I looked at the coin in my hand, which immediately lost its tarnish and became a shiny coin.

"That didn't take long," I noted as Sir Rose cleared his throat.

"He has a way of doing that; he probably scared the shit out of them. They must have just made it to the front gates."

"Sir Rose." I smiled. "Language."

We all snickered as he blushed. A thought formed in my mind: We had three things to do. First, we needed to get the devices the Council gave us on the section of the table needed. Next, we needed to get to the roof and help as much as we could. Lastly, we needed to get Phil and use the portal to get back home.

If any of those things didn't happen, it was likely we would be stuck in the past, at risk of changing Camelot's very history.

I turned to Sir Rose. "Take Tristen to the overwatch. We'll be right behind you; I want to talk with Gabby and Petro for a few minutes."

"I'm not sure that's wise," Sir Rose cautioned.

"This is one of those things that doesn't need to be known by those in this time. It could cause issues," I advised, and he reluctantly motioned for Tristen.

"Draw your sword, young man. Morgana is not to be underestimated." He pulled his blade with a *shink.*

After a round of fist bumps, the two left the room. I walked over quickly, closing the door. "Petro," I started, "are we alone here? No ears or eyes?"

Petro sniffed the room, taking a quick lap before landing on my shoulder. "All clear, boss. What's the plan?"

"The round table is three floors up. Did you guys notice no one was in there other than the servants who entered? I doubt they're still there. I would bet they're hiding," I noted as Gabby motioned for my infinity bag.

She quickly pulled out four ancient black stone squares with unfamiliar etchings on them. "You're probably right. We set these up, help with these skelabats, and leave."

"You make it sound easy," I reflected.

"Well, I'm sure it won't be." Gabby half smiled.

"Boss, we need to get going," Petro huffed, flying over to the door. "I can hear all kinds of stuff out there."

We followed without saying a word. Within five minutes, we were again standing in the same room, looking at the round table. Luckily for us, Petro and I had been around the massive object on several occasions. With no one around, it was time to get to the robbery of all robberies.

"That section there," I pointed. The interesting thing about the table was that while they were similar in build, each section had a unique personality. A slight difference in carvings, or in this case, a keyhole directly in the middle.

According to Dr. Freeman, this section was literally the key to activating the table's abilities. Gabby quickly placed the four squares on its corners.

"That should do it. We just need to activate it."

Reaching down, I pushed my will into each of the small objects separately. They glowed briefly, only to shift back to their initial dull black exterior.

"How do we know if it worked?" Petro asked.

"Ana Vlad said it would." As the words left my lips, the table slowly started to dissolve into a transparent version of itself, followed by the sound of gears grinding. Apparently, the table was warded, and we had just set something off.

"We have to go now," I barked. "It's not gone, so the ward hasn't fully activated."

Not wanting to find out what the ward did, we ran out of the room just as a massive set of iron bars slammed into the entrance, sealing the space. Pausing, we looked back as a servant peeked out from another set of bars on the other side of the opulent room. They had seen us, and after the dust settled, the gig would be up.

"Well," I grumbled, "no coming back now." Looking one last time at the table, the section we needed disappeared.

"Let's boogie, boss," Petro urged as I looked at Gabby.

"We can just leave," I said. Gabby cocked her head so hard her ear touched her shoulder.

"Really? Here I thought you were a hero. If we take, we give." She was quoting the ancient Vampire creed, which referred to taking life-sustaining blood from humans and, in return, giving them protection and care.

"Alright. We take care of the bats, then leave. We can't risk getting too involved."

"You do know Phil is at the gate. I'm sure we're already pretty involved," Gabby justified.

We finally erupted onto the overwatch to find a scene of chaos. Tristen was slinging magic into the massive flock of what I now understood were undead bats. Even Krampus would be jealous of the skeletal flying creatures.

A handful of archers slung arrows while Sir Rose ensured the blade of his sword kissed any of the creatures that came too close. King Ban was on the edge, directing the archers. Not needing an invitation, we immediately went into motion.

Petro's helmet formed over his head as Gabby leapt to the opposite side of the overwatch, covering the area Sir Rose could not reach. I, on the other hand, figured it was time for some fireworks.

Running to the waist-high wall, I made the mistake of glancing down. There, surrounding the castle, was an army of the undead; it was clear they had somehow lowered the front gates. What was more concerning was the massive elephants with large decks built on their backs heading that way. They were obviously full of fighters.

A group of knights was holding off hundreds of undead warriors. Without my enhanced vision, the entire scene below would just be a blur of chaos.

"Sir Rose, Tristen!" I yelled, getting their attention. One of the bats swooped down, only to be slashed in half by the knight. "Everyone, back to the entrance walls. Tristen, get behind me."

Everyone blurred into motion. To my right, Petro darted away from one of the bats that was chasing him as an archer lined up a shot, shattering its skeletal wings. A mix of rotted flesh and magic was all that was keeping the creatures afloat.

King Ban motioned his men to fall back, and in a flurry of motion, they disappeared into the castle. Ban turned before leaving. "We will go help the others at the gate. May God be with you."

Nodding, I tapped Tristen on the shoulder, who was still slinging magic. He looked stressed yet excited to be in the fight. When his magic hit the creatures, they turned to literal dust. That likely meant something, but I would try to figure it out if we made it through the evening.

"Sup?' Tristen asked. The exertion of pushing his magic was

evident in his breathing.

"I'm about to give it all I've got. If anything happens, or any get through, I need you to—" We both ducked as a bat dive-bombed us, only to be hit by an arrow. "I need you to stop them. If I look back, I need you to place your hands on my back and push your will into me. You got that?" I asked.

He slowly nodded. "Is that safe?"

I shrugged, still balling my will and focusing it on the wave of hellfire I was about to cook the surrounding sky with.

"We're both gods in our own ways, kid. I've tried something like this before. Think of it like letting me borrow some juice. We can do this."

He shook his head while I turned back. It was time.

Out of all the things we had apparently invented during this trip, unleashing hell was about to be our pièce de résistance. A pull in my guts started burning my insides. I was about to go supernova differently than when we had been stuck in the belly of the massive spider with Caddie, the only possessed, kickass seventies Cadillac DeVille in existence. This time, I was concentrating everything I had in a continuous shotgun blast of death.

"*Gahhhh!*" I yelled, unleashing said hell into the skies.

Red flame lit the entire castle grounds, the vambraces on my forearms melting instantly, dripping globs of molten metal on the ground in front of me.

"Yeahhh!" I continued yelling as massive columns of hellfire erupted from my hands, coming out into two large spires of flame.

Looking up, it was as if the sky was on fire. Upon further inspection, it was. Between the humidity and wall of skelabats burning, hellfire was lingering in the fog of war.

The sound of a thousand freight trains visiting the past echoed from all directions. I could feel the heat in my mouth and my churning guts. It felt like I was also on fire and about to explode. When I had done this inside the Spider of Doom, it had been a one-time focused blast.

Every pore on my body was on fire. Feeling my effort coming to an end, I looked up one more time as a burning, crumpled bat crashed down in front of us. Even though I had scorched the initial wave, they were still coming. If the army below wasn't going to get through the main gates, the bats sure as hell were.

Good thing Tristen stood at the ready.

"Hey, kid," I huffed, cocking my head back, my energy quickly draining. "Game time."

Tristen's hands started glowing as he stepped forward. We had already agreed this was a gamble worthy of the greatest card player.

"Hold on," Tristen yelled, the sound of my onslaught overtaking his words. The truth of the matter was, he knew how powerful he was.

Turning back to surveil the carnage, I could feel a cooling pulse rippling through my body. My hellfire stuttered, slowly starting to pulse. Sparks flew from the columns of hellfire as I took a deep breath.

"You ready?" Tristen asked.

"You mean you haven't started?"

Before he could reply, he fully pushed his will into me. Stars took over my vision as the hellfire flowing from my hands engulfed my arms. Sparks streaked the hellfire as lightning crackled through the sky. Whatever he had pushed into me was working its way through my body.

Waves of pain pulsed through my body as our magic combined. They weren't fighting; they were learning to work together.

The last thing I remembered before falling to my knees and passing out was someone's arms grabbing me around the waist.

CHAPTER 38

Afterglow

Stars danced in my mind as I slowly realized I was still alive. Muffled words were spoken while the light breeze of Petro's wings on my face started to slowly bring me back to reality. My arms burned, a searing pain drenching my back.

"Boss! Boss!" Petro was yelling. I slowly lifted my arms, Gabby's scent filling my senses as my eyes started to come into focus.

"Hey," I slurred. My mouth felt like I had swallowed a pile of burnt sand.

"Max," Gabby pleaded, pulling her arms from my waist and kneeling in front of me. "You there?"

"Me?" I huffed. "Yeah. Not so sure about my body."

"He's alive, God's above! Boss, you were all like, *woosh, woosh,* then all like, *yeah,* then all like *rahhh,* then—" I cut him off.

"I get it. What happened?"

Gabby grabbed my hand, lifting me up. "You happened," she said, pride beaming from her face.

"Is it safe?" I asked, just as Sir Rose came into focus.

"Yes, for now," he replied, looking over the wall.

"Is it over?"

Sir Rose turned. "No."

Tristen was still sitting on the ground. While he was fine, his hands were burned. Another knight was wrapping them in clean cloth.

"You okay, kid?" I asked.

"I think so." He nodded. "You?"

It was at that time my back decided to let me know just how it was feeling. Where Tristen had placed his hands burned like a thousand daggers being driven through my skin.

"My back hurts. My arms are burning, and I could use a day off." I smiled, not letting it reach my eyes.

"About that, boss. You're going to need to get that looked at. It's kinda nasty."

I knew better than to ask further, figuring I had added to my all-you-can-eat buffet of scars. Looking down, I saw my leather armor, while intact, was charred, and any metal that had been left on my body was deformed and scorched. Around us, burned remains lay in smoking piles of death.

"The town's on fire, and it's all my fault, isn't it?" I asked Gabby, who nodded.

"Whatever you did . . ." She paused. "I've never seen anything like that. Are you okay?"

"Yeah. I'm a little gassed, but I can manage. I'm not sure how much more hellfire I can sling around, though," I replied as she bit her lips; she looked like she was about to cry, something I had yet to see a V do.

"Hey, babe," I followed. "It's about time to get out of here."

She sucked back in her feelings. "We don't let these people die here today."

"That's my girl," I said, looking at the rest of the knights on the roof. I hadn't noticed the looks of amazement and, in some ways, fear on their faces. While brave, what they had just witnessed was a thing of nightmares. They thought, and rightfully so, that I was a demon of sorts. Well, partly a demon.

Sir Rose, also seeing this, turned to the knights. "Max and his companions are here to help us by Merlin's hand. For the king!"

The men all looked at each other. "For the king!"

Petro, of course, added his two cents' worth. "For the king! Badabing!"

"Some things never change," I said, helping Tristen up.

"That was something," Tristen said, holding up his hands. "Guess it will be a lonely night."

"You sure you're not related to Petro?" I asked as Petro buzzed over.

"You can get a sock—"

"Nope," I interrupted Petro, who frowned. Tristen, meanwhile, picked up his sword with a wince. The burns on his hands, while not severe, would keep him out of the fight.

Sir Rose turned from the wall overlooking the castle. "Something's happening at the drawbridge."

Everyone made their way to his side, looking down. The massive drawbridge was slowly closing, piles of the undead resembling ants falling into the moat. On the far side, the elephants were backing up so fast that the large structures built on their backs were swaying, sending their riders falling off.

"They have them on the defense," I said. This, of course, was the wrong thing to say, as that signaled the gods themselves that it was time to shit on our parade.

Out of the now dark skies, a deep blood-red glow pulsed, followed by the sounds of enormous flapping wings.

"It's the Anger!" several of the men shouted.

"Gods and graves," I grumbled. Reaching down, I felt for the coin in my pocket. I had—No, *we* had a decision to make.

I turned to Gabby. "This was in my dream."

"Something is telling me we're supposed to be here," she said, holding her cool hand to my face. I loved her, and it was clear she loved me. "If we can get this Anger person out of the way, it looks like the others can handle this till Arthur and his armies get here."

"Sir Rose?" I asked.

He nodded. "The devil himself couldn't stop that army."

"I wouldn't be too sure about that," I joked. It landed flat. "Just kidding."

A shriek worthy of the angriest god echoed in the distance. Wings pierced the dark, clouded night sky as everyone froze. A knight walked forward. "It's a dragon. We must ready the spears."

"That's no dragon—it's a real demon; the kind we all need to worry about," I noted. "Get everyone off the overwatch. Spears will just piss this thing off. We need Merlin."

Possibly feeling his name being called, Merlin snapped into existence beside us. "The time is here to stand and face this beast."

"You mean we must stand and face this beast." Petro wasn't asking; he was telling the truth as he saw it.

"Perhaps, perhaps not." Merlin kept saying that phrase, leaving everything up to chance, though I had a feeling he didn't leave much of anything to chance.

"Well, before it burns down what you have of an army, let's go say hello," I suggested. Everyone started backing up except Merlin, Gabby, Petro, Sir Rose, Tristen, and myself. I turned to the group left standing at my side. "I'll make you all a deal. You all stand back at the doors, and if I need help, I'll let you know." Merlin turned to walk back. "Not you, hotshot."

"Hot shit?" he inquired as I shook my head.

"Hotshot," I huffed. "Never mind. You stay by me; I'm about out of juice, if not completely. There's a reason I saw this in my dream."

A stream of reddish hellfire lurched from the beast's mouth above the clouds, scorching one of the towers with several large spears waiting to be launched.

"Merlin, can you get its attention?" He raised an eyebrow as everyone finally made it to the doors leading into the castle.

Spreading his arms like an eagle in flight, Merlin sucked in what seemed to be all the air surrounding the place. With a massive exhale, his words rattled the very foundation of the castle. "ANGER!"

The creature snapped its attention directly at us. "Yeah, that did it," I said as he slammed his staff into the ground.

"The rest is up to fate, young Max. Let me ask you, in the future, am I only remembered in books?"

"You, hah," I let out a nervous laugh. "People name their kids after you. Well, weird people. Movies, songs, games. You know it."

Merlin smiled. "I have no idea what any of those are, but they sound like an honor."

Two glowing red eyes homed in on us as I steadied myself. This wasn't Merlin's time. Slowly, I mustered what was left of my will, unbinding from the celestial gauntlet. Merlin stared at it as it slowly formed around my arm.

"What trickery is this?" he asked as I slid it off.

"Plan B. For you, that is. Put it on."

He nodded. Sniffing the air, his eyes widened. "This is celestial."

"It is. We don't have much time here." I could see the familiar female figure of the demon now charging toward us.

Sliding it on, Merlin gasped as it melded with his body. Looking unsure about the gift, he again turned his focus to the problem at hand.

"Get behind me," I urged while he side-eyed me.

"Not today, young man. We are blood; we stand together." I found it ironic he hadn't in our earlier fights, but he knew this was something different.

We set ourselves as the winged creature—flapping its massive wings—slowed its advance. It was well aware that Merlin and I were on the overwatch. In some sort of a standoff, the creature hovered in the air, no longer using its wings. I could have sworn I heard Petro yell, "Boobies," behind us.

The woman's figure was tight and alien, with scales overlapping her skin. Enormous wings adorned with claws and bone swayed in the dark night. Whatever fighting was occurring below was now in full swing. While the drawbridge had been raised, several of the undead had already made their way behind the castle walls.

After a few seconds of staring, I noticed small blobs of e-core dripping from the beast, forming large creatures once they fell to the earth, similar to when Bo let his e-core puppy loose on unsuspecting victims, such as Phil's boots when we first met.

"Grab the staff," Merlin ordered. I could feel him pouring energy into it. Unable to make out the creature's face, I reached over and held his staff, which he was charging with Etherium.

Before I could pull my hand back, the creature spit out a stream of hellfire, engulfing the entire battlement. Blinding red hellfire swam over our bodies as I pulled Merlin behind me, forming a bubble of hellfire around him with some of the energy I had pulled, effectively cutting him off. While he would be slightly medium rare, he would survive.

As quickly as it started, the fire was over, but the creature had dropped two blobs onto the ground, which promptly shifted into black versions of hellions.

Before I could react, Sir Rose ran from the door with his sword in hand. "Stop," I barked, to no avail. He would fight. That's what the man did.

"You . . ." the female voice scratched. "You will die."

"That didn't seem to work," I yelled back. It was clear the Anger was confused as to why I wasn't a pile of melted bones. I glanced back at Merlin, who was on his knees. He had been blasted by a thousand-degree hellfire. While he looked unscathed, he was dealing with the shock. Even iconic wizards had a limit to what they could physically take.

The sound of fighting rang from Sir Rose's side as I tried to keep my focus on the problem at hand. Truth be told, I had no clue what to do.

"You..." The voice again flowed out of the creature. "You will pay for what you did to my pets." She was referring to the bats.

Pulling what energy I had gained from Merlin's staff, I slung a ball of hellfire at the demon. Without moving an inch, the creature let it bounce off its chest, looking down.

Turning toward Sir Rose again, I started to see he was struggling. "Merlin, you got to get up, buddy. I could sure use a hand here."

Before I could turn my focus back on the demon, Gabby, Tristen, and Petro burst out of the doors, joining the fight. Two more globs of e-core slammed into the far end of the battlements, forcing the group to move further away. This was good.

"What's wrong? Never fought one of your own?" I yelled again. This time, the creature was not having any more of it, lunging forward with its mouth open. It was going to eat us.

Death came in many forms, but they said your life flashed before your eyes before you died. I had died once—sorta died, if you wanted to get technical—and could confirm this was true.

Tensing my body, getting ready for the inevitable, I closed my eyes. I had nothing left to give—nothing truly magical, that is. I, of course, had packed a dissolution grenade. Not just any dissolution grenade but one strapped to an actual grenade.

The contents of my infinity bag were my secret to keep.

Quickly pulling the pin and cooking the grenade off, I perfectly launched it into the Anger's open mouth. An explosion rocked the entire castle as I dove, grabbing Merlin as we skidded across the hard stone floor.

With my speed and reflexes, getting out of the way of a flailing, flying demon dragon was something I could do. My back screamed as Merlin huffed under my weight. As suspected, the fight had moved to the far end of the battlement, saving the others. If they had stayed in the doorway, they would have been killed by the impact; the Anger had slammed directly into it.

Yeah, I was getting pretty good at this stuff.

Dust covered the space, and I suddenly realized the once massive creature was no longer there. Merlin and I slowly stood, taking several steps back. I could hear Tristen yelling in the background.

"No!" he screamed. I turned, only to hear a shuffle of stone coming from the dusty area where the creature had landed. Seeing a brilliant flash of his magic, I figured he had things under control. We had bigger problems on our hands.

Merlin again planted his staff on the ground as a woman walked out of the dust. Naked and moving slowly, she shook her head, holding it down not to show her face.

Merlin threw his staff up, ready to strike, but I pushed it down. Something was off about the situation. Something wrong, and even worse, something familiar.

"Who are you?" I asked the woman, who shook her head one final time. The sound of bone getting back into place snapped before she finally lifted her head.

There, standing in the midnight dust, was Lilith. My grandmother.

Her eyes burned into my soul as we both stood frozen in place. Merlin glanced at the both of us before speaking. "What is it?"

"Tend to the others. It sounds like something happened," I said, not taking my eyes off Lilith.

"But—" Merlin started, but I held up my hand.

"Leave now, or I promise she will kill all of you," I urged, knowing they were no match for her.

Merlin slowly backed off as I opened my mind. I knew how to talk to her, and being family, she would instantly know once I made the connection.

"Hello, Lillith . . ." I whispered in my thoughts. Her head

cocked to the side, her gaze hardening.

"*How can this be . . . ?*" she hissed back. Her voice was familiar but different, even in my mind.

"*We are one,*" I replied, seeing how she would react. She was, after all, thousands and thousands of years old, if not more.

"*How?*" she again asked.

"*I am your grandson. The grandson of Thomas Gabriel Sand, son of Merlin.*"

She looked momentarily confused, but she quickly regained her focus. I knew for a fact she walked away from this fight even after we left. That is, if we ever did.

"*Yes . . .*" she replied. "*You are of another time. You are a scourge on these lands and time.*"

"*Yeah, I get that. You need to leave this fight to the others and go home to your father.*"

The funny thing about talking in the old head movie was that it had to look awkward from the outside. While our bodies were standing there, frozen, we were having a grand old chat.

It was becoming extremely clear why, in the future, she acted the way she did toward me. She had known all along, and when I said all along, I meant even when we'd first met. Hell, she'd known when I was born, probably keeping an eye on me the entire time.

Once again, I needed to have a little chat with grandma when I got back.

"*Why?*" she asked.

"*Because I'm afraid of what will happen if you don't. I know why you're here, and I know what must and must not happen. If you activate the table, they will come—the Old Gods.*"

"*Let them come to their death,*" she hissed.

"*Earth is not ready; the Under is not ready; you are not ready—but you will be.*"

A smirk grew on her face as she took several steps closer to me. "*We will see. Why are you here?*"

In times like these, I always leaned on the truth. She would know if I was lying. *"To take what you need to draw the Old Gods into a fight. And it's already done."*

Her smirk changed to a scowl. She looked up into the sky before leveling her eyes on me again. *"I see. That means I have no need of this place. Yes, the table will draw them here, but it will also force them to a level battlefield."*

"What does that mean?" I asked, slightly concerned with what she was saying.

"You fool. It can send them to the Everwhere if used properly, a place where we have been harvesting an army of souls since the Great War. The path of blood to gain such an army created many heavens and hells. I am here to save this wretched race of dogs."

This was news to me. While I knew putting the table together and activating it would draw the Old Gods to Earth, they already knew where we were, and it was just a matter of time. The fight over the Pillars had guaranteed that. But now, knowing this, if the table could indeed send them to the Everwhere, it would be possible to pull enough forces and power together to take them head-on. I needed to get this information back home.

Everyone had always assumed they would come to Earth, but with the Everwhere on the table, it would be another situation altogether. The Over, the Under, the Plane, and everything in between would be able to convene there.

"Leave now; I will not ask again. While I won't fight you, the others will." As the words left my thoughts, the sound of a thousand horns blew in the distance. King Arthur had finally made it back.

"Let them. I can see who you are—or aren't. There will be a time when our paths will cross again, but until that time, my work here is done."

I stared at Lilith with more focus. Her eyes hazed over momentarily. *"What are you doing?"* I asked.

"*Time, young Max. I must not be worried about these things,*" she pushed into my mind. I grimaced as her voice became more distant and omnipotent. "*I see now the path I must take.*" She was clearly pulling from my memories.

"*Stop,*" I demanded. She nodded. Whatever she had done was complete.

"*No need to worry, I was just poking around a little. I see we will meet again.*"

Shaking my head, I reflected on the first time we met. She'd acted as if she didn't know who I was at first. It had all been some type of twisted game she was playing. The more I reflected on the entire situation, the more I realized she'd allowed us to take the younger children. Lilith had been in control the whole time. Even more, she had also flushed out Darkwater, if I peeled more layers back on everything that had happened since the start of the entire mess that had occurred since the Balance.

Lilith took several more steps closer, now within arm's reach of me. She held her hand to my face as she took in my features. "*I will be seeing you . . .*" she breathed out, cutting our mental link.

Her hand turned to ash first, then her body faded into nothingness. I stood in the ashy dust, staring into the horizon as Petro zoomed in front of me.

"Boss! Boss! What happened?"

"I . . ." I didn't know what to say as he zipped directly in front of my face.

"We got to go to the others. It's Sir Rose—he's hurt bad."

Nodding, I knew there was nothing left for us to do here. Again, the horns blared, and cheers could be heard from below.

"What's happening?" I asked while he screwed his face up, wanting to get back to the others.

"There's an army of burning zombie things coming. Looks like when you set them on fire in that valley, they started heading this way and kept setting other zombies on fire. It's a zombie barbeque out there. The army that just showed up is cutting through them like a line cutter at Disney World."

With those words, I turned and sprinted toward the others.

CHAPTER 39

Hold Me now

Sir Rose sat propped against the wall with Tristen kneeling beside him, holding out a cup of water. I glanced at Gabby, who had a sizable gash on her cheek. No words were needed as she shook her head. Sir Rose would not see the return of his king.

Tristen had tears streaming down his face. He had formed a father-son type of bond with the man and, by the looks of the surrounding area, had taken out his pain on everything within reach.

Hand on his abdomen, the noble knight was holding in his literal guts in one last show of defiance. I joined Tristen, kneeling down and putting my hand on his shoulder.

"It's okay; we'll stay here with him. We're done here," I whispered, reaching down for Sir Rose's other hand. While weak, he still had the grip of a dozen men.

"Max," Sir Rose breathed out, his spittle now mixed with blood.

"We're here. You—" I almost choked up. Not only was he a new acquaintance, but he was, in a way, family, as was Ed. Our merry band of misfits had formed a family of friendship. "You were brave; if it wasn't for you, I would not have been able to take on, Lil—the Anger," I corrected myself.

"My work here is done." He smiled. "Tell me of my family again."

"Edward Rose is one of the bravest men I know. Noble, just like you. He's kind and, like you, willing to do what it takes to help others. He is a knight."

"I see." Sir Rose's breath was steadying. I could tell he was envisioning Ed.

"Yeah," Petro added. For once, the prince of the Pixies knew now wasn't the time for his usual banter. "He gave me a job and helped me become who I am: a prince."

Sir Rose's pained smile widened. "And a prince you are, my lord. This makes my heart full."

Gabby spoke up this time. "He is in love with an amazing woman. You would blush if you saw her."

"Like his father; yes, the love of a good woman is the most powerful of magics."

"I will tell him about you," I said as he reached under his chest plate, pulling out an amulet. I recognized the design—it was Ed's family crest.

"I had this made for my sons, but they are in foreign lands. Can you ensure this goes back to my family?"

I nodded, taking the amulet. I couldn't help but lean over and hug the man. He patted me on the back. "Enough of this. I am to be celebrated. I know I will not see the sun again."

Merlin finally joined us after recuperating from the literal oven roasting he had endured. Again, Gabby looked at him, and Merlin closed his eyes in understanding before also kneeling down. It was clear from his expression that there was nothing he could do. I stepped back.

"My old friend." Merlin smiled. "Always the one to show off."

Sir Rose rolled his eyes in jest. "You should be talking, you old crusty wizard." They had been fast friends, and had spent a lifetime of fighting side by side. Sir Rose coughed, and Merlin held his hand to his chest, letting a light-green glow calm his breathing.

"We will see each other again, under another night sky." Melin turned for a second, holding back his emotions.

"It would be my honor."

Merlin, having heard Sir Rose's comment about never seeing the sun again, pulled himself to his feet. I noted the burn marks on his arms and face; most normal men would have died under that type of heat.

Slamming his staff on the ground, a yellow glowing ball of light grew from its end, illuminating the entire area. As the ball grew, Merlin pushed it into the sky above us. Seeing Sir Rose's dulling eyes fix on the light, Merlin pulled a white dove from under his cloak, setting it on Sir Rose's hand. The knight smiled as the dove looked into his eyes.

I glanced at the amulet, realizing it was a dove holding a cross and a sword behind it as it took flight. It was the Rose family crest, one I had seen many times.

Tristen shook his head as Sir Rose shifted his focus on the young man. "You, young man. You have been of great service to the king, a servant of the house of Ban and Arthur. Today, you become a knight." He coughed as Merlin again eased the man's lungs.

"I—" Tristen spoke. "You need to get better, then show me how to be a knight."

Sir Rose's hazy eyes shifted as he placed the dove on his shoulder, wincing at every move, trying to hold himself together. "My sword, Lord Abaddon."

I had never been called that before, and for some reason, it felt as if I was being told more than I knew. I reached over, picking up his sword. The weapon's weight was more than I expected, being made of solid, shiny cold iron.

Knowing he couldn't hold it, I placed it in his free hand, holding it up. "Kneel in front of me, boy, to make you a man," Sir Rose commanded. The bright orb of light overhead continued to expand as rays of gold beamed down on the historic scene.

Tristen did as instructed while tears of anger and sadness streaked his face.

"I hereby christen thee, Sir Lancelot, Knight of the Round Table and holder of my honor. Your title rings true as a true servant of the king. You will be his greatest warrior, a deity among men. I have one creed for you." His voice was getting strained, and I could feel him loosening his grip on the sword as I guided it to Tristen's other shoulder, the shock of the words and his now given name taking hold of all of us.

Tristen nodded as Sir Rose continued. "You are to tell no one of your power and keep it in your favor for all time. That is the only creed I ask of you."

"I swear to it," Tristen replied—or by this point I should say, Lancelot. I let the thought linger as the hard truth of what had just happened landed directly in my chest. The young man we had brought to the past with us to bring home would not be leaving. No, in fact, he would become one of the most storied knights in all of history: Sir Lancelot.

Sir Rose smiled, finally letting his grip go. "Go with God, or whomever you see fit, but ring true your name and creed."

"I will," Tristen whispered as Sir Rose looked into the light one final time after nodding at the dove and took his last breath.

I looked over to see Petro perched on Gabby's shoulder, covering his face. They were both crying. I had never seen a V cry; blood streaked her cheeks. Their tears were the blood that ran through their veins.

I handed Tristen Sir Rose's sword. "You're not coming with us." It wasn't a question. Tristen—Sir Lancelot—would stay, regardless of what I said.

"No, I'm not." Tristen stood a little taller, sounded a little more certain, and his chin hardened just enough.

Petro hovered in front of him as Tristen held out his hand. "You read the books, kid, right?"

"No, not really. That's just what you all talked about. Who doesn't know about Excalibur," Tristen replied. He was a knight, and with that, he would not tell a lie.

All the things Lancelot ended up doing flowed through my mind. We never sat around and talked about Lancelot's affair with Lady Guinevere and him being the downfall of King Arthur.

"Hey, kid"—I pulled out my coin—"listen, don't be tempted by what isn't yours." While I couldn't fully tell him the truth, I would leave him with those words.

Merlin cleared his throat. "We have much to do here. Morgana is still on the field of battle." He stomped his foot. "Let's get on with the goodbyes."

I smiled, now knowing I had Merlin's blood coursing through my veins. "Goodbye, old man. Listen, there's something I need to tell you." I was about to talk to him about Tom.

Merlin held up his hands. "Pancakes."

I screwed my face up. "Pancakes?"

"Yes, pancakes. You've given me quite enough to digest."

"Yeah, pancakes," Petro barked. "You better not jack that shit up!"

"Brave prince, I would never do such a dastardly deed." Merlin smiled at Gabby. "You, young lady." He walked over to her, grabbing her hand. He looked back at me. "You know you could do better."

Gabby let a fang slip. "I suppose, but I think he's pretty okay."

"Suit yourself. But I must say, such beauty is often wasted on a fool. It's a good thing I would never have such folly in my bloodline." Gabby leaned over, hugging the old man.

"Merlin," I interjected, "tell the king what happened here and look after the kid."

"I think he's no longer a kid." Merlin smiled. "Go now, before you muck everything up."

Rubbing the coin, I pushed my will into it; it was time to leave. I was just hoping Phil wasn't using the bathroom again.

You thought I forgot about that at the Crystal Castle? Never . . .

CHAPTER 40

There's No Place Like Home Other
Than Taco Bell After Midnight . . .

Phil finally stopped complaining when we entered the Postern. We had apparently sucked him through the gate while the celebration was just kicking off around the gate. According to Phil, he, Lash, and Gelf had found a barrel of ale on the way down the gate tower. With Arthur's armies arriving, every knight in the tower had been calling for what Phil called "a victory lap."

The truth of the matter was the fight was still raging, they had simply done their part. He was also pissed about not being able to say goodbye to everyone, but when we finally told him about Tristen and Sir Rose, he stopped.

Like a pissed parent finding their child coming home through their bedroom window, James lifted his head off a table that had been placed in the middle of the room with a chair and computer. The one thing I hadn't taken into consideration over the past couple of days was the amount of time that would have passed back home.

"You scared the shit out of . . ." James froze, seeing the condition we were all in. My armor was charred and in tatters, and Gabby and Petro were covered in various sticky substances that even a porta-john would question.

"James, looks like you got the night shift," I said, seeing the digital clock on the shelf reading one o'clock in the morning.

"What the hell happened to you? And where is Tristen?" James was starting to get his body in motion, pressing a red button on the desk. Phones didn't work in the Postern.

"About that. I think it's better to tell the whole group. How are things here?" I asked as Petro buzzed forward.

"How long have we been gone? Casey said I had better not stay out late, and I was totally good," Petro buzzed, landing on the desk.

"Four months. The table showed up an hour or two ago. Everyone went to verify it's good before heading this way. We thought you would be a little longer," James informed us.

"Shite, you didn't know if we would come back at all," Phil huffed. "Bruther"—he turned to me—"you might want to change."

"Yeah." I nodded, walking to the shelves. Beside my pants and shirt, Tristen's clothes sat as if they were a memorial to the past.

Catching onto this, James shook his head.

"He's not dead," I said, stripping off my armor.

Ed, Jenny, Angel, Frank, Tish, the Pixie crew, and Doctor Freeman burst into the Postern, voices booming as everyone converged on us. If you've ever tried to listen to the radio while someone else's stereo was louder, with someone screaming at you and a plane flying ten feet overhead, that was the level of noise in the Postern.

"Right!" Ed barked. "Enough. Everyone, calm down. Max, where is Tristen?"

Gabby, Phil, Petro, and I all glanced at each other. "He stayed. He's alive."

"Why?" Ed quickly snapped back. I found their concern for him interesting, considering the rest of the situation.

Time to pull the Band-Aid off in one swift pull, I thought, shaking my head. This was going to be a hard pill for them to swallow. "He's Sir Lancelot now."

"What?" Dr. Freeman asked.

"That's right. He was knighted by . . ." I paused, looking at Ed. "Ed, we need to talk later, but . . ." I reached down, picking up the amulet Sir Rose had given me from my pile of discarded armor. "Here."

Ed dangled the amulet in front of him, his face softening. "Where did you get this?"

"It belonged to the person who created your family crest." Seeing the confusion on his face, I continued. "Your great-something grandfather was a Knight of the Round Table."

"Yeah, and one hell of a warrior!" Petro added. In reality, his death hadn't fully set in yet.

Seeing Ed still confused, I grabbed the amulet in the palm of my hand, lowering it into his. "He helped us. We met him. He . . . He sacrificed himself to save us."

Ed held the amulet tightly as he nodded. "Right, I don't understand all of this, but we will have time to discuss this later. What else happened?"

"Well, I need to talk with Oscar. And . . . Lilith was there." I hadn't even told the others this news yet. "I'll need to talk to her too."

"What?" Trish interjected. "She was just at the Council halls verifying the last section of the table."

"It's a long story, but what do you know about the Anger?"

"I see." Trish nodded as I refocused my thoughts. "Enough to understand."

"Listen, about the table, it's hard to explain, but there is a way to use it to pull the Old Gods to the Everwhere instead of here. It's what it was made for. Does that make sense?"

"Of course," Doctor Freeman spoke up. "It would make sense. The Council wants the table to send them back when they come. Why not use it to divert them? Genius." He paused. "How?"

"Lilith will know. In the meantime, I have a trip to take," I said as Gabby turned to me.

"What? We need to get to the Council," she fussed; she didn't want me to leave.

"It can't wait. You guys can handle that and let everyone else know what happened. Hell, they will probably not believe everything," I said, smiling at her. Angel stepped forward, grabbing her hand.

"Come on, let's get you fueled up. You look like you've seen a ghost." Angel was doing the math in her head: I needed to do something important, and Gabby wasn't about to let me out of her sight.

Gabby nodded. "I see you had to pull out the big guns." She grabbed my hand. "Be safe."

"I will."

The chatter from the group of Pixies cut in, and they turned to see that Casey and Petro were in a full-on make-out session. Neil was making gagging noises while Macey and Lacey were trying to pull them apart.

"Well, bruthers, some things never change." Phil clapped his hands.

"Yeah, enough, you two," Frank huffed, flicking them. They came to a stop as they both wiggled their eyebrows.

"Totally worth it, bro," Petro said, squinting his eyes. "Flick me again, and I'll pix your underwear drawer." This was a common threat when a Pixie actually liked you and taking an eye was simply too much.

Frank let his fangs slip. "Anytime. I don't wear them."

"True," Angel said as she walked out with Gabby.

Trish, having been silent for the most part, cleared her throat. "Why do you need to see Oscar?"

"His father, Lash. Oscar was from that time—and so was Tom. It's hard to explain, but I need to see him," I said as her eyes widened.

"Lash? He was alive?" Trish stepped within an inch of me.

"You were the queen he was talking about. Didn't you know he had a son?" I asked as she grinned. He had never mentioned his queen's name.

"That sly fox—well, cat. He was sent on a journey and never returned. He must have been busy along the way." Hurt, warmth, and caring all flowed through her eyes. I wondered if Lash was also friends with Amon. Again, this was a conversation for another time.

The past was as confusing as the future. Time was, in many ways, starting to prove itself to be an endless loop of coincidences—something that Gramps was adamant wasn't a real thing.

"Right," Ed finally said, turning to the larger group as I stepped back. "We have a lot to catch up on, but more importantly, we need to talk with Lilith. Max, I know you're going to wherever it is you said you need to go, but a lot has transpired since you were all gone, so make it quick. Hell, I'm surprised the Council hasn't shown up yet. They want you all at the Council halls as soon as you—"

Ed stopped talking as I walked through the Seekergate in a snap of ozone, quickly shutting it behind me.

CHAPTER 41

Hello Again

Trees rustled as the sounds of birds chirped in the calm British countryside. Not only did I need to clear my head, but I needed to see something for myself. The Lady of the Lake was an Elemental, and with that, would very much still be alive.

From all the history books I'd read, King Arthur had thrown the sword back into the lake, where it had, of course, been found by Goolsby's past relatives. It was one of those odd loop scenarios, I thought to myself as I considered the sword. If we went back in time to get it and then took it further back in time, where was it? Lost? Or stuck in an endless loop of time?

From what I could remember, the books and stories had gotten it all wrong: the true size of Camelot, who Lancelot was, and everything else I had witnessed.

In the background, a cow grunted.

"Hey there, stranger," a familiar but older voice spoke from behind me.

There, standing not five feet away, was Tristen.

"Long time no see," I joked while he nodded. He was wearing a large brown robe that looked to be from the time we had just left.

"A very long time. I must confess, I am happy to see you." Tristen smiled. Time and age sat on his face like a mask. Something wasn't right.

"Why haven't you come to find me?" I asked as he waved his hand over the water, opening the same entrance we had once entered through.

"I have been and, well, will be here until things change. And that time is now. You see, I cannot leave this meadow pond. The only reason I am up here"—he pointed to the ground—"is because of you being here."

"You do know your folks are a pretty big deal; we might have to chat them up." I smiled. "I take it she wants to see me."

Tristen nodded. "Yes, very much so. We can discuss the rest later. It's good to see you, old friend."

I walked the familiar path like I had done it yesterday. The bodies that once haunted the cavern leading to the underwater keep were no longer there; time had turned the bones to dust.

Walking inside the familiar keep, Nimue stood in front of the fireplace, the recognizable smell of food wafting from her stew pot. "Max."

"Nimue," I replied, bowing slightly.

"No need for pleasantries; we got that out of the way a long, long time ago. We've been waiting for this day to come. Time has forgotten us in many ways." She dropped a copy of the screenplay for the movie *Excalibur* on the table. "Though in many others, they haven't."

"I see you have some eyes on the outside. Listen, I know this is going to sound weird, but something told me to come here. I remember you telling me to come, but I didn't want to wait."

"Very wise. Merlin was right about you. Why are you here then? Other than to see this place again for your own sanity?" Nimue was making a good point.

"You wanted to see me?"

"Hah," she cackled. "I've wanted to see anyone for centuries. Yes, I knew you would come."

"What happened with everyone? Lash, Merlin." I looked at Lancelot, not speaking his name. "Morgana?"

She picked up what looked to be the original manuscript for *Excalibur*, chucking it into the fire. I had, in fact, watched the eighties movie.

"Not this. Well, for starters, Tristen—or dare I say, Sir Lancelot, was not the suitor he was accused of being. It was another—a craft." She smiled at Tristen. "As for Merlin, well, he lost his mind. He died in a fire at night in his sleep. He had a long life and saw many things."

"How long?" I asked as she bobbed her head, pouring me a glass of ale.

"Don't bother yourself with these things. Now, as for the rest of the story, you need to understand that some things are best left untold. Lash continued his journey, and Gelf . . . Well, Gelf became part of another story. Let heroes be heroes and enemies be enemies. Now, I have something for you." She lifted a cloth from the middle of her fireplace, exposing Excalibur.

"I don't understand. The sword was lost in a time loop, or whatever you call it."

"You don't need to understand. Many lives were lost breaking that loop. But that is a story for another time. It's time for you to go, but there is one more thing." We both took a sip of our drinks. "You have two moon cycles until they arrive."

"Two years? How do you know?" I asked as she pursed her lips.

"You have been given enough information. Tristen, on the other hand, has given me much; company and friendship for many moons. Please send my regards to Hades and let him know where his son is; he will be able to unbind him from this place," Nimue said, walking to the entrance door.

It was time to leave.

I reached out to shake Tristen's hand. "I'll come back soon."

Tristen smiled, opening the top of his robe, exposing his chest. In the center, a slit through his heart where a blade had been sunk into his chest lay ragged. "Yes, please do. We have much to catch up on. And if Hades can't get me out of here, can you bring the others?"

"You bet. Here." I handed him one of our communicators, but he shook his head, knowing it wouldn't work.

"We will see each other again. Please, tell my father. Oh, and Merlin gave me his gauntlet after you left. It's one of the reasons I'm still here." I had forgotten about leaving it with him. Truth be told, it was likely what saved him during the broiling he survived.

"Why are you both still here?" I asked.

"I can never leave." Nimue frowned. "As for Tristen, he was stabbed in the heart with Excalibur. Arthur and Merlin parted ways after that. He cannot leave unless taken. Arthur bound him to this place by striking a deal with Morgana, the very person who controlled the craft that took the heart of his precious Guinevere. A most foul agreement. Only a true god can heal the wound. Even an immortal is not immune to Excalibur's blade."

"I'll go see him. I just have one more stop."

I saluted, turning back to the dark path to the surface.

CHAPTER 42

Grandma

Smoke wafted from Lilith's cigarette as she crossed her legs, her red lipstick leaving marks on the end of her cigarette filter. Trish had motioned the last of her customers out of FA's, so it was just good old grandma and myself.

Setting down two glasses of Magnus, Trish walked back into the kitchen. I'd finally taken a shower after returning from England and hadn't missed a beat getting to Lilith.

"Nothing to say?" I asked as she took another drag of her smoke.

"I believe you stopped believing me years ago, child."

She wasn't wrong. "I'm not going to threaten you anymore about playing games. I get some of it, I do. I mean, after what I saw, you could have ripped us to shreds when we first met."

"Hmph. 'The Anger.'" She held up quotation marks in the air. "Yes, I can be rather convincing. But you found a way."

"Sorry about that."

"Don't be sorry. I would have eaten you." Her mood shifted. "I know how much time we have."

She was talking about the message Nimue had given me.

"Yeah, two years."

"Yes. Enough time to deal with the problem at hand."

I took another sip of Magnus. "Problem at hand?"

"Yes, Goolsby said you haven't been by to see the Council yet. Must I always tell you everything?"

"You know what? Yeah. For once, yes."

She smiled. "While you were away and slightly before, there were a string of sensitives being killed by supposed regulars. That picked up after you left. It reeks of Darkwater, and there have been reports of him being back. He's trying to start a divide, and possibly looking for someone."

"Tristen?"

"No. As soon as you left, the creatures searching for him did as well. They were the leftovers from the knights of the Old Gods."

"What happened?"

"I had a little chat with Titania. Needless to say, she wasn't too happy and handled the situation herself. She is set to meet with the Council next month."

"Gods and graves, a lot has happened."

"Indeed, it has. I also know you need to go see Devin."

I leaned back. "Why aren't Gabriel and the celestials involved in all of this?"

"They will be soon enough, and when they are, we will all be thankful, as always. They like being dramatic—they *are* dramatic, you just don't know it yet." Seeing my face, she huffed before continuing.

"They're handling the big stuff: negotiating, working behind the scenes. I suggest you spend some time with them." She paused. "On second thought, don't. They are dreadfully boring."

"You know something? You aren't half bad when you're not starting wars and killing people."

"Even I have to have a hobby. Max, the time for all this cat and mouse, as humans say, is over. I'm here to help. I have a meeting with Goolsby and his wannabe crusaders tomorrow. You should come along."

"You seem to be spending a good bit of time with old Gooley pants."

She shuffled in her seat. "Well, someone has to. Take the time we have to prepare yourself. Focus on Darkwater; he is still a part of this."

I started thinking about everything that had occurred, including having Excalibur in my truck. It was like putting a puzzle together, except all the puzzle pieces were the same color.

For the rest of the night, we ate and drank, talking about the times of King Arthur and Merlin. For once in our odd relationship, we sat as family.

EPILOGUE

A dull yellow light illuminated the hazy room where Darkwater and a group of people sat. The rest of the space was covered in ominous shadows.

He leaned forward.

"Is it done?" Darkwater asked, already knowing the answer.

A hard-faced woman leaned forward as well. "No. But the news cycle is packed with pandering to the anti-magic crowd. It's just a matter of time."

"Is it." He wasn't asking but rather making a statement.

A large figure put his elbows on the table, showing his thick face. Pulling his hood back, a bold man started to talk just as Darkwater pulled out a pistol, shooting him between the eyes. The blue, enhanced round punched through the man's forehead, as his head snapped back.

"We need to ensure the knife is twisted. Pick up the pace; I am here to authorize phase two," Darkwater advised the group.

"Sir," the woman spoke again. She was clearly the only person at the table with the guts to do so.

"Go ahead."

"You're asking us to attack regulars. Are you sure?"

Darkwater snapped his fingers as several cloaked figures walked in, dropping bags of cash on the table. "Hire an army. There are plenty of people up for the job. Start this war and distract the others."

"Yes, sir," the woman said, leaning back into the shadows.

Darkwater stood. "We are on a schedule. If we can get the Council to focus on a war with humanity, we can bring on the Old Gods. The rest of the planes will fall under their own pompous weight, and we"—he spread his arms—"will take this realm for ourselves."

Darkwater smirked, happy with his speech. To him, the Old Gods were just an inevitable speed bump, one he would see both sides destroy each other for his own gain. The only roadblock in his plan was his lack of understanding of just how powerful the Old Gods and celestials were.

As he saw it, they would kill themselves to prove a point. Egos, as with everything, had been their initial downfall.

The ego of a god was something that even the weight of the universe couldn't hold down.

NOTE FROM THE AUTHOR

Hello, folks, and thanks for joining our merry band of misfits once again. As you have read, the stakes are higher, and we are getting close to the epic conclusion of the first of many arches in the Max Abaddon series. We are just getting started.

If you've been with us from the beginning, you will see many loose ends being closed and just how important that table Max first kicked his boots up on in Tom's office actually was. Never fear, Max and the team will be back for another adventure in MA9. We are about to come face-to-face with the Old Gods.

This book sets the table for many things. While we didn't get to see all of King Arthur's time, you now understand many of the breadcrumbs that have been laid out since the beginning. MA9 will be another ride, but next time, we will find the crew on their home turf.

End the end, I hope this book shows you that we all have a little magic in us.

Always remember that time connects us to everything—our past, our future, and our beginning. Everyone's true family started with a man in a field in medieval times, a cavewoman collecting furs, a worker building the great pyramids (or aliens, depending on who you ask), or a famous person we will never know we are related to. We are all connected by one thing: time. Don't let time manage you; manage time. If you can do this, you will be as strong as the mightiest mage. You can control the magic of your own time. The here and now. We all have a little magic in us.

www.ingramcontent.com/pod-product-compliance
Lightning Source LLC
Chambersburg PA
CBHW030958260626
47169CB00002B/592